PIRATES
OF THE
OUTRIGGER
RIFT

PIRATES
OF THE
OUTRIGGER
RIFT

For Jodie –
May you encounter
pirates only in
fiction. Thanks
again! You rock!
Best,

GARY JONAS & BILL D. ALLEN

47NORTH

Text copyright © 2013 Gary Jonas and Bill D. Allen
Originally released as a Kindle Serial, October 2013.

Published by 47North, Seattle

www.apub.com

ISBN-13: 9781477849248
ISBN-10: 1477849246
Library of Congress Control Number: 2013944241

Cover illustration by Chris McGrath
Cover design by Inkd Inc

We dedicate this romp to Poul Anderson, Harry Harrison, and Douglas Adams.

EPISODE ONE

CHAPTER ONE

Sai Collins adjusted the collar of her jacket as she boarded the public tram. She was still uncomfortable in the standardized Nebulaco suit. The uniform made for first-level execs like her was ill fitting, but it was a badge of respectability. At first it made her feel like she was going places, but she knew better now. This was the last time she would have to wear an exec suit. Her career was over before it had really begun.

Six months ago she had been living on the streets of a bustling starport town on planet Raken, earning her living by dubious means. But when the opportunity arose for her to move to Nebula Prime and work for Frederick Casey at Nebulaco, she had pounced on it.

Corporate home worlds were the place to make your fortune, but doing business here came with a price. No man, government, or god was greater than the corporation. Everything served the corporation in one way or another, or it was eliminated. So far, the trade-off had meant that she hadn't gone hungry in a while, so she couldn't complain.

The only neutral areas on the corporate planets were the starport free zones, where the galactic law of the Confed ruled and corporate security had to maintain a mostly hands-off approach. It was a necessary arrangement—an embassy area of sorts—to ensure free trade routes and service areas for commerce no matter the species, the government, or the corporate sponsor. The trade served the corporations and was the source of their revenue, so starports were an oasis of what little liberty remained in this part of Manspace. She would be returning to that oasis with relief as soon as this last bit of business was concluded. It had taken her awhile to see through the polished façade, but she now knew the corporate world wasn't for people like her. The back alleys were safer and populated by more honest thieves.

She rode the tram uptown to an elite leisure zone in Opportunity City from the beehive-like apartment buildings where those of her pay class had to live. The thought of leaving this life to go back to the streets was a mixture of regret and relief. She had never truly fit in. Security Director Casey had set her up with a job in an obscure accounting unit as a front; her real mission was obtaining data from locked systems and recovering whatever Casey needed. He paid well, but he was merciless. Failure was intolerable, and he always got what he wanted, even after death.

When the news announced that Casey's body had been found that morning, it meant more than the loss of a paycheck and the end of a career for Sai; it meant one more mission for Casey as instructed. She was on her way to meet a man who would give her the details.

The meeting place was a bistro between a row of tall, uniform apartments in the residential sector and the silver towers of Nebulaco's central offices. It was not her sort of place. The customers were the up-and-comers who wanted to be seen as such. She would have been far more comfortable in a greasy diner on the other side of town. But it hadn't been her call.

She walked up to the maître d'. "I'm meeting a man named Kendrick."

He gave her that look—the one she'd seen most of her life from people who thought they were better than her, which seemed to include everyone. He checked the display on the podium before him. "Yes, he said you were coming. Mr. Kendrick is already seated. Come this way."

She followed him through the dining area past tables of couples and small groups, all wearing strained smiles and acting like they were really letting loose. If not for all the stiffs, the place would have been cozy. Out the window, there was a wonderful view of Opportunity City's skyline towers gleaming on the cliffs overlooking the poisoned and stormy sea.

Kendrick's table sat near the kitchen in the back of the bistro. Loud, with no view, but thankfully with fewer watching eyes. Sai took a moment to use the skill Casey had coveted. She extended her mind and senses to do a quick check for electronic surveillance. Everything seemed fine. Kendrick stood as they approached. The maître d' pulled out her chair, waited until she took her seat, then turned back toward the front door.

Nathan Kendrick was young and handsome, like most junior execs, but his eyes wouldn't hold her gaze. "I'm glad you were able to meet me so quickly."

"I knew it was urgent," she said.

"Would you like a drink?" he asked as he seated himself.

"No. I'm fine. If you don't mind, I'd appreciate you getting to the point as quickly as possible. I would have preferred to handle this in the free zone."

"Well, I need a drink," Kendrick said. He flagged down a waitress. He ran a hand through his hair. His eyes kept darting toward the entrance.

"Why are you so nervous?" Sai asked.

"Don't worry about it," Kendrick said.

The waitress came to the table. She wore a smile that never reached her eyes.

"Scotch," he told her.

"Very good, sir," the waitress said. "Anything for you, ma'am?"

Sai shook her head.

After the waitress departed, Kendrick began. "Sorry you're out of your element, but it might attract attention for me to go slumming on that side of town. I can't take the risk of raising any eyebrows. You, on the other hand, appear to be simply another pretty girl trying to get ahead in the corporation, working after hours. Besides, someone like you should appreciate the opportunity to experience the finer things."

"Someone like me?"

"I know who and what you are." He gave her a stern look. He wasn't very good at it. The flop sweat on his forehead undermined the effect.

Sai considered him for a moment. He was obviously a little drunk. She wondered what his game was as she leaned back in her chair. "I don't know what you're talking about, Mr. Kendrick. I work in accounts payable as a clerk. I've been there for six months. I worked at an offworld branch office before that."

"If you were just a clerk, Director Casey wouldn't have even known your name."

Sai smiled. "Maybe I *am* that kind of pretty girl and Director Casey had a wild side. It's certainly none of your business either way. We're both here to do a job. I was expecting a call as soon as I heard Casey was dead. You said a name that has meaning to me to prove that you were legit."

"Dirion," Kendrick said. "Who is he? Your lover? Your pimp?"

Sai stood up and put a finger in Kendrick's face. "Don't mess with me, little worm. I don't give a damn where we are, I'll hurt you."

"Now, now, don't make a scene. I have a reputation to maintain," Kendrick said.

"You're just lucky we aren't on my side of town. I'm here because I respected Casey's wishes, not to play games." She started to walk away.

"Leaving would be unwise," Kendrick said. "You know he wouldn't have made it that easy."

Sai stopped and stared hard at Kendrick.

"Word is that he killed himself," he said.

"He wouldn't have done that."

Kendrick shrugged. "I don't know what happened to him. I don't care. I hated the old bastard. But I don't want anything to happen to *me*. Casey left instructions for both of us. I did my part because I didn't like the alternative if I failed. I'm certain you wouldn't like the alternative, either."

Sai returned to the table and sat down. "Then let's get it over with."

Kendrick looked around. He retrieved his briefcase from beneath the table, hesitated a moment as he looked around casually, then opened it. He withdrew a small metal box and handed it to her. "I was instructed to give you this, along with some credits to book passage to Raken. There's enough extra as a healthy payment for you as well. Inside you will find a sealed and coded courier pouch with a datastore and some instructions on where and when to deliver it."

Sai rotated the box in her hands but did not open it. She met his gaze. "And what is the 'alternative' if I don't?"

"Director Casey was thorough, and viciously efficient. He put in guarantees. I have a simple set of instructions. Other people have instructions to carry out in the event I fail to perform my duty. There would be consequences. Believe me, I would have avoided this if I could. Casey had something on everyone. He was a coldhearted brute, but he knew how to make people do what he wanted."

Sai noticed that his hands were shaking and sweat was beginning to break out on his brow again.

"There is nothing off-limits to such a man. You knew him, Ms. Collins. You know what he was capable of. I don't care if you follow your instructions or not, but I surely followed mine to the letter."

Sai nodded. She knew she didn't really have any choice, but she didn't have to like it.

"Okay, let's get this taken care of," she said, and pulled a credit stick out of her pocket. Her fingerprint activated the device, and glowing green numerals displayed a pitifully small amount. She tapped the privacy mode so Kendrick wouldn't see the balance.

Kendrick nodded. "Ah yes, payment." He withdrew a stick from the open briefcase. It was gloss black with a silver "N" stamped across it. He put his fingerprint to it, then keyed in a transfer sequence on the face of the stick. He reached over and swiped it across the front of hers. The glowing numbers displaying the deposit grew respectfully large.

The waitress returned with a drink. Kendrick took it from her and she started to walk away, but Kendrick raised a finger and she paused. He upended the drink, swallowing the amber beverage in one gulp. He handed back the empty glass.

The waitress raised an eyebrow. "Another, sir?"

Kendrick nodded his head and waved her away.

He leaned toward Sai. "One more thing. I am to impress upon you that you need to follow the schedule and be at the drop-off point on time. Don't be tempted to run off with the payment. As I said, Casey was thorough. He employed some very dangerous people. Have no doubt that if you don't deliver, there will be consequences. Make sure there are no mistakes. Get away fast and quiet."

"The sooner this is done, the better I'll like it."

"Good," he said, smiling. "You have no idea how glad I am that this is over." He took the linen napkin from the table and wiped his forehead.

"Oh, it won't be over for a while," she said. "I'm sure whatever is in that pouch has got to be important. Important things go missing and people notice. I'd suggest that you lay low and quiet. Someone will come looking."

His face paled. "But . . . how could they possibly find me?"

Sai rose to leave. "Take some free advice. Grow a pair, Mr. Kendrick. If you're worried about getting caught, stop acting so damned guilty."

She left him and exited the restaurant, eager to change clothes and get this part of her life behind her.

* * *

Mike Chandler sat in the pilot's seat of the *Marlowe*. A Scout-class ship, the *Marlowe* was too small for trading, too slow for racing, and too ugly for a pleasure craft, but it suited Chandler just fine. It had enough room for him to live and to store the tools of his trade. He was a special investigator. It sounded impressive, as if he were in charge of protecting Confed senators or capturing smugglers. Usually it meant he was checking out bogus insurance claims or setting up security systems for paranoid middle-income wage slaves. So much for glamour.

He'd been contacted by an agent of Lord Randol, a corporate noble who owned a large percentage of Nebulaco. Randol had a job for him and wanted to meet in person. Chandler agreed in part because you generally don't say no to a corporate lord, but mostly because he was running out of credits.

He entered orbit around the third moon of the planet Trent. Chandler transmitted his ID code to Randol's traffic controller. Access to the moon was tightly regulated. A sensor grid blanketed the upper atmosphere.

The communicator crackled to life with the voice of the controller. "You're late."

Chandler pressed the communicator. "I don't normally make house calls. Does he want to see me or not? If not, I'll just forward the bill for my time and be on my way."

"Lord Randol doesn't like to be kept waiting."

"Neither do I. Just give me landing coordinates and we can all be happy."

The controller grumbled, but in a few seconds the coordinates for his destination were uploaded to his navcom.

He broke orbit and began his descent. The private moon, once barren, had been terraformed into an oasis of living things—grass, trees, hedges—and stocked with exotic songbirds. There were gravity generators to keep your feet firmly on the ground and the atmosphere from flying off. Just the place for a corporate lord to call home.

Chandler piloted the small ship down through the atmosphere and locked onto the guidance beacon. Randol's controllers took over and brought the *Marlowe* in.

As he descended, Chandler looked out over the estate. Green grass carpeted the rolling hills. Paved walkways crisscrossed lush gardens. He also noted the assault cannons tucked in among the petunias. Randol obviously liked his privacy.

Two security guards met Chandler when he exited his ship and escorted him to a processing area. Typical drill: retina, DNA, full molecular scans. They took him to an office occupied by a muscle-bound guard in a fancy uniform sitting at a desk. The placard on the door read CAPTAIN JORGESON. "So," Chandler said, "are you the ringmaster in this circus?"

Jorgeson glared and dismissed Chandler's escort. "I'm the officer in charge of security here. I expect to be treated with respect."

"I expect a lot of things, too, but I find that I tend to get disappointed pretty often. How many more hoops do I have to jump through to see His Majesty?"

Jorgeson grunted and nodded his head. "A wiseass. Let me tell you something, Mr. Special Investigator. I think the old man has finally lost his mind, hiring gutter trash like you. But he's the boss. Just pray you don't piss him off or you'll have me to contend with."

"Ooh, it's a date. Anything else?"

Jorgeson pointed a finger at Chandler. "Watch yourself. Don't get sticky fingers. Don't go exploring, and don't think for a minute that you can pull anything over on Lord Randol. We've had our share of con men; they follow money. I know how to deal with them."

Chandler smiled. "I bet you do."

Jorgeson shuffled him out the door where the same two guards awaited him. They left the security area and took Chandler outside, marching him along a stone pathway through a section of garden toward Randol's mansion. Trees bearing unblemished fruit rose in perfect symmetrical patterns. The grass grew in a perfect blanket without a single bare spot or weed. The sky was the perfect shade of powder blue. It was perfectly sickening. It made Chandler long for a handful of crabgrass seed. He was definitely out of his element.

Randol's mansion was a rambling structure, patterned after the Roman villas of Ancient Earth. It, too, reeked of perfection. Alabaster pillars held up the massive lintel. There were words carved across the front, written in a language Chandler couldn't read, but he figured they said something like, *We've got ours—screw you.*

A balding man wearing a servant's uniform waited for him at the entrance. He gestured for Chandler to enter. The guards took up positions at the door and allowed Chandler to continue alone.

Chandler stepped into the foyer and looked around. "La . . . dee . . . da."

His entire ship could have fit into the front hall. The servant followed, closing the doors behind them. Chandler shook his head.

"I am Aland," the servant said. "I will escort you to Lord Randol. I hope the trip was not too unpleasant."

Chandler chuckled. "More unnecessary than unpleasant. We could have done this by holo."

"That is not for me to say, sir. I am sure that Lord Randol has his reasons."

Chandler stepped past Aland into the foyer and looked around. "So how many people live here?"

"Lord Randol and his daughter, Helen. However, she is leaving this morning to continue her education offworld."

"Humph. Must be cramped."

Aland either didn't hear or pretended not to.

"Of course, the household staff has separate quarters."

"Of course."

A mural covered the ceiling, depicting a man tearing a fistful of stars from the heavens. No doubt it represented the first of the

Randol clan, back when their blood was a bit thicker and they were more like the rest of humanity. Not the same, of course—they were never the same, always a touch better.

Suspended from the ceiling on a golden chain was a giant chandelier of dark, ruby-colored crystal. It looked like a frozen cascade of blood. Columns lined the circular room, corridors led off in three directions, and twin staircases spiraled upward to a second level.

"Wait here a moment, sir, and I shall announce you," the servant said, and walked down the hall.

Just after Aland disappeared, a woman rushed forward from a side corridor and collided with Chandler. "Watch where you're going," she said.

Chandler stepped back. The woman looked about twenty, with soft, flowing blonde curls and the kind of creamy skin that only the rich can afford to keep. She wore a short, sheer peach-colored dress that draped off one shoulder and left the other bare. Her legs were finely sculpted from her calves to her exposed thighs. Her skin was as pale as the alabaster columns. She looked at Chandler with a slightly annoyed expression. Her eyes were deep blue.

"You must be Helen," he said.

"Who are you?"

"I'm here to see your father."

"You didn't answer my question," she said.

"You're right. I didn't." Chandler grinned.

Helen opened her mouth as if to speak, then laughed. "Why are you seeing Father?"

"I don't really know yet. Maybe you could tell me. Do you know what your father is up to?"

"I don't involve myself in business matters. Besides, I've been too busy getting ready to go off to Driscoll University. I leave in a few hours."

Driscoll University was reserved for the richest and the most connected, although it advertised itself as a school for the best and brightest. "Great school," he said.

"It sounds like a bore to me. I don't like to be bored." She moved closer, into his personal space. "What about you?"

"Ahem." Aland returned just in time to break things up. "This way, sir," the servant said.

"Does he always move so quietly?" Chandler asked.

"He specializes in sneaking," Helen said. "It was nice to meet you . . . whoever you are. Maybe we'll meet again sometime."

"You never know. I might show up at a frat party or something. I'm a champion beer chugger."

She smiled, then walked past Chandler and Aland.

Chandler watched her walk away, enjoying the view.

"This way, sir," Aland said.

Chandler didn't move. "Wait for it."

Just before taking a turn in the corridor, Helen glanced back to see Chandler still grinning at her. She quickly looked away and disappeared from view. But Chandler had seen her blush.

"Gotcha," he said. "Quite a fiery young woman."

"Yes, sir," said Aland.

"Does she always welcome visitors like that?"

"Mistress Helen is a very good hostess, sir."

"I'd say so. Strong and smart or just a rich harpy?"

"I am afraid I cannot comment, sir."

"Of course you can't."

They arrived at a solid oak door, carved with grapevines and fat naked babies with wings. Aland opened it and gestured for Chandler to enter. "Lord Randol waits within, sir."

Chandler stepped inside. Aland remained in the hallway and shut the door behind him. The room was a massive library. Rich wooden shelves filled with books covered three walls, floor to ceiling. A roaring fireplace stood in the center of the rear wall. The mantle sported a miniature sailing ship from another century. A ladder on wheels stood ready in one corner. An ancient rolltop desk and several wing-back chairs sat upon a huge rug in the center of the room. In one chair sat an elderly man, deeply engrossed in a book—an antique studying an antique. He wore a conservative business suit. On his right hand he wore a ruby ring worked in the shape of the Randol family crest, a bloody fist.

As Chandler stepped forward, Randol peered at him over the book, then smiled. "Ah, Mr. Chandler."

"That's me." Chandler said, and took a seat without being asked. "This is quite a spread you have here, although I think you should have gone for the turquoise sky. It's in fashion this season."

"My, my." Randol closed his book. "You're every bit as insolent as I'd heard."

"My reputation precedes me."

"Yes, it seems that you were once contacted by Lord Oke, and he was not satisfied with your job performance."

Chandler shrugged. "Okay, I'll bite. So why did you call me after that kind of endorsement?"

"Let me ask you a question first. What exactly was the task Lord Oke wanted you to perform?"

Chandler stared coldly at the old man. "Sorry, that's confidential. If that's why you've asked me here, I'm afraid we're wasting each other's time. The last thing I need to do is get involved in a feud between lords."

Randol gave a dry laugh. "Relax, young man. That's not why I brought you here. I already know about Lord Oke's issues and indiscretions. I know that your task would have involved the destruction of a few innocent people's reputations. What I'm interested in is your response when he tried to hire you."

Chandler leaned back in his seat. "To put it bluntly, I told him to shove it."

"Precisely."

"So what?"

"The point is that Lord Oke offered you a large sum of money and it wasn't enough for you to violate your principles. The fact that you even possess principles sets you apart from many of your colleagues."

"I can't argue with that," Chandler said, spying a decanter filled with amber liquid on the desk next to him. He nodded toward the bottle. "Is that for guests?"

"It's thirty-year-old brandy. Would you care for a taste?"

"All right, but no more than a liter or so. I'm trying to cut down."

"Shall I summon Aland to pour?"

Chandler shook his head and grinned. "I think I can manage." He rose, jerked the stopper out of the decanter, and poured himself two fingers. "Want some?"

"No, thank you."

Chandler shrugged and returned to his chair, taking a gulp of the brandy and wincing.

"You were talking about principles," Chandler said. "Mine, such as they are, aren't for sale."

"A rare quality of which I have need. I distrust any man who can be bought, even if I'm doing the buying."

Chandler gulped down another swallow. "I don't know. I've always thought that every man has his price. For some people it might be a chunk of money, for others it might be different, like getting to keep all their fingers and toes intact for another day, or getting to take a few more breaths of oxygen. Sooner or later everyone has a breaking point. Anyone will turn on you if the pressure is too high. I've always avoided trusting anyone with anything I couldn't afford others to know."

"I don't need a superman, Mr. Chandler, just an honest man, and I think you're the closest I've got."

"Okay, we've established that I'm a saint among men. What's the job?"

"I need you to meet a courier, retrieve a package, and pay for it."

"A pickup? You have Jorgeson. Why do you need me?"

Randol sighed. "It's a matter of utmost confidentiality. There are certain people, powerful people, who would like to obtain what I'm entrusting to you. I need it protected."

"What about Nebulaco Security? Can't the company handle this?"

"I can't trust anyone within the corporation."

"So these 'powerful people' are corporate? Are you feuding with another lord?"

Randol shook his head. "No, it's nothing like that."

"Okay, then what is it like?"

"To put it directly, Mr. Chandler, I'm willing to pay you ten thousand credits in advance. That's what it's like. I expect confidentiality. Due to your history I feel confident that you won't betray me. But I am not prepared to divulge everything to you. It's for your own safety as well as mine."

Chandler finished his drink in one large gulp. "Well, the pay is good. I'm used to two hundred credits a day plus expenses. I'll take the ten thousand as a retainer. We'll call the difference a bonus since you seem inclined to pay it, but I'm a freelance professional, not an employee." Chandler rose and poured himself another round. "Bonus money or no, I do things my way. You're just another client to me."

"Fair enough." Randol rose and extended his hand.

Chandler looked at it like it was a dead fish. "Not yet. I need to ask a few questions."

"Very well." Randol clasped his hands behind him. "Ask away."

Chandler swirled the brandy in his glass, watching the play of the amber liquid against the flame of the fireplace. "What's the courier carrying?"

Randol squinted at him. "Nothing illegal or difficult to conceal. I will say this much: she's carrying information on a datastore in a password-sealed courier pouch. Any attempt to open it without the proper password will result in its immediate destruction. It's for my eyes only. I have my secrets, too, Mr. Chandler."

Chandler nodded. "I'll buy that. I suppose that goes for the identity of these 'powerful people' you've mentioned as well."

Randol was silent.

Chandler walked over to examine the rolltop desk. He rolled the lid partially down, marveling at the craftsmanship. He turned back to Randol. "Why can't this courier make the trip alone? She hops on a ship and makes the delivery. No delays, no complications."

Randol nodded slowly. "Normally, I would agree. However, in this case I feel that I should take special precautions. You don't know where the courier is coming from, and the courier doesn't know where the package is going to. This offers certain protections to all parties."

"You think you have a security leak that would expose your sources."

Randol shifted his weight and looked away from Chandler. "There is that possibility."

"I see. Does anyone know about me? Other than the household."

Randol shook his head. "No."

Chandler took a sip of brandy. "As to them, what about Aland and Jorgeson?"

"All Aland knows is that you visited me. He has no idea why. Jorgeson organized everything, so he is fully informed. He was going to perform the job himself, but I felt that I needed someone from the outside. He's too well known and too close to me. He seldom leaves the Trent System. His movements would have been watched."

Chandler placed his empty glass on the desk. "Where am I supposed to meet this courier?"

"On Raken, Hemdale City. It's a corporate town. There's a tavern popular for clandestine encounters of this sort. Jorgeson will brief you on the details." He reached into his pocket and withdrew a small transponder key. "You'll need this. The courier was given a unit in her package that's coded to this key. I don't know anything about the courier except that she is female. She knows nothing about you. This will help you identify each other safely." He handed it to Chandler.

Chandler pocketed the small black device. "I don't like walking into a situation where I don't know all the angles, and I may regret this. But you have a deal."

They shook hands, sealing the bargain.

Randol smiled. "Excellent. Aland will have your retainer for you when he shows you the way out."

Chandler felt he'd just sold a bit of his soul, but at least the lien on his ship would get paid on time. This month.

* * *

Nathan Kendrick returned to work as if nothing had ever happened. He went through the motions of normalcy, and when it was time for him to leave, he sighed with relief. He had pulled it off. It was going to go away and he didn't have to worry anymore.

Director Casey's death and the immediate promotion of Vincent Maxwell as new security director were causing chaos in the corporation. The rumors were that Casey had been selling information about shipping schedules, cargos, armaments, and escorts to the underworld. Talk was that he'd been caught and he'd killed himself. Guilty or not, Casey was dead, and with his death, Kendrick's orders had gone into effect.

He remembered when Casey first called him into his office. Kendrick was scared. He'd been skimming some money, just a little here and there to help out with the bills. Everyone in the corporation had some sort of secondary racket going. It wasn't that big a deal. But he felt certain that Casey was going to either fire or imprison him when he discovered his secret. To his surprise, Casey gave him a set of odd instructions to perform in the event of his death. He was supposed to retrieve a package hidden in Casey's office and follow the instructions included with it. He was even given the access codes so it would be easy. Casey warned him that if he didn't do what he was told, other parties would expose him. But if he made good on Casey's instructions, he would be paid a hefty fee.

Casey called it his insurance policy. Kendrick didn't know the specifics, but based on Casey's reputation, he was sure that the contents of that courier pouch were going to make someone pay dearly for Casey's death.

He walked to the tramway station casting nervous glances over his shoulder. He eyed every stranger and tried to control his breathing. Foolishness, paranoia, but still he listened for footsteps following in the shadows.

The ride home was uneventful. He entered his apartment building, watching for anyone out of place. His heart still thundered in his chest. He was almost done. Just get to the apartment and get some sleep. Tomorrow he'd go back to work as if everything was fine, and perhaps it would be.

He took the elevator to his floor, but when he stepped off, he saw that his apartment door stood wide open. He could see furniture overturned and his possessions strewn about.

He backed away and tried to step back into the elevator, but the doors had closed and the car was gone. He turned toward the stairs. The doorway was already opening, and a man dressed in black walked slowly forward. Two others stepped out of his apartment and moved toward him. One man took a drag off a stimstick. His eyes were hard and gray.

"Hello, Mr. Kendrick," the gray-eyed man said, allowing pale-blue smoke to escape from his lips.

"What do you want? I don't—"

"Save your breath." The man turned to his compatriots. "Search him."

The men shoved Kendrick against the wall. One kicked his legs apart and patted him down. He shook his head.

"Nathan, we're going to take a little trip. The new boss wants to meet you."

CHAPTER TWO

Jacbar's, a dark, hole-in-the-wall club, sat near the docks in Opportunity City on Nebula Prime. Spacers loved it because there were few dirtsiders and no tourists. Jacbar himself used to be a spacer. He'd made a living as a free-trader until pirates ambushed him just outside the Deneb System. He lost a hand, an eye, and his ship. The hand and eye didn't matter much, but he loved that ship. Now he kept bar, a scarred, brooding man behind the counter who knew the ways of pilots and fate.

Sai entered the smoky place. Jacbar looked up, still polishing a glass. He smiled and eyed her figure, then placed the glass on the counter.

Sai walked to the bar and sat on a cushioned stool, ignoring the stares she attracted. Jacbar didn't pay them any mind, either. He simply walked over and stood before her, hands splayed on the counter as he leaned toward her.

"And what can I do for a lovely lass like you?"

"I need a ship," Sai said. "I need to book passage to Raken and I need to leave right away."

"Good luck. Business is booming here. Most of these pilots have plenty of cargo and they don't bother with passengers. That's what the commercial liners are for."

"There has to be someone," Sai said. "There always is, but I need someone I can trust as well."

Jacbar raised an eyebrow. "Well, there's Keller, but he's a mercenary bastard. You can trust him just as long as your money holds out, but he'd chuck you out an airlock if you owed him a credit. Let's see, there's Hank Jensen, his word is his bond, but you don't want him."

"Why not?"

"He's a good man," Jacbar said. "But he's on a bad luck streak. Call me superstitious, but it might be better to hire Keller."

"Bad luck or not, I need someone I can trust, not someone I have to buy off. Is Jensen here?"

Jacbar sighed. "Yeah. See that gent nursing a beer in the corner booth?"

The man was in his midthirties, built like a middle-weight boxer—large chest, strong arms, and a slender waist. He sported a thin mustache and a shit-eating grin.

"That's Jensen?"

"Yeah. He used to be a loud and cheerful son of a bitch, but the last few years have been hard on him. His last two runs were a bust. He'd take the devil to a prayer meeting if it paid well enough, but you might have trouble keeping him sober." Jacbar took a frosted mug from the cooler beneath the counter and filled it with beer.

"Thanks for the tip."

"No problem. Here," he slid the beer across the counter to her. "On the house. It's ladies night."

"Thanks."

Sai took the mug and walked over to Hank Jensen's booth.

"Hey there," she said, with a slight grin.

Hank looked up from his drink and smiled. "Ah, darlin', you will excuse me if I decline your favors tonight," he said, raising his hands.

"You don't—"

"No, no," Hank said. "It's not that I don't have the inclination. I just don't have the finances."

"I know about your money problem," Sai began, sliding into the booth next to him.

"Saints be praised! A charitable woman!"

"No, you don't understand. I want to hire you."

"Darlin', this gets better all the time," he said, wrapping an arm around her shoulders.

Sai stiff-armed him away. "Mr. Jensen, let's get a few things straight. I'm not some starport tart, and I'm only interested in your ship. Not you. I need passage to Raken."

Hank sighed and cradled his beer in his hands, staring into the amber liquid. "Alas, another broken heart." He took a drink, then turned back to her, all business. "Unfortunately, my ship lies in dock without a drop of fuel in her and no money to buy more. I spent half my assets on this brew before me and I'll wake up tomorrow wishing I'd spent it on food."

"I have money, Mr. Jensen."

"I'm sure you do, love, but it would take five times the price of a commercial fare to fill her up."

"I may be willing to pay you that much. If you can get me out tonight."

Hank took another drink and nodded. "In a bit of a hurry, eh? And what sort of luggage will you bring along? Lots of funny little crates I can't open?"

"No baggage. Only me."

Hank stared at her.

"I'll ask you one more time, Mr. Jensen. Then I'm going to offer the job to Keller. Have you received any better offers tonight?"

"All right, I'll do it. Keller's a bastard." Hank smiled. "The price is a thousand credits. I'll need the cash up front."

"Half now, half once we're on Raken."

"But darlin', I've got to fuel my bird before we can leave."

"Half payment will get you enough to take us to Raken and back four times."

Hank smiled at her and finished his beer. "You drive a hard bargain, my dear. What's your name?"

"Sai," she said, pulling out her credit stick.

Hank took a stick out of his pocket and let her transfer the payment to him.

"Where's your ship?" she asked.

"Dock B, berth ten. Meet me there in an hour."

Sai nodded, then stood up. "I'll be there. You just make sure you spend that money on fuel for the ship and not on liquor or stims. If you aren't at the dock, I'll come looking for you." She pulled a whisperblade from her waistband and flicked it on for effect. The blue fire of the plasma blade bathed her face in light. It was a wicked weapon in the right hands. Normally, the user had a control gauntlet to help guide the weapon in midflight, steering it to the target with tiny maneuvering repulsor beams. Sai didn't need a gauntlet.

Hank pointed at her untouched beer, his eyes reflecting the blade's glow. "You gonna drink that?"

* * *

Vincent Maxwell surrounded himself with beauty. His new office sat on the top floor of the highest building in Nebula Prime's capital city, and an immense window offered a view of the evening skyline, decorated with lights and activity. He stood watching as, in the distance, a cargo ship blasted from the starport, streaked into the sky, and illuminated the heavens with fusion fire.

Casey, the previous tenant, was a hard, Spartan individual by Maxwell's standards and had no sense of style, so Maxwell was having it redecorated. The formerly mundane room was going to be transformed. He had a vision of adorning it with rich wood tones, imported marble, and art of the highest caliber. He would have just enough lighting for efficient work. For now, the room would serve its purpose, but not with the level of style he wished for.

His massive desk, however, was already installed. It suggested strength. Its mirror-polished obsidian top sat on a dark granite base and was supported by four Ionic columns of white marble swirled with green mineral traces. A large black cat perched atop it.

The delicate, soft music of stringed instruments floated around him like smoke from a fine cigar. The faint lingering scent of jasmine hung in the air. It was a start.

A chime sounded. "Enter," Maxwell said, turning to face the doorway.

Nathan Kendrick entered Maxwell's office, his eyes darting back and forth at the luxurious surroundings. He wore a navy blue suit with the Nebulaco insignia embroidered on the right breast pocket, the uniform of a junior-level exec. Kendrick patted his disheveled hair and took several deep breaths.

"Mr. Kendrick, I trust the trip across town was comfortable." Maxwell walked behind his desk and took off his jacket, hanging it on the back of his chair. He sat, steepled his fingers before him, and studied the man. The cat moved from the desk to Maxwell's lap.

Kendrick stood sweating before the broad desk. There were no other chairs in the room.

"Fine. Very comfortable, thank you for asking, Mr. Maxwell—sir."

Maxwell smiled. His dark hair was streaked with silver at the temples, giving him a distinguished air. "Good, good. But please, call me Vincent. You see, Nebulaco takes great pains to ensure the comfort of its employees. We love them, and all we ask in return is loyalty."

Maxwell paused, allowing an awkward, silent moment to pass for Kendrick. He sat behind his ominous desk, calmly stroking the fur of the sleek cat. The cat purred loudly. "Can you define 'loyalty' for me, Mr. Kendrick?"

"Uh, certainly. It's the quality of faithfulness, the steadfast allegiance to . . . well, whatever you're loyal to . . . sir . . . I mean Vincent."

"Very good. Yes, I'd say that's an adequate definition." Maxwell leaned back in his chair. He stroked his chin with his index finger and appeared to study something off in space just above and behind

Kendrick's head. "I have a problem—one dealing with loyalty. I'd appreciate your assistance."

"Yes, sir," Kendrick said. Sweat beaded on his forehead.

"Splendid. I'm afraid that we have a traitor in our midst, Mr. Kendrick." Maxwell scratched the cat's chin and allowed his words to sink in for a moment. "Would you happen to know anything about that?"

"No," Kendrick answered quickly. "Of course not, sir."

"Vincent," Maxwell corrected.

"Sorry."

Maxwell waved his hand. "Really now, Mr. Kendrick, I was told that you were quite the amateur sleuth, and that you make a hobby of accessing certain secure areas. There is no need for humility."

"I don't know what you mean," Kendrick said. He shifted his weight from one foot to the other.

"Oh? I hope you understand that we all have a responsibility to be on guard. I'm sure you're aware of our recent difficulties with piracy. The reports all suggest the pirates are controlled by one man: Thorne. Obviously he couldn't be raiding our shipments so successfully without inside help."

"Sir, I don't know anything about security. I'm in accounts receivable."

"Interesting. An important item is missing, an archival datastore with classified information that could lead us to the mole. You do have access to the storage area, do you not?"

"Well, yes, but I—"

"Tell me this, Mr. Kendrick. Why does a junior exec need access to a high-level security area? Why would Casey have assigned that clearance to you?"

"I don't know what you mean, sir."

"Really? Then it seems we have a mystery."

Kendrick swallowed, then cleared his throat. "I don't know if you're aware of this, but I did have an arrangement with former Security Director Casey."

"Do you mean the man charged with espionage? The one who took his own life before he was arrested? If so, then let me remind you that *I'm* the new director."

"That's not what I mean, sir. I mean I've never done anything on my own. I've always been loyal to the corporation . . ."

"You worked for Casey? How is it I've never even heard of you until today?" Maxwell dismissed the thought with a wave of his hand. "You must be aware of the nature of the charges against Casey. Perhaps you were actually working for Thorne all along."

Kendrick jerked back as if he'd been slapped. "I can't believe that."

Maxwell shook his head. "Isn't it obvious? You've been duped. The missing archive is the only evidence against Casey that couldn't have been tampered with. Whoever possesses it holds the key to this whole damned mess. It was our chance to prove him innocent, or guilty."

Kendrick's face was ashen. "But . . ."

"Listen, son. I understand. You were doing what you thought was right. I liked Casey, too. He seemed like a good man. I don't want to believe that he was a traitor, but without the data we can't prove anything. I need that archive. Now, you have to do the right thing and tell me everything you know. It's the only way we can start clearing all this up."

Kendrick nodded.

"Okay then. We're on the same side here. Did you take the archive?"

"Yes. I received orders from—"

"Do you still have it?"

"No."

"Do you know where it is?"

"I gave it to an employee."

"Named?"

Kendrick swallowed hard. "Sai Collins."

"Do you know where she is?"

"No, I mean, I know she left for Raken, but I don't know where she is now. Honest. I was only following orders, sir. I—"

"Guards!" Maxwell yelled, sending the cat scrambling off his lap.

Six men burst into the room dressed in black combat exo-armor and bearing holstered pulse pistols. They surrounded Kendrick.

"He's our man. I want this little worm grilled until he bleeds out every shred of what he knows. Do a full deconstructive brain-scan and download the results to my classified file. No one else has access until I examine the data."

The men took hold of Kendrick, who tried in vain to fight them off. They restrained him in seconds.

"Please, no! Listen to me! I told you everything I know! I—"

The doors closed behind the men as they dragged Kendrick off. Silence.

Maxwell called the cat back to him. It gave him an annoyed look and walked off. Maxwell smiled; he had something to report to the council.

* * *

Hank Jensen grinned as the small woman exited the bar. She was a tough one. He couldn't help liking her. Maybe she was his salvation, but more likely, like most women in his life, she would turn out to be the devil incarnate. Either way, he couldn't turn down money right now.

He went over his options. Nearest he could figure, he didn't have any. A free-trader's life was always a gamble. How could he have known that the market for Polytungstan would collapse almost overnight? How could he have planned around that rebellion on

Carthas? It wasn't his fault. It wasn't fair, but fair or not, those two financial disasters had broken his back.

Still, he had to admit he'd reaped the benefits of chance and fate often enough in the past. You had to take the bad with the good. That was the price of freedom.

Jacbar, the bar owner, was one of the lucky ones. He got out with enough in savings to start a business. Most free-traders ended their lives in starport gutters. The odds were always with the house.

But there were the exceptions, those trader lords who struck it rich. They were fabulously wealthy, living in pleasure palaces on the rim of Manspace, free from corporate interference. The call of El Dorado still lured men to their deaths.

Hank wished, maybe even daydreamed, but didn't believe that load of shit for a heartbeat. He was content that for at least a while longer he would be free to roam the spaceways, master of his own destiny. The ride was what interested him, not the destination.

He checked the time on the comlink at his wrist. It was late. There was a lot of work to do before he spaced out. He activated the unit to call the one woman he loved. "Elsa, it's Hank."

A voice answered from the wristband. "Who else would it be? What's up?"

"We have ourselves a gig, honey. A passenger. I'm fixing to make a deposit right now. We blast out of here in an hour."

"What's the destination?"

Hank hesitated. "She says we're going to Raken."

"Oh no. Tell me you didn't," Elsa said.

"What?"

"You know what I mean. You said 'she.' This is another one of those hard-luck cases, isn't it? A damsel in distress?"

"Honey, I am the original hard-luck case. We can't afford to be too choosy. I haven't eaten in so long my stomach thinks my throat's been cut. I'm so poor that—"

"Enough! Just make the deposit and I'll handle the details. It's just that I have a bad feeling about this."

Hank grinned. "Are you sure it isn't jealousy?"

"I should say not! You're the most egotistical man I have ever known. You, my friend, are not the great prize you think yourself to be."

"Ah yes, but you love me anyway, don't you?" Hank switched off the com. Things were finally looking up.

He ordered another drink and started contacting the dockmaster to deposit funds to pay for his berth fee and fuel. After that he'd call his creditors. He was sure they'd be surprised that he was actually making a payment instead of an excuse.

CHAPTER THREE

The docks stretched for several kilometers. They were arranged like spokes shooting out from a central hub. Spaced evenly down the spokes were the individual berths, flat concrete segments crisscrossed by conduits and cables, highlighted here and there by spaceships rising majestically to the sky.

Protected walkways ran underground with blast doors leading to the outside at every berth, open until the time of launch.

Sai stood for a time, then began pacing back and forth at the blast doors to dock B, berth ten. She'd been waiting an hour and a half.

"Shit!" she said for the hundredth time.

She heard someone whistling down the walkway. Sai ducked in the threshold and readied her blade. The echoing tunnel prevented her from locating where the sound was coming from.

Then she heard singing.

" . . . *The next thing I heard was that lonesome sound, the drive kicking in, as they left the ground. And that's how my baby spaced out . . .*" It was Hank's voice.

Sai put away her whisperblade and stepped out of the doorway, hands resting on her hips.

Hank saw her and waved. "Hi, honey. Sorry I'm late."

"Where were you? I've been waiting for over an hour!"

"I had to take care of some business that got a little more complicated than I thought. We can leave in a few minutes."

"What about the fuel?"

"Already loaded. I paid the dockmaster to send one of his guys over and do it earlier," Hank said, walking to the ship and keying the door mechanism. "Any more questions?"

"No, let's just get off this damn planet."

The door opened. "After you, darlin'," Hank said, motioning for her to enter.

Sai gave the exterior of the ship a once-over before going inside. It was a squat, well-worn Pioneer-class scout ship, renovated for use as a trading vessel. "Can you even get this shit bucket off the ground?"

"What? My *Elsa*? Why she's as fine a ship as I've ever flown. Sturdy as a rock."

"Rocks don't fly."

"Look, if you'd rather wait for a commercial liner, that's fine with me, but the deposit is non-refundable."

Sai grumbled, but she followed as Hank led her up the ramp to the inner airlock. They cycled through and stepped into the cramped living quarters, which consisted of two sleeping bunks, a nutrition station, and a small workspace. Mostly it was cramped because of the trash that littered the floor and the piles of dirty laundry.

"Oh my," Sai said. "When's the last time you cleaned this place?"

"Clean?" Hank said, as if he'd never heard the word.

Sai fanned a hand before her face and wrinkled her nose. "It smells like something died in here."

Hank shrugged and walked forward to the cockpit.

"We need to get going. You can sit up here with me if you promise not to touch anything."

Sai followed him.

"Take a seat." Hank punched a few buttons and the engines thrummed to life.

Sai sat in the copilot's chair. "Thanks."

She watched as he deftly checked status lights and ran through pre-launch checklists. He moved efficiently, with military precision.

It was obvious that the man was in his element. Perhaps there was more to Hank Jensen than his drunken buffoon act.

"Clearance codes coming through. You'd better strap in," Hank said, fastening his G-harness.

He hit a bank of switches, and the engine's dull throb cranked into a high-pitched whine that set Sai's teeth chattering. Hank pushed the nav-control, and fusion fire erupted from the exhaust ports. The ship shot skyward as the G-forces slammed her back in her seat.

Out the front viewport, Sai watched the ground retreat and rush by in a blur as the ship shot up and forward, apparently on automatic. She scanned the control console, reaching out with her mind to sense the control circuits. The finer points of the navigational controls eluded her, but the computer interface was remarkably sophisticated. She scanned deeper. Complex patterns flashed across the control net. Her mind reached out to the circuitry and began to sort through the pathways of impulses.

"Stop it!" Elsa said, her voice emanating from the com.

"Oh my God," Sai said.

"What's wrong?" Hank asked.

Lurking beneath the navigational controls, the life support monitors, the hydraulics and cables, Sai detected a sentient entity. "What kind of hardware do you have controlling this thing?"

Hank stared at her. "It's some surplus military gear, why do you ask?"

"It's more than that."

"Why do you say that?" Hank shifted uneasily in his pilot's seat.

"I just know. This isn't a normal ship."

"I don't like her," Elsa said.

"Elsa, you aren't helping. Go back to plotting our course."

"She's a cyber-psi, and she has no respect for privacy!"

Sai had dealt with this all her life. When people discovered she was a computer telepath, they were uncomfortable and guarded. But usually it involved privacy of their bank accounts, or personal writings and images; this was the first time that she had actually entered another entity's mind. She had never experienced anything like it. Part of her felt ashamed because she truly had invaded Elsa in a way that was inexcusable.

"We all have our secrets it seems," Sai said, speaking toward the ship's console. "I am truly sorry. I had no idea that you were . . . *you*. Tell you what. You keep quiet about my secret, and I'll respect yours. I don't want to cause you any problems."

"I suppose in light of the circumstances, I should go ahead and formally introduce you to Elsa," Hank said. "She can't hide from you. Elsa, meet Sai."

"I would say it's a pleasure to meet you, but I'm still mulling over that shit-bucket comment, and I don't take kindly to uninvited guests snooping around in my thoughts."

"Again, Elsa, I'm sorry. I didn't realize. I won't do it again."

"See that you don't. I'm not as easily distracted by a pretty face as Hank."

Hank smiled and shrugged. "Elsa's program is based on an actual scout, a woman who patrolled the Outyonder during the Psi Wars. I knew her then. She was a friend. And now, she's a hell of a lot more than just a ship: she's my partner."

"Unfortunately, it seems like I'm mostly a silent partner. I must say that I would occasionally like to have a bit more say-so when Hank tries to make the occasional boneheaded move—such as taking on this run. You, little miss, are trouble."

"Now, now," Hank said. "Don't get catty. You two are going to have to get along."

He didn't speak again until they were free of Nebula Prime's polluted atmosphere. "Okay," he said. "We'll have you on Raken in no time. If you want to catch a few hours' sleep, there's an extra bunk."

"Clean sheets?" Sai asked.

Elsa piped in. "Don't count on it."

"Hey," Hank said. "I changed those sheets last year."

Sai reclined the copilot's chair. "I think I'll just stay here, thanks."

"Wise decision," Elsa said.

Sai closed her eyes and spent the rest of the uneventful flight napping.

* * *

Chandler arrived at Tyree's Emporium on the planet Raken for his rendezvous with the courier early enough to take a walk around the block, searching out of habit for anything that raised a warning flag: a conspicuous stranger hanging around a street corner, an occupied parked floater, a pedestrian who did a lot of walking but never seemed to get anywhere.

It paid to be cautious in his line of work. The job covered the rent, but it could also make a man dead.

On the job, some dicks liked to wear leathers and exo, which made them stand out like a corporate lord in a slum. Chandler favored the opposite strategy. For this job, he wore oil-stained tech-crew coveralls and a weathered jacket to blend in with the crowd and avoid attention.

He reached into his jacket pocket and repositioned his blaster, which weighed him down like a tombstone. He glanced at his watch. It was important to stick to the timetable.

Dusk, and the streets were busy, as usual. Day or night didn't matter: the ships came in at all hours, and thirsty, horny spacers poured into the city like wild dogs. Raken enjoyed the bounty of being a crossroads world where several major trade routes intersected. Hemdale City had the planet's largest starport, and the wildest Starman's Quarter to go with it.

Whorehouses and gin joints appealing to human and alien tastes were boom industries. Tyree's would be raking in the credits tonight.

The streets were still slick and reflective from the afternoon rainstorms. Floaters swooped overhead as the pedestrian traffic made its way across the pavement below. Colored lights danced from the street signs, and music blared from several bars. Savory and not-so-savory aromas from sidewalk food vendors teased and assaulted his senses with exotic meats and spices from across the galaxy. One stand offered a particularly exquisite-smelling snail the size of his fist, swimming in garlic sauce, which might have tempted Chandler except that he knew those critters lived on the droppings of something unspeakably vile.

As Chandler walked along a back alley, a hairy bisteen wearing drellskin pilot leathers staggered by arm-in-arm with a human female. The woman's hair was dyed blue, with lipstick to match, and she wore expensive leathers. The bisteen stopped suddenly and doubled over, vomiting a green mush.

The woman stepped back and covered her mouth and nose.

The bisteen spoke between heaves. "What's your problem?" He wiped his face with a hairy paw and reached for her.

She turned and walked away from the alien pilot.

"Your loss," the bisteen snarled, stumbling away down the street.

Chandler avoided the pair and walked out of the alley.

He looked up as the sun threw the last of its light across the red clouds and struck the sign, featuring a glowing green caterpillar wrapped around the word "Tyree's." One of the caterpillar's arms stuck out and raised and lowered a long, thin pipe to and from the bug's smiling lips. Every third puff, the caterpillar blew smoke rings that floated above its head and formed the word "Emporium" magically in the air.

Tyree's stood at the edge of Starman's Quarter and attracted a wide range of interesting guests. Apparently the local execs loved to slum there.

Chandler crossed the street toward the entrance and stepped through the winged doors into the smoke-filled bar. As he entered the room, his eyes scanned the crowd. Typical collection of spacers, down-and-outers, whores of multiple sexes scattered around, with a few exec-types trying to look spiff and, even though Tyree's didn't specialize in non-human activities, a couple of aliens. He couldn't make out an obvious courier anywhere, and the transponder key in his pocket was still.

The dimly lit club spread out in a circle. A catwalk lined with booth tables stretched around the circumference. Before him, a short staircase dropped into a central pit that held more tables, most of which were occupied. In dead center stood the bar, with six bartenders mixing drinks and quite a crowd lined up before it.

Chandler took a seat off to one side, facing the door. He checked his watch. If everything went smoothly, it wouldn't be long.

A slack-jawed waitress in a black dress sidled up to him. He told her his poison and in a few minutes she returned with a double Blackjack.

Chandler took a sip of his drink and considered his current situation. He'd already spent a portion of the retainer, making one more payment toward the *Marlowe*, his combination transportation, office, and home. In another three years, he'd own it outright, just in time to haul it to the junkyard.

He observed the patrons. Something nagged at him about the guy at the bar wearing the tattered trench coat. The man's hair was messed up and he needed a shave. He held his drink with both hands, cuddling it like a baby. But something didn't seem right.

Just then, he felt the transponder begin to vibrate in his pocket as a woman entered the bar. Her long blonde hair spilled over her shoulders and rained down the back of her black jacket. Under the jacket she wore a silver half shirt that exposed her taut belly. Her skin-tight mesh pants tucked into her boots at the knee. She didn't look like a spacer so much as a girl who wanted to be *with* a spacer. He shook his head. Way to stay low-profile.

Spacers looked at her and smiled. Some of the down-and-outs looked, too, but knew they didn't stand a chance with her.

Chandler watched as she stepped carefully down into the pit. He rose to intercept her. The man in the trench coat rose as well. Only then did Chandler realize what had bothered him about the man. His boots. They were polished to a military shine in contrast with his disheveled appearance.

Then Chandler noticed that two others like Mr. Shiny Boots, from different parts of the room, began moving in. Something was going down.

The girl noticed all of them moving toward her. She turned and bolted toward the exit.

"Stop!" Shiny Boots yelled, pulling his blaster and aiming it at her back.

Chandler didn't have room to draw in the closeness of the crowd, so he tackled the man. The blaster discharged and struck the wall above the courier's head. Chandler wrestled with the man as she continued to run.

A pair of dirtsiders entered the bar, laughing over some joke. She darted between them toward the door as the other men opened fire. Energy bolts cut down the two laughing men where they stood, sending blood and bones flying amidst the bright flashes and high-pitched belches of the weapons. The stench of smoldering flesh filled the bar.

Chandler twisted the blaster from Shiny Boots' hand and hammered his jaw with a solid right cross. The man went limp.

Chandler rose to sprint for the door, turning to cover his escape with a few rounds of blaster fire. Before he could get off a shot, he was blindsided by a chair. The lights went out in a flash of pain.

* * *

Sai pushed through the doors and cut to the right just as they exploded into splinters. She ran. She felt the transponder still buzzing in her pocket. Since they might be able to track her with it, she pulled it out and dropped it on the pavement.

She had caught a glimpse of the man who must have been her contact and had seen him fight with one of her attackers. She doubted he had any chance of making it out of the bar.

Before Sai could reach a turnoff, she heard booted feet clacking on the street behind her. People panicked as the heavily armed team stormed out of the bar.

Behind her, she heard one of the men shouting into a comlink, "Green Leader to all units! We're in foot pursuit northbound from Tyree's."

As she ran, pedestrian traffic grew thicker. Sai shouldered her way through the crowd. Energy bolts flashed and people cried out, tumbling to the ground to avoid death. Her pursuers fired recklessly.

Sai gained some ground, thankful that the team didn't seem to have anyone ahead of her. The men had to stumble over the prone bystanders. Even so, she barely made the corner as the energy bolts slammed into the stone wall behind her.

A taxi hovered near the curb. The old cabby stared at the approaching chaos, cigar dropping from his lips.

"What in the name of—"

Sai raced to the taxi, pulled open a door and jumped inside. "Let's get the hell out of here!"

"What?"

She whipped her whisperblade from her jacket and flipped on the power. She held the deadly glow of its blade centimeters from the cabby's right eye. "Go! Dammit, go!"

The cabby hit the engine and pulled up and away from the curb.

"Can't you go any faster?"

"I'm going as fast as I—"

An energy bolt slammed into the back of the cab, cut through the back seat next to Sai and burst through the front seat.

The cabby fell face-first into the dash, blood seeping from the corner of his mouth.

"Damn!"

Sai rolled over the seat, kicked open the door, and pushed out the cabby's corpse. It fell onto the road ten meters below. She took hold of the control lever and slammed it into high gear, turning onto the next street so fast that the anti-crash system took over and shot out an extra booster to send the cab up and over the oncoming traffic.

The cab bounced violently on a magnetic cushion over the vehicles. Sai jerked the lever to the side, overcompensating, and the cab dropped suddenly down onto the sidewalk so hard that the metal actually hit the concrete, sending off a shower of sparks.

People leaped out of the way as she careened around the next corner. She whipped the cab into a dark alley and parked it for a moment to consider her options.

She suspected that, while the men chasing her were on foot, they probably had transportation nearby. She'd never learned to drive a floater on manual, and if she let traffic control take over she'd be a sitting duck. The cab wasn't exactly inconspicuous.

Sai had to ditch it, create a diversion, and slip away unnoticed. She exited the vehicle and shut the door behind her. Closing her eyes, she concentrated on the floater's guidance system, creating within her mind an image of the programming pathways. The cyber-psi link began to form, merging her will with the data stream. She brushed past the limited security system and manipulated the guidance control. She executed a subroutine, then severed the link. The cab floated upward and entered the flow of traffic.

It didn't get very far.

Three blocks away, a sleek black sedan intercepted the taxi as it raced along. The sedan slammed into the side of the cab just as the vehicles approached a sharp corner around a tall building. The cab careened into the steel-and-glass structure, then exploded. Wreckage and fire rained down upon the street. The sedan banked and came back for another look.

Did they see that the taxi was unoccupied? If so, the search and destroy mission would continue. If not, they would think she was dead.

Sai knew it was best to play it safe and assume the worst. She needed to get to Dirion. He would know what to do.

She began walking toward Dirion's place, limping a little at first, but soon the pain was gone. Sai did her best to stick to the shadows or to mix in with groups where possible. Perhaps they hadn't seen her escape. Something bothered her. Something at the edge of her senses, but she figured it had to be the adrenaline. After a few blocks, her breath came easier and she thought she was safe.

She was wrong.

CHAPTER FOUR

Angus Brock eased his floater back into the flow of traffic and checked the position of the girl again on his monitor. He had been waiting outside Tyree's for her to show, and as soon as she had, he'd let his little friend loose on its mission.

The tiny nanite observer flew silently behind her. It had dogged her every move since she had stepped into the bar. Even now it buzzed, gnat-like, behind her as she took back alleys to her destination in the slums of Hemdale City. His monitor showed the view from just behind and over her shoulder where the nanite floated.

He had to admire the woman. She was sharp and tough. The Nebulaco Security force had bungled the job, jumping the gun before they were in proper position to cut off her escape. Rank amateurs. They were soft from bullying the weak and passive. It was obvious that they didn't have combat experience.

Brock had plenty, and he didn't want any more if he could help it. He had transferred into the Confed Secret Service from the Marines three years ago. This latest assignment didn't sit well with him.

He'd been working undercover for six months, starting with odd jobs and infiltrating the pirate Thorne's network of informants, spies, and muscle. Brock was trying to find out how Thorne was getting so much detail on shipping routes and cargos, how he was avoiding armed escorts so easily.

By demonstrating his skills at surveillance, Brock had so far found it easy to move up in the ranks of Thorne's organization. To date, this latest job was the most elaborate. Nebulaco Security had been chasing the girl he was tailing and they were tearing the hell out of the free zone to get her. Heads would roll over that one once the Confed heard about it. And Brock was going to make sure they heard plenty when he reported in to his handler.

Even though the girl was a thief, he was sorry that she would likely die. She'd been smart, and she played the game well. At least he didn't have to do it; his job was merely to track and report. He couldn't break cover. There was too much risk.

Where was she running?

Making a detour around a traffic accident, he keyed a query into the secure comlink to operations. He had to hand it to Thorne—the pirate had one hell of an information network. Brock was learning more about it every day. Each successful mission brought him closer to the secret of who and what Thorne actually was. Obviously he was more than just some hijacker preying on trade ships. The organization was too precise, too elaborate.

In moments he had his reply. A stream of data filled his monitor. The girl was ID'd as Sai Collins. Prior to accepting a job with Nebulaco, she had been a datalifter and courier who worked for a freelance oracle named Dirion.

Thorne's information from the underground also said Dirion's place was in the direction she was headed. It made sense. She needed a place to hole up.

Twenty minutes later he was parked across the street from some run-down apartments. He pulled back the nanite just before she entered the building. If Dirion was like most oracles he would have surrounded himself with scanners and security systems. No sense in letting him detect Brock's observer.

He lowered the window on his floater and released more nanites to circle the building in case she took a back way out.

Sighing, he clicked his comlink. Time to report to Thorne's people and earn his keep.

* * *

On the outside, the shabby apartment building looked like any other in this part of town. Built in the booming days of early exploration, it had once housed the best brothel in the sector. Now the building was abandoned except for the top floor, which was occupied by one man—Dirion. Sai felt reassured as she entered the familiar home of her adoptive father. If anyone knew what to do, he would. He had taken her in from the streets years ago after her parents died and left her alone.

She eased her way along the hallway. It was covered with peeling, water-stained wallpaper, but she knew that beneath the shabby façade lay sensors, scanners, probes, and automatic weaponry. There was enough security gear in the building to outfit a corporate stronghold. If Dirion didn't want to see you, you'd best stay well away from his home. It was a deadly mistake to come uninvited.

As far as she knew, she was the only one who ever visited Dirion. He dealt in information and handled all his business over the Grid. Dirion was the best freelance oracle on Raken, a powerful man, but in person he was vulnerable.

Sai opened the door to the inner sanctum. In the dim light, she could see him sitting on the cybernetic throne that permanently connected his mind to the Grid. A ring of neural probes encircled his bald head like a crown of thorns. His pale, nearly nude body was horribly emaciated, ribs sticking out in sharp relief. His limbs were vestigial organs, unfeeling and unused for decades.

"Hello, my little Sai," came Dirion's voice from hidden speakers. "I'm relieved to see you. I was afraid you wouldn't make it."

Sai collapsed into the dusty chair opposite him. "I take it you picked up on the mess over at Tyree's?"

"Who could miss it? The Grid is buzzing about it."

"Who were they?"

"Nebulaco Security."

"Damn," she said. "I can't believe they'd waste their heavy hitters on little people like me. Even risking trouble with the Confed to do it."

"You obviously have something they want very badly."

"Director Casey had something on everyone. There's no telling what it is."

"Do you have the package with you?"

"Yes." She opened her jacket and removed a black case.

"Can we open it?" Dirion said. "If we defuse the issue by releasing the secrets on that datastore, we can possibly get the heat off."

"No. It's sealed and code protected. The contents would be destroyed if we tried to open it. Nebulaco might want the data destroyed, or maybe this is vital data they need. Either way, I know the intended recipient wants what's inside. I'd have corporate security *plus* the client after me at that point. I have to finish the run somehow."

"Without knowing to whom it should be delivered, that could be a problem," Dirion said. "But let's examine what we know and see if we can extrapolate an answer."

Sai smiled. Dirion was true to form. Always the analyst. "We don't know much."

Dirion chuckled. "But we do. We know that at one time this information was most likely in the possession of Frederick Casey, the deceased security director for Nebulaco."

"True," Sai said.

"We know that just prior to his death, Casey was implicated in a scheme involving piracy of Nebulaco trade shipments. Supposedly, Casey's subordinate, a man named Vincent Maxwell, intercepted some communications that exposed Casey."

"And then Casey killed himself," Sai said.

"An implicit confession to some. But dead men can't mount a defense against any allegations, whether they're true or false."

"So how does this relate to the datastore in the courier pouch?"

"A dead man has no interest in further protecting himself, so I doubt it's evidence against Casey. A dead man has no need to increase his riches so I doubt it's more information for the pirates. What would a dead man want if he were falsely accused of a crime?"

Sai considered it for a moment. "Vindication? Revenge?"

"Very good. The logical conclusion in my estimation is that the contents of that pouch detail the truth about Thorne and the piracy against Nebulaco. But not the whole truth. If Casey had all the answers he wouldn't have waited to act. But he was close enough to be a threat, so he was removed. I'm sorry, Sai. But this information is hot and they won't stop until they get it."

"It's not your fault. I accepted the risk of working with Casey, running his data operations here and there when he needed my touch. I have to see this through. Let's look ahead. What do I need to do first?"

"First, I may have identified your intended contact. I have a report that a man named Mike Chandler was taken into custody at the scene. Nobody else was arrested."

He pulled up a holo image of Chandler. Sai nodded. "I saw him at Tyree's. He saved my life."

"He's a freelance operative. They're holding him in lockup, so he's likely undergoing interrogation. I'm putting a tracer on the data and sending you his comlink info. If his status changes you'll get an update. I believe he may have a powerful ally, but at this point, since he's in custody, he isn't a viable option. You can't complete the drop to him."

Sai began to pace the room. "So who was he working for? Who was the end customer? I need to get this thing off my hands."

"Odds are it's one of the corporate lords at Nebulaco. They could make the most of the data and act on it within the corporation."

"But it was Nebulaco Security who attacked me. If it's going back to the corporation anyway, do you think I can just contact them and give it back?"

"There's a power struggle going on. Their own security director either killed himself or was murdered. They wouldn't think twice about taking the pouch and then silencing you. We have to get the package to the lord who's trying to get it, but we need to figure out which one. If you go to the wrong person, this could blow up in your face."

"More than it already has?" She sighed. She felt as if she were being buried alive by the reality of the situation. Why was this happening to her? Why wasn't anything ever easy? "Okay then, what's the plan?"

"Let me check the starport databanks for transport. We need to get you off Raken."

"To go where?"

"Anywhere but here for now. You can lay low until I determine to whom the package needs to go."

"Do a search for Hank Jensen. He's the pilot I traveled with earlier today. He's an arrogant bastard, but I trust him."

"Trust is rare. Searching now."

As Dirion sent his senses through the Grid, Sai got up to go to the kitchen. "I don't suppose you have anything to eat in here anymore, do you? I'm starving."

"Sorry, all intravenous. I didn't bother restocking after you left the nest. Of course you're welcome to a vein full of saline with lipids and glucose on the side." Dirion's voice followed her to the speakers installed in the kitchen.

"No, thanks." Sai poured a glass of tepid water and drank it while Dirion's circuitry hummed around her.

"I think I've found your ship. Hank Jensen is still in port. I'm showing that he just made a credit purchase at the Silver Dollar Saloon, a spacer club in the Warehouse District."

"I know where that is."

"You'll need some traveling money," Dirion said. Sai heard a faint hum as a credit stick ejected from the side of Dirion's chair.

She walked over and took the stick. "You don't have to do this."

"Take it. I wish it could be more."

"Thank you. I never seem to be able to tell you how much I appreciate you. I love—"

An alarm sounded from one of Dirion's communication stations.

"Sai, you need to leave . . . now," Dirion said. "I've been monitoring the security channels. There's an attack squad coming this way. They have orders to kill, and they know you're here."

EPISODE TWO

CHAPTER FIVE

Angus Brock sat in his floater, parked in the shadows outside the stronghold of Dirion the oracle. The nanite observers he had placed around the building were still functioning and had reported no activity since the girl had gone inside. She was trapped.

He watched a sleek black sedan float to a stop at the curb. Four men clutching pulse rifles piled out—a Nebulaco Security heavy weapons squad. That didn't take long, he thought. The flow of communication between Thorne's underground network and corporate security was efficient. Why was Thorne so interested in Nebulaco getting this girl?

When they began marching straight for Dirion's building, Brock cursed. No combat sense at all. They were going to screw it up and get killed. He couldn't just let it happen without at least warning them. He exited his floater and rushed toward them.

"Hello there, officers!"

They froze and turned to face him.

He put on his most innocent grin. "I'm just a concerned corporate citizen trying to help. I don't mean to be rude or anything, but I just thought you might want to know that building over there is owned by an oracle."

There was no reaction.

"Oracle," Brock repeated. "As in stronghold. As in you might want to be a little more stealthy."

One of the men approached him. "Listen, bud, we don't need some civilian telling us our job," he said, stabbing Brock in the chest with an armored finger. "You need to back off and get out of the way."

Brock put both hands up and stepped back. He read the name stenciled on the man's breastplate armor. "Sorry, Lieutenant Larson, just trying to help."

Larson spoke into his comlink. "Red Team Leader to control. We are executing. Okay, men, let's go!"

Brock waved. "Have fun, Sparky!"

The team rushed across the street and into the building with little more than a cursory weapons check. Brock leaned against a light pole, cleaned his fingernails, and waited for the show. He knew it wouldn't be long.

A few minutes later, he saw lights flashing in the windows of the building as apparently random pulse-rifle rounds shot every which way. He heard faint screams. Shortly thereafter, Larson staggered out of the building, his face covered with dirt and blood from numerous wounds, uniform in tatters.

"Gee," Brock said. "Did he put up much of a fight?"

The man dropped to his knees, spent pulse rifle clacking to the pavement beside him. He spoke into his comlink. "Control, this is Red Leader. Red Team is gone. We need backup and medical. Send Blue Team to my location."

Brock knelt next to Larson and helped him apply direct pressure to a bleeding flesh wound on his lower leg. "As I was saying, Lieutenant Larson, oracles are known for heavily defending their bases of operation. Perhaps you might have been better off calling for backup before you stormed the building like a complete idiot."

"Fuck you."

"No thanks," Brock said. "Personally, I would have stationed men around the building to make sure no one could escape, then take a couple of guys and apply a few well-positioned shape charges. Eliminate the targets without risking the traps. But that's just my opinion."

Another team arrived about ten minutes later along with three ambulances. They ran to Brock and Larson.

"Here's the situation," Brock began.

The Blue Team leader ignored him. "What happened, Larson?"

"It was a trap. I figure the best thing to do at this point is to apply a few well-positioned shape charges. We'll blow the bastards to kingdom come!"

Blue Leader nodded and gave him a thumbs-up. "Right. Come on, men!"

Larson struggled to rise and go with them. Brock tapped him on the shoulder. "Make sure you use concussion charges instead of that incendiary stuff or you'll have an inferno on your hands. This whole block will go up."

Larson shoved him. "Don't tell us our business. We're professionals." With that, he limped into the building behind Blue Team.

Brock shook his head and leaned against the pole again to watch the circus continue.

* * *

Fire exploded into the night sky, the building burning uncontrollably as Sai shouldered her way through the large crowd already gathering to watch the spectacle. A short-haired woman clutching a young boy blocked Sai's path. The woman pointed and gasped as the fire progressed.

"I'm glad we don't live there," the boy said.

Sai maneuvered around the mother and son. An empty pit opened in her stomach. She would never see Dirion again.

"Move aside, people!" a voice called over a broadcaster. Emergency vehicles tried to lower themselves to work the blaze, but the crowd didn't seem to notice them. The people stood entranced by the fire.

Sai pushed her way through the throng, tears blurring her vision. She looked back at the destruction wrought on Dirion's home. The entire top section of the apartment building had blown up. Nothing remained above the fourth floor.

Earlier, Dirion had given her instructions and hurried her out the back exit to the stairs that led down to the street. As the door had shut behind her, she'd had no idea that moments later the building would erupt into flame.

Dirion was dead. He was gone. She reached out and braced herself against the wall of the building closest to her.

His death was all her fault. She had led her pursuers right to him. She nearly doubled over, but she had no time for tears. No time for grief. Dirion wanted her to forge on. All she had left was her life, and even that wouldn't last long if these people didn't get out of the way. She had to get off Raken.

As she struggled through the crowd, a face caught her attention. It was the security man from the bar who had first spotted her. He watched the blaze progress along with his men, all still wearing their trench coats.

Sai moved on, trying to keep low and out of sight. Just as she reached the corner she heard one of them shout, "There she is! All units, this is Green Leader. The girl's alive!"

Damn! She turned the corner, hoping to outrun them, slowed as they were by the crowd. She started toward a muddy back alley, trying to lose herself among the onlookers. But they were watching the fire, blocking her path. Frustrated, panicked, she tried to push between two large men.

"Watch it, lady," the biggest one said, irritated.

"Then move!"

He turned sideways and let her pass. "You have a problem," the man said.

Sai slipped into the shadows and ran past trash incinerators and winos, hearing the thunder of booted feet running behind her.

"She went this way!"

Energy bolts slammed into the walls around her, spraying her with debris. She rushed down an alleyway, diving for the first doorway she saw. It was locked.

"She's in that alcove!" They were closing in.

Sai pulled the whisperblade from her jacket pocket and activated it, plunging the plasma-edged weapon through the lock, easily melting and cutting the deadbolt. She kicked the door open and hurried inside. She shoved the door closed, but it couldn't be secured. Damn.

The dark room was dusty and filled with old furniture. In the dim light she spotted a workbench off to one side. She dragged the bench over to hold the door closed. With the door blocked, the room was pitch black, her eyes not yet adjusted. She moved through the room, sweeping her hands before her to try and find another exit. She hit a wall at the same moment the guards began pounding on the door.

She moved faster along the wall and found a staircase just as energy bolts pierced the door, sending slivers of wood flying. Sai rushed up the stairs to the roof. These buildings weren't spaced too far apart; perhaps she'd be able to jump to safety.

The squad pushed through her barrier and began searching the lower level.

"Here's a stairway," someone said.

Sai cursed. A stack of chairs stood on one of the landings. She kicked them over to slow their progress and continued climbing.

When she finally made it to the roof, she found it old and in disrepair. It sank slightly under her weight. Carefully, she tiptoed to the edge and peered over. It was a long drop.

She hurried around the perimeter of the roof, searching for some way down. No luck. Across the way, the roof of the Bryant Hotel was her only chance of escape, but she wasn't sure she could make that jump.

She heard the men coming up the stairs. She was out of time. She activated the whisperblade and prepared to throw. Her cyber-psi senses reached out to touch the weapon's control circuits and she activated the flight controls.

She threw the blade, sending it sailing to cut deeply into the roof behind her, further weakening the structure. She controlled its path, manipulating its tiny repulsor beams, making several passes. She heard the squad tossing the chairs out of the way as they climbed.

At her mental beckoning, the whisperblade returned to her hand. She hoped it would be enough. "It's now or never," she whispered. She moved back, took a deep breath, and glanced toward the doorway from which the first of the men burst onto the roof. She ran toward the edge of the building and jumped.

Time suspended as she flew through the darkness. She landed hard, her momentum carrying her into a shoulder roll.

She glanced back and saw the rest of the squad pour through the doorway, heedless of the weak roof. She turned and rushed toward a door on the far side of the hotel. Suddenly, she heard a crash as several of the men fell completely through. The others froze where they were, then took aim at Sai on the other roof.

Sai dove for the cover of the entrance. Energy bolts chipped the bricks. She threw open the door and rushed inside.

She sprinted along the carpeted hallway to a lift and pressed the down button. She paced the floor, waiting for the doors to open. She decided that once she got to the ground floor, unless there were more men waiting, she would head for the Warehouse District of the Starman's Quarter. She needed to reach the port tonight and get off this rock before they could tighten the noose.

Finally the doors hissed open, and she stepped into the lift. "Ground floor," she said. The doors closed, and she felt the lift descend.

* * *

Brock stared at the path of destruction and shook his head. What a bunch of bumbling idiots! They were here to stop one girl and what happens? They burn half a city block, killing dozens of innocent people, but not the girl they were looking for. Worse yet, the damned explosion took out his nanites so he had lost track of the girl, too.

Larson listened to a report on his comlink, then turned to the other security men. "Green Team has her cornered in a building three blocks away. Let's get over there and end this thing," Larson said. "We can't let this woman get away. It's personal now."

Brock wondered if they were going to blow up that other building, too.

The haggard remains of Blue Team hesitated.

"What's the problem?" Larson asked.

One of the men gestured at the sea of people between them and their car. "Are you kidding? We can't get through that crowd."

Larson sighed. "Why do I always get the incompetents?" He moved to the edge of the crowd. "Security! Make way, people! Coming through!"

Nobody moved.

He yelled again, but still no one moved.

"I don't believe this." He pressed a button on his comlink. "Green Leader, this is Red Leader. We're having trouble reaching you. It's going to take some time for us to get there. Do you have the situation handled yet?"

"Hell no, it isn't handled. I lost three men when a roof collapsed, and the target got away. We've lost her."

Brock couldn't keep the grin off his face. Professionals—what a joke. This assignment was over. They had promised him that if he showed aptitude on this task, he would be moved up the ladder. Brock suspected that the fact that he was the only one who wasn't an idiot on this backwater planet would be enough. He needed to get closer to determine the true power structure of Thorne's organization. So far he had been shuffled through a series of flunkies and middlemen. He'd been given Grid contact addresses and drop boxes. But nothing had given him much insight.

He was due to report to his Confed handler soon. Obviously this event on Raken was more than a simple act of corporate theft. Thorne was either controlling or actively cooperating with Nebulaco Security. That connection was deep and obviously hadn't died with Director Casey. What was the courier carrying? What was the connection with Thorne? When he returned to his vehicle he'd prepare a coded transmission. Maybe Confed Secret Service could sort it all out.

CHAPTER SIX

Nebulaco Security Director Maxwell sat at the head of a conference table surrounded by the holographic forms of Nebulaco's Council of Lords. Their ghostly images interacted with each other in the shared virtual environment of the cathedral-like room and were now engaged in heated debate.

The council consisted of Lord Oke, a young man with a weak chin who seemed more interested in how his hair looked than the problem at hand; Lady Hemming, a big-boned middle-aged woman with steel-blue eyes and a stern countenance—as always, she was in outrageous costume, today appearing in a pith helmet and bush jacket, but because she was a corporate lord, Maxwell knew better than to tell her how foolish she looked—and finally, there was Lord Randol, who seemed the most focused and reasonable of the group.

Maxwell smiled calmly.

Randol looked at him. "What exactly have you been doing, Maxwell? Sitting in your new office all day counting your new salary? Why hasn't progress been made in the hunt for this missing data that you insist proves Casey's guilt?"

"Milord, I have confirmed that former Director Casey had an elaborate intelligence network within the corporation that was assisting him in his clandestine pursuits. I've just begun interrogations on one of his agents, who has already admitted that he stole the data per Casey's standing order. I have every confidence that we shall retrieve the data as the investigation progresses."

"What possible motive could Frederick Casey have for preserving data after his death?" Randol asked.

Maxwell shrugged. "Obviously it wouldn't help him, but perhaps it was a mutual agreement he had established with his accomplices. There are almost certainly more conspirators involved in this plot. A quick removal of the evidence would facilitate their escape from justice."

"And what of Thorne?" Randol asked.

"Thorne is not some sneak thief or pickpocket. He has excellent resources and, apparently, the ability to vanish without a trace. Even our reward money hasn't enticed anyone to provide information concerning his whereabouts."

"And why is that? How is it that a vicious pirate could win the hearts of the common people? You'd think they'd jump at a reward," Randol said.

"Either through loyalty or fear, no one seems willing to provide credible leads."

"Could it be that our security personnel are bullying the people too much and Thorne seems to offer an end to that harassment?"

"Lord Randol, in one breath you accuse me of being too lax in my duties and in the next you claim that I am too forceful. Could it be that I am neither?"

The other lords laughed. Oke stood and spoke, his voice feminine and detached. "Well, I for one am in favor of the methods used by our new security director. He has produced commendable results. If nothing else, his exposure of Casey is laudable."

Randol scowled. "I still have concerns."

Hemming adjusted her pith helmet and rolled her eyes. She was conferencing from a jungle on the planet Zaan, where she was on some sort of hunt. "Gentlemen, let us also remember that it was Maxwell who originally brought this Thorne to our attention and practically begged us to provide him with more resources to fight the problem at its onset. Now Thorne has grown from a minor annoyance to a major threat."

"Milords, the situation also appears to be unique to our corporation. Since we are being specifically targeted, perhaps this is an indication that our competitors may be financing Thorne," Maxwell said. "Galaxia Inc., Asta Enterprises, Three Star . . . none of our corporate rivals are suffering as we are."

Oke spread his hands. "Let's face it: Thorne has brought us to our knees. We are as diversified as possible. We manufacture everything from spaceships to lingerie, but unless we can get our product to market, this corporation does not make money. My financial advisers report to me that some divisions of the corporation will become insolvent soon if the situation doesn't change. In order to stay in business we need to maintain safe shipping lanes."

"The Confed is supposed to provide that protection. We certainly pay enough into the system," Hemming said.

Maxwell shook his head. "The Confed has regular patrols, and they have expanded their escorts, but there are simply too many shipments to protect."

"Strange that the ships under escort are never the ones attacked," Randol said.

Maxwell turned to look directly at Randol's avatar. "Milord, you wouldn't think it strange if you factor in a corrupt security director who was obviously providing the details of which shipments would be guarded."

Randol shook his head. "I still don't believe it. And I won't believe it until I see this so-called proof that you can't seem to locate."

Maxwell smiled. "I'm confident it will be obtained soon. With the traitor gone, we can continue to utilize the Confed, and we can also hire private mercenary ships as guards without fear that our plans will be exposed. However, the larger issue remains, as Lord Oke pointed out, that we need an influx of capital. Heavily armed convoys are expensive."

Oke stood to take the floor. "We really only have one option. In order to raise the necessary capital we must simply sell off some of our stock holdings. While it's true that we shall hold less, a small sell-off won't matter. No one has a block of stock that can compete with our holdings or we would have heard of it, and certainly no one person has enough to claim a lordship on the council."

"But our dividends will diminish as well," Hemming said. "We have a certain living standard to maintain."

"You're both being ridiculous," Randol said.

"We won't have any dividends at all if we keep losing money," Oke said. "This gives us a chance to reinvest, and it buys some time to eliminate Thorne. Hopefully, when the company recovers we'll be receiving larger dividends than we do now, even with fewer shares."

"Interesting," Hemming said. "How much are you proposing?"

"Perhaps a five percent block from each of us. Does that sound acceptable?" Oke said.

"You want us to give up fifteen percent of the corporation?" Randol said. "Are you insane? With the outstanding shares already out there, that would leave us owning less than fifty percent of the corporation. Utter stupidity."

Oke turned red. "Lord Randol, there is no reason to be insulting. It's a reasonable suggestion. Although the stock may be out there, it is dispersed among throngs of minor investors. There is no credible threat to our authority."

"This sounds like an excellent opportunity," Maxwell said. "A massive influx of capital would solve many of our problems."

Randol glared at him. "Director Maxwell, please limit your comments to the subject of your expertise, which is simply security. You are not a lord and have no right to an opinion on this matter."

"Please accept my abject apologies, Lord Randol. I meant no offense." Maxwell lowered his eyes and bowed to him.

"Lord Oke, when you have more information, we'll discuss this further," Hemming said. "Until then, is there any other business to discuss? I have a hunt to attend."

* * *

Helen Randol sat before the information terminal in her cabin aboard the *Aurelius* and examined her schedule yet again. It seemed that she was destined for the next two years to be saddled with a never-ending series of classes consisting primarily of useless material.

It was well understood that as the only daughter of a lord, and therefore a future lady herself, Helen did not need to bother with a formal education in order to live extravagantly. However, if she wanted to one day lead the corporation rather than simply be a leech who drained the coffers of her apportioned share, she knew she'd have to apply herself to her education.

Her father took such things seriously, and so did she, which made it doubly frustrating to see the litany of worthless courses such as Rigelian Comparative Anthropology. Could they actually be serious? How would that be of any use in running the affairs of a corporation?

She turned off the course schedule and chose some music. Soft blues tones filled the cabin. She lay down on her bunk and sighed. She stared through the viewport next to the bed into the darkness. She dimmed the lights in the room until the fainter stars became visible.

She would endure her time at the university. She would suffer the pompous nattering of her fellow students as they went about their daily nonsense, the vacant flattery of those trying to win her favor, and the machinations of those trying to rise on the social scale by bringing her down. She would endure it because of her father. She needed to be strong to take her place in the corporation so she could prevent it from falling under the influence of idiots like Oke and his ilk once her father was too old to continue.

Ever since Helen's mother died, she had tried to take care of her father, and she had learned early on that the best way she could do so was by learning how to succeed him. The corporate world was brutal, and it had taken its toll on him over the years. He had survived buyout and takeover attempts, controversy and treachery. But the biggest threat so far had been the pirate Thorne and his raids on their shipping lines.

She knew her father and former Security Director Casey had suspected that there was a traitor in some prominent position within the company, and they organized an internal investigation to identify him. Somehow everything had turned upside down with the loss of Casey. Part of her wanted to delay attending the university, but her father had argued against it.

"So do you think there will ever be a time when there isn't a crisis? What then? Will you ever go?" he'd said.

She had agreed, begrudgingly. But as she lay on the bunk in her dimly lit cabin and faced the prospect of the next two years, she had second thoughts.

The sound of music was suddenly replaced by the blare of a warning klaxon, and a red emergency light flashed in the room.

Helen looked out the viewport. She could see something flash, then flash again, and she realized that it was a rapidly approaching ship firing upon the *Aurelius*. A ball of plasma engulfed the ship, turning the viewport white. The ship shuddered and Helen was tossed across the room.

The lights went out and the normal sounds of cycling air and the hum of ambient engine noise ceased, leaving behind a cold, empty silence. Helen crawled back to the viewport and watched the ship close in. It was mottled and pieced together, armor plating sloppily welded here and there across the bow. Pulse cannons and plasma guns bristled from every available mountable surface. Someone had smeared black and white paint on the nose. It was a nod to an earlier time, a classic calling card—a skull and crossbones.

Pirates.

Helen had been trained from childhood how to deal with attacks. As the daughter of a lord she was always at risk. She kept a handgun and a jump bag in her cabin. She grabbed them immediately, racing along the passageways toward the life pods. Often pirates would ignore those who escaped in pods because there was no profit in retrieving them and no gain in destroying them. Occupants of the pods might rest in suspended animation for years before being found, but Helen was sure that her father would send a Confed search party for her. If she escaped in a pod before the pirates realized she was aboard, they would likely be happy with capturing the yacht.

No one challenged her as she rushed down the corridors. As she approached the engine rooms she heard someone in a side corridor ahead. She drew her pistol and cautiously went forward. There was a man in the coveralls of a crewman picking up the contents of a bag he had just spilled. It contained gold ornaments and silverware. She pointed the gun at his back. "So helping yourself, eh?"

The man put his hands up and slowly turned around. She read the name tape on his coveralls. "Radje? Mind telling me what you're doing?"

"Sorry, Your Lordship, milady, but . . . well . . . I figured it was better than them pirates getting it."

Helen sighed and shook her head. "Fool, let's just get out of here before they find us. The gold won't do you any good if you're dead." She waved him forward with the gun barrel.

Radje lifted the bag. "Can I keep it then?"

"I don't care. Just hurry!"

The escape pods were just ahead at the next intersection. Six pods with open doors awaited. Helen headed toward the first open pod door.

"Hold it!" a voice commanded. Helen turned to look and saw a man armed with a pulse rifle taking aim. She moved to fire and would have made the shot, but Radje bumped against her as he dove into the open pod.

Her shot went wild as the pod door closed with Radje inside. The pod immediately launched.

The pirate with the pulse rifle didn't miss. The shot took her in the chest.

CHAPTER SEVEN

"Why did you attack my men?"

"I told you," Chandler said. "I walked toward the bar to get a refill and some guy pulled a blaster on me. What would you have done?"

Chandler sat restrained in an interrogation chair being worked over by Nebulaco's finest. After he was patched up from being blindsided in the bar, they brought him to the detention center for questioning. That was at least three hours ago. He was tired, thirsty, hungry, and he thought he had a mild concussion.

The room was a gray box, and he sat in the middle of it under a lamp hot enough to bake cookies. The lead interrogator, a dark man with one eyebrow named Sergeant Cox, had the personality of a hemorrhoid.

"They were Nebulaco Security men on special assignment. You blew an important operation."

"They didn't identify themselves. I had no idea what was going on. Besides, I was in the free zone. Corporate Security isn't even supposed to be there."

Sergeant Cox sighed and massaged his temples. "Why did you help the girl?"

"What girl? You keep talking about a girl. I don't know any girls on this stinking planet."

Cox got up in his face. His breath smelled like old cheese. "Don't play games with me, Chandler. I want answers or you're going to spend the rest of your life in a deep, dark hole that smells like your own shit."

There was a knock on the door. Cox walked over, opened the door, and spoke briefly with another man. He returned white.

"Mr. Chandler. I am very sorry for the misunderstanding," Cox said. "There has been a mistake. I apologize, and I am to express my regrets and extend to you every courtesy of the Nebulaco Corporation." His hands shook as he removed the restraints from Chandler and helped him up from the hot seat. "I hope you'll have it in your heart to forgive us."

Chandler shook his head. "What?"

"I had no idea who you were. Those field officers gave us misleading information. We'll have you out of here immediately."

Chandler grinned through his bruises. The ass-kissing continued for another ten minutes, all the way out the door, where he found a limo waiting for him. He looked behind him and wondered how many people had left the place in style, not counting those who left in a box, of course.

The door to the limo hissed open and Randol nodded to Chandler. "Get in."

Chandler slid into the seat beside him. The limo smelled like it had just come off the showroom floor. It had a fully stocked bar and a plush interior. He looked at the old man for a moment, then raised his arm and moved it backward through Randol's body. The image flickered, then re-formed as Chandler pulled his arm back from the holo. "Didn't think so."

"Somebody talked," Randol said.

"No shit. What do you need me for? You should be the detective."

The limo pulled away from the detention center and rose in a lazy circle toward the traffic flow.

* * *

Sai trudged through the rainy streets, past the shanties and closed shops of the dilapidated West Side. It may have been risky to walk those streets, but there were fewer people to dodge, and this way she could sneak back into Starman's Quarter and possibly avoid detection. Nebulaco Security had no doubt alerted the taxi companies and public transports by this time.

She glanced upward and saw the beacon lights of the starport through the mist of falling rain. The lights cut sharply through the darkness, radiating into multiple spectrums. They beckoned wandering starcraft home to port, back to a safe haven. The Silver Dollar wasn't too far away now. Hopefully, she could find Jensen, leave quickly, and try to find a safe haven of her own.

She heard something behind and above her. She whirled around. Movement up high. The hum of flywires cut through the white noise of the rain. Three men flew toward her out of the darkness, each clad in black and red. It was a street gang. Sai recognized the colors: Tenel's bunch—the Flyboyz.

They glided gracefully toward Sai. Each man had devices grafted to his forearms that shot molecular wire-lines with static hooks on the ends. They fired the hooks ahead to lock onto an array of anchor points the gang had mounted throughout their territory, then glided forward on the wires. As they approached the end of their lines, they released and retracted the trailing hooks and shot them forward again for another great step. Fire, glide, release, fire—they flew toward her like angels of doom.

Sai crouched low and tried to disappear into the shadows, but one of the Flyboyz let out a shrill whistle and Sai knew she'd been spotted.

She ran for it, hoping to find someplace where she could more easily defend herself. Here on the street, she was wide open. To make a stand would be suicide.

This just wasn't her day.

Sai looked back to check their proximity, but she could no longer see them. Before she could turn forward again, a booted foot shot out from nowhere and kicked her in the back, driving her face-first into the curb.

The three men laughed. Sai pushed herself to her feet. She spit blood and wiped her split lip with her hand, glancing briefly at the crimson stain on her fingers.

The Flyboyz landed, surrounding her.

"Nice night for a swing," she said.

The smallest of the three kicked Sai full force in the stomach. She doubled over, retching in pain.

"That's it, Tork!" the second Flyboy said. "Give it to her!"

The third, clearly the leader, stood well back from the others, saying nothing—only watching.

Little Tork strutted before Sai. "Who are you, bitch? What are you doing in our sector?"

Sai looked up, rubbing her stomach with one arm as she tried to catch her breath.

"I'm Taj," Sai lied. "Tenel knows me."

"Tenel knows everybody so that don't mean shit to us. You got caught in our space so you gotta pay. You got credits? Or," the little man smiled, "do we take it out in pain?"

Tork released his flywire like a whip and cracked it down on the pavement beside Sai. He arced a loop of the molecular wire, and it sliced cleanly through the curb. Sai glanced down and watched the curb slide into the gutter.

Her eyes glazed for an instant as she reached out with her mind toward the trio. Her cyber-psi senses traveled the twisted paths of the circuits that tied them to their flywires. She could see the psychedelic fire of electrical impulses at the bases of their brains and the electro-neural pathways to the flywire bands. She readied a data command. Already, she could see the second Flyboy standing by, command sequences poised to attack.

Tork kicked her again, this time in the face.

"Speak up!" he said. "What's it gonna be, babe?"

Sai rode out the wave of agony. Strange, she thought, how the smallest assholes always have the biggest mouths.

"I don't have any money. If I did, I sure as hell wouldn't be sitting out here in the rain." She rubbed along her bruised ribcage again, this time grasping the whisperblade, hidden out of their sight.

Tork grabbed her wrist and pulled her to her feet. His hand slipped under her jacket as he yanked her close. "I guess that means tonight's your lucky night!"

Sai stared deep into the Flyboy's eyes.

"Could be," she said smiling, "but not yours!" She whipped the bright, humming blade out of her jacket in a cross draw, and Tork's severed hand flopped to the ground.

He screamed.

Sai dove to the right and mentally sent the command sequence.

"Whisperblade!" shouted the third Flyboy, who had kept his distance. He backed farther away to get full use of his flywires and tried to fire, but couldn't.

Sai threw the whisperblade at the second, who still hadn't grasped what was happening. The whisperblade flew like an angry hornet.

The Flyboy saw it coming and tried to duck behind a waste disposal unit. The whisperblade hissed and whipped around the corner to its victim.

Sai heard the shriek but didn't see the blow. In an instant, the knife flew back to her. The blade gleamed, but the handle was covered in blood.

The final Flyboy stood on the curb across from Sai. They stared each other down, thirty paces apart.

Tork still screamed unintelligible prayers as he clutched his stump.

Sai relaxed her combat stance. "All I want is to be on my way," Sai said.

"Then go," the leader said.

"I'm sorry about your friends. I didn't choose this fight. I didn't want any of this to happen."

"It could have gone the other way." The man gave her a sweeping gesture indicating she was free to pass.

Sai relinquished her control of the flywires and gave the man a small salute.

He gave her a nod, then moved toward his fallen comrades. Tork wasn't screaming anymore. Sai looked over and saw that he had passed out from shock and loss of blood. His body lay in a heap. The rain washed his rich red blood down the sidewalk into the gutter.

She continued toward the docks of the Starman's Quarter. A few blocks down the road the comlink vibrated on her wrist. It was the status update on Chandler that Dirion had set up. The man had been released. Sai cut into an alcove and keyed in the com number Dirion had obtained for the man. She might be able to make the delivery after all.

* * *

"I understand how you feel, Mr. Chandler," Randol said.

"No, you don't. Let me hit you in the head with a chair and have some asshole yell at you for a few hours. Then you'll begin to have an idea about how I feel. Only I don't have a mansion where I can go home to feel sorry for myself."

"At least you're getting to go home."

"Sorry," Chandler said with a sigh. "It's been a long day. Thanks. I do appreciate you saving my skin. But you know this is a stupid move if you want to keep your name out of this mess," Chandler said.

"I hired you because you had the integrity to keep my secrets. I assume you didn't reveal anything to your interrogators?"

"I am the most pitiful victim of circumstance that you can imagine."

"Well, had I not acted when I did, you would've eventually been taken in for a deconstructive scan and they would have discovered every detail of your mission. As it is, they can suspect and surmise all they wish, but that's far preferable to solid evidence."

"Not to mention that I would've been an empty husk at the end of it."

"In any event, the situation has changed. The courier is no longer my primary concern. My private yacht, the *Aurelius*, was attacked by pirates a few hours ago. My daughter, Helen, was aboard. It can't be a coincidence."

"Is she all right?"

"Shortly after I learned of the distress call and the attack I got a simple anonymous message: 'We have her.' Nothing else."

"Listen," Chandler said, "couriers, security teams, pirates, and kidnapping. I want to help you, but I can't work in the dark. Tell me what's going on. If you're not prepared to do that, drop me off here. I'll help myself to a pocket full of these little bottles of booze and I'll be on my way."

"It's complicated."

"It always is," Chandler said.

Randol nodded. "Five years ago I sponsored Frederick Casey to the position of director of security. I thought he had great potential—all-the-way-up-the-ladder kind of potential. When the pirate Thorne started the attacks against Nebulaco, Casey recognized early on that there must have been a leak high up in the corporation. I was the only lord he trusted to keep in the loop as his investigation progressed. Neither Oke nor Hemming inspire confidence."

Chandler nodded. "From all I've heard about them they're idiots."

"Please, Mr. Chandler. They are lords and deserving of a modicum of respect for that fact alone."

Chandler shrugged and Randol continued.

"Casey was sure that the only hope of success lay in an internal investigation. The Confed patrols were ineffective. Thorne doesn't just wander around looking for targets. For the last three years, every raid has been a directed strike. A quick surgical action in and out, almost no chance of being caught. All of our Trojan horse missions—heavily armed ships disguised as merchants—have failed. In any event, we also realized that there was great potential for personal danger. Therefore, we established a protocol for any and all evidence that he had obtained to be delivered to me upon his death."

"And I take it that Casey is dead and the courier woman has this evidence?"

Randol's hologram nodded. "An allegation was brought forward that Casey was the one leaking information to Thorne. Before any hearing or review of the evidence Casey was found dead. Reportedly a suicide."

"I take it that you aren't buying it."

"It's ridiculous. He must have gotten too close and the traitor killed him," Randol said. "I need someone I can trust to help me, Mr. Chandler. There isn't a soul working for the corporation that I rely on completely. I've been betrayed too many times."

"I can see that. Your courier was ambushed at a secret meeting. The route of your yacht was compromised. Yeah, you're in trouble. But we do have a few things to look for. Typically, pirates aren't wasteful. The ship would be too precious to destroy, and since they obviously know who your daughter is, she is likely safe enough for now. They'll hold out for a ransom. The question is, how much would you pay to get your daughter back?"

"Mr. Chandler, I may be ruthless in aspects of business, but I would give up everything for my daughter."

Chandler bowed his head for a moment, then met Randol's eyes and held them. "You realize that no matter how much you give up, they're unlikely to release her alive."

Randol shifted uncomfortably as if the thought had been pounding in his brain, but he refused to acknowledge it. He looked away and closed his eyes. Finally, he turned back to Chandler. He nodded. "That's where you come in."

Chandler's comlink vibrated. He looked at the source information. "I don't know this ID, but it's coded urgent." He hit the button to take the call. The viewscreen displayed the image of the girl from the bar.

"Chandler?" the girl said. "We were supposed to meet earlier at Tyree's."

Chandler looked up at Randol and smiled.

"The mysterious courier. I'm glad to know you're still alive."

"I'd like to finish my run and make the drop. Can you meet me somewhere?"

"I'm on my way to the dock. You can try to meet me at my ship, the *Marlowe*. It's berth twenty-seven on dock D. I can be there in about an hour."

"Got it."

"Someone sold us out, so there may be people watching. If for some reason you can't make the drop . . . hold on." Chandler muted the circuit and looked up at Randol. "What's your secondary location?"

"At this point, all attempts at stealth are pointless. Just have her bring it to me directly."

Chandler nodded and unmuted the com. "If you can't deliver it to me here, take the data directly to Lord Randol of Nebulaco. Book passage to Trent. Lord Randol is on the third moon, Mordi. Ask for his security head, Jorgeson. Randol will be expecting you."

"Thank you," she said.

"Be careful. You're a lucky one, but sooner or later luck runs out."

Chandler ended the call. "Well, that simplifies things. If I get the package, I'll hand deliver it to you on Trent, then while your people go over it, I can start working on finding Helen."

"The floater can take you back to your ship, but feel free to utilize it as you will while on Raken. In addition, I'm setting up a meeting for you with Vincent Maxwell, the head of Nebulaco Security. While I don't fully trust him, he'll have more information for you about the

Aurelius." A credit stick slid out of a slot on the console. "If you need to purchase equipment or supplies, simply use this. I will be available if you need to contact me."

Chandler snagged the chip and grunted a reply.

"Good luck, Mr. Chandler," Randol said as his holo image faded, leaving Chandler alone in the limo.

Lords and security, couriers and betrayals. Confed patrols and pirates. This whole thing was spiraling out of control. But, other than a bump on the head, he couldn't complain about much. The pay was good. He cocked open an eye and looked around him. The fringe benefits were excellent so far. Chandler reached for a miniature bottle of Blackjack, cracked the tiny seal, and took a drink.

Still, it made him uncomfortable to be running with the big dogs. He was more the cheating-husband locator, the insurance-scam investigator. All this was over his head. But, in spite of the fancy trappings, there was a rat somewhere. He was a good rat catcher no matter how far uptown the rodents lived.

He reached forward to the override control panel. He had some stops to make for supplies. He intended to see how good Randol's credit was. If he was taking this on, he wanted to make sure he had what he needed to survive.

* * *

Maxwell stormed through the hallways of the security building toward his office. People carefully avoided him, rushing to move out of his way, fearful of his infamous temper and barbed tongue. It would be unhealthy for one's career to attract his notice at such a time.

Maxwell burst into his office and slammed his fist into the control that sealed his doors. "Son of a bitch!" he screamed. "Pompous ass! How dare he treat me like a lackey!"

Maxwell grabbed a delicate crystal sculpture from his desk. It had been created by a blind artist from Rigel, a member of a species whose artisans devoted a lifetime to construct a single, perfect masterpiece. It took him a fraction of a second to shatter the object against the nearest wall.

But even as he watched the shards of razor-sharp crystal explode and dance, glittering to the floor like tiny fireflies, he knew that it was true. He was only a lackey. He was the hired help. No matter how he struggled, no matter how high he climbed in the corporation, he would always be expendable. He would always be employed at the whim of the Council of Lords.

What made them any better than him? They held their position through an accident of fate. A genetic lottery. They were the pampered and worthless descendants of those who had founded the megacorporations. They had, for the most part, never worked a day in their lives, and if they had, it could hardly be called work. More like play-acting, as if it mattered whether they succeeded or failed. They had never missed a meal, never had to worry about the sound of booted feet passing by their door.

His intercom buzzed. "Confed representative wants to talk to you, sir. Line three."

"Tell them I'm busy," Maxwell said.

"But they've been calling every fifteen minutes. It must be impor—"

Maxwell cut the connection and stood there fuming. As if dealing with the lords wasn't enough, he had the Confed breathing down his neck, too. Unlike the lords, they could be pushed aside for a while.

Maxwell had fought for everything he had ever obtained. But no matter how talented, no matter how intelligent or ruthless, he could never escape the lords and their mocking condescension. No one could rise to their level. It wasn't an even playing field.

No new megacorporation had been created in almost two hundred years. Smaller corporations existed in remote parts of Manspace, but only because they were too insignificant to be any threat. Once they grew large enough to attract the attention of one of the megacorporations it meant that there was significant money to be made, and they were invariably devoured as the megacorporations collected the profit.

In order to survive, a corporation would have to be created quickly, suddenly, with massive growth and momentum. It could catch the lords by surprise, perhaps tearing out a place for itself before their ancient and bureaucratic system could react to the threat.

Yes, the man who could achieve such a coup would have the potential for even more. He would have to beat the megacorporations at their own game, break them down, conquer them one by one like Alexander the Great or Napoleon, and give the lords something to fear for the first time in their lives.

He sat at his desk and called his operations command. It was time to check on the progress of the apprehension of the courier. They had followed up on the information from Kendrick, and he hoped that this would tie up loose ends related to Casey, perhaps even give him what he needed to shut up that fool Randol.

When Maxwell saw the pale frightened face of his Raken security commander, Gerard, he knew it was bad news. "Tell me what happened. I want details."

The man stuttered through the story.

Maxwell groaned.

"Our patrols are searching for her, sir. I'm certain we'll get her back."

"Listen here, Gerard, I want that courier caught, but more than that, I want that datastore back intact."

"We're working on it, sir."

"That's not good enough."

"Yes, sir."

"I want you to do a full deconstructive mind probe on Chandler. He has to have valuable information."

"Sir, I regret to tell you that we no longer have Mr. Chandler in custody. His release was ordered by Lord Randol. We had no choice."

Maxwell smiled. "Really? Well then, of course I understand, Gerard. We serve at the pleasure of the lords. I'm sure there was a very good reason."

This was wonderful. Better than Maxwell could have hoped for. His nemesis on the council was falling into his hands.

"Gerard, I want you and the rest of Green and Blue Teams out looking for the girl. I don't care how long it takes. Call in all the assistance you need. Use all measures necessary. And that imbecile, what was his name? The sole survivor of Red Team?"

"Uh, that would be Larson, sir. Ray Larson."

"He's fired. Tell him to be on the first shuttle offplanet or we'll arrest him for trespassing on corporate property."

"Yes, sir."

"Who is the lead interrogator on Raken?"

"Sergeant Cox," Gerald said.

"Have him contact me immediately. I have a job for him." Maxwell cut the connection.

He walked across his office and poured himself a cup of coffee from the refreshment station. He returned to his desk, sat down, and took a sip of the strong, hot brew as he sorted his thoughts.

Randol's undying devotion to Casey was sickening. He'd added an outside element to the equation, a private security agent who provided enough interference for the courier to escape. A foolish mistake traceable to him. Just the sort of thing that Maxwell had hoped for.

Maxwell keyed a request for Mike Chandler's dossier into the computer. A moment later, a holo materialized over his desktop. Words hung in the air beside the image of Chandler's license.

Michael Chandler: Parents were industrial workers. Chandler ran away from home to join the Confed and served ten years in Marine Special Forces. Twice decorated. Promoted and demoted numerous times, usually due to insubordination. One incident with a colonel's wife. Entered civilian life as a personal security expert.

Maxwell then pulled up Chandler's financial records.

"Here we go," he said.

The only asset Chandler possessed was equity in an aging Scout-class ship. Habitually behind on payments. Yes, there were possibilities here.

Perhaps this Chandler would listen to reason. The old man obviously wouldn't. Perhaps an unpleasant experience with Nebulaco Security coupled with enough financial incentive could turn Chandler into a true asset.

CHAPTER EIGHT

Sai followed the signs toward dock D, berth twenty-seven, where Chandler's ship was waiting.

As she approached the last turn, she stopped and took a right into an alleyway. She moved behind a building that housed a closed gift shop. She didn't want to walk into a potential trap.

The alleyway was dark, and the rain had caused puddles of collected filth to pool in the chuckholes. She quietly moved around the back of the building to the next alleyway, which opened onto the entrance of berth twenty-seven.

Hiding behind a large crate, she withdrew her whisperblade and activated the remote. She threw the blade high, up and out of the alleyway, guiding it into a graceful curve into the street and past the gateway to berth twenty-seven. She watched the display on the com unit on her wrist, which transmitted video from the camera on the whisperblade. She guided the unit forward, keeping it high enough to avoid easy detection.

Corporate Security had arrived before her. She saw six men hiding behind the entrance. Three on either side. Three were armed with blasters but didn't seem particularly alert. One stood smoking a stimstick, and another was taking a leak against the wall.

Still, she didn't want to fight six armed men. She would have to abandon the idea of making the drop. Even if she could navigate past the security goons, she didn't know whose side this Chandler guy was on. He sounded genuine, but he might have sold out to

Nebulaco. He might be working with them to create these traps and maybe that so-called arrest was completely bogus. It didn't matter; she needed to get out. It was time to go to the Silver Dollar Saloon and hire Hank Jensen to take her offworld.

She commanded the whisperblade to return.

"Don't move," a voice said quietly behind her.

She froze. In the corner of her eye she could see movement as a dark figure circled around her.

"So you thought you could get away from me?"

"I thought I was doing a pretty good job."

The man laughed. "Stand up and put your hands on your head, and don't move one little muscle because I would hate to have to kill a fine young thing like you."

She did as she was told.

"I'm Sergeant Cox. Security Director Maxwell sent me here personally to find you. I'm not like those idiots who work for me. I left them over there exposed, but I decided to keep at the edge of the perimeter. I figured you were too smart to barge in on our trap, but just stupid enough to at least try to contact Chandler once he was released."

"What do you want?"

"No games. I want the package you were supposed to deliver to Chandler."

"Who's Chandler?"

"Don't insult me! I'm not a moron. Chandler can get away with it because he's the favorite of a lord, but you are nothing but dirt! I want that package!"

"What if I don't have it?"

"In that case, you and I are going to have a lot of fun. I am very, very good at interrogation. Luckily, we have a lot of leeway at Nebulaco. Since what's good for the company is good for everyone, we can do what we want to people who try to hurt the company. I like interrogation. Who knows? Maybe you'll like it, too."

Sai saw the whisperblade behind Cox. She guided the whisper-blade toward him.

"Maybe I will," she said in a husky whisper. "Are you going to spank me if I'm bad?"

Cox grinned. "You're very naughty, aren't you?"

At that moment the whisperblade came flashing down. He dodged to the right and the blade missed him, but it slashed through his blaster.

Sai rushed forward and kicked Cox in the crotch. Then she followed up with a combination to the gut and nose. Cox's head snapped back with the power of the blow and he fell back, unconscious.

Sai spat on his fallen form and gave him a gratuitous kick in the ribs.

She went through his pockets, took what few credits he had, and checked his ID. It matched his story. He was Sergeant Luther Cox, Nebulaco Security.

She activated the whisperblade again and used it to cut his pants off. Not that she was vicious. After all, she didn't cut off his dick. She'd just taken enough shit for one night and it was nice to give some back.

Retreating down the alleyway, Sai headed toward the Silver Dollar Saloon. It was back to plan B.

* * *

Helen heard a voice in the darkness. "You're lucky you were recognized."

She opened her eyes and saw the speaker. He sat on a stool just outside the bars of the brig with his feet up on a table. He wore dirty clothes and scuffed combat armor. "The pulse rifle was on stun."

Helen's head hurt like hell. She lay on a bare metal bunk in a small cell. She still barely had control of her extremities from the aftereffects of the blast. Her nerve endings burned and tingled. It was as if she were being slowly electrocuted.

"You're going to be a bit twitchy for a while, but no permanent damage. We want you nice and healthy for Daddy."

"Where are we?" Helen asked.

"Not on your pretty little ship, for sure. We're on Thorne's ship, the *Naglfar*. We're headed to the base, where you're going to have a nice little cell there of your very own. I'm sure that Daddy wants you back pretty badly, so we figure on getting some good coin for that perky little ass of yours."

"My father isn't as weak as you might think. He's not one of those delicate cowards on the council. He's going to take this out in blood."

The pirate laughed. "Well, you'd better hope he plays nice. He can get you in one piece, or one piece at a time. We know how to do this, sweet thing. The price keeps going up, not down. He's a business-man. I'm sure he'll make the wise choice."

* * *

When Sai walked into the Silver Dollar, Hank was standing in the middle of a group of six men. He had a tankard full of dark beer that he was waving wildly as he spoke. "—and then we were struck from behind by a torpedo."

"Hank!" Sai called.

He stopped his story and turned his head in her direction, squint-ing. "Sai? Issat you?"

"Yes, Hank. I need to speak to you."

Hank turned to his fellows. "Pardon me, boys, but the lady needs me." He winked, then turned and staggered toward her.

"Oh shit, you're drunk!"

"You have a knack for stating the obvious, my lovely little blade-wielding wench," Hank said. "Heh, I guess I ain't that drunk after all. I just said a mouthful there, didn't I?"

"Hank. I really need to get offplanet quickly. Come on. There were some problems."

"Problems? Well, honey, we all got problems, but it gets better. Take me for example. Yesterday I was flat broke, and today I got the sweetest deal I ever saw on Denebian pantor melts—I mean mantor pelts. You know—furs. I just gotta wait until tomorrow night to take possession and I can triple my money anywhere in the Greensward. The guy was desperate for credits."

"Hank. There are some people after me. I need to get away. I'll pay twice what I paid before."

His smile faded when he focused on her face, seeing that she had been injured. "What happened to you?"

"Long story," she said.

"Sure, sure. I can help you out. We can blast out of here tomorrow night."

"We need to leave today. Now."

"Sorry, no can do, honey. I finally made a decent score. I have to see this deal through."

Sai looked around the room. She wasn't too impressed with the options. "Do you have anyone you'd recommend?"

Hank closed one eye, squinted with the other, and staggered in a circle to look around the room. "Nope, all worthless bums who'd rob you the first chance they got."

There were some laughs around the room.

"Come on, be serious."

A man standing at the bar turned in her direction. "Ah, lass, he is serious, ya see. We are pretty much that a-way when it comes down to it. Just business, o' course."

Hank laughed, but he quieted when he caught the look in Sai's eyes. "Come here, let's sit down a moment in a more private place. Maybe we can figure something out."

They moved to a quiet table in the back.

"What happened?" he asked.

"My delivery went bad. It happens sometimes." She looked over her shoulder, then leaned close. "I can pay you well, very well. Drunk as you are, I would still rather not take a chance on someone else if at all possible. Can you pilot like this?"

Hank stiffened. "Of course! I'm even better when I've got a bit of lubrication. Besides, to tell you the truth, Elsa does most of the work on the takeoffs and landings. But I can't leave any earlier than tomorrow night."

"But I have to leave now."

"Darlin', can't you just lay low for a bit? Maybe hide on board? But do not, I repeat, *do not* clean up my stateroom again. I can't find anything now."

"Things are too hot right now."

"Corporate?" he asked.

"Yes. I think there's a corporate hit team looking for me."

Hank nodded, appearing to sober somewhat. "You're in a fine state, then. There's many that would agree to take you just to turn you in. It won't take long for the company to send out a bounty notice to the docks."

"Then you understand my problem."

Hank grumbled. "Yes, I understand it. But damn it! I can't leave early. I just can't. I appreciate you taking the chance on me darlin', I needed the break. But I'd be pissing it away if I let this deal fall through. This shipment will put me in the black for a good, long time if I don't do something stupid. This is also a matter of survival. I don't want to end up sleeping in some starport gutter. Besides, we just got here. I have to refit the ship and refuel. That takes time."

Sai nodded. "I understand. I'll find someone else."

As she got up to leave, Hank stood. "Sai, I said you can hide out on the *Elsa*. Even Nebulaco Corporate Security doesn't have the balls to order a ship-by-ship search of the entire port. The trading guilds would have a conniption fit."

Sai shook her head. "Don't feel bad, Hank. I know what I have to do. I appreciate the offer, but I have to go."

"But, Sai . . ."

She knew he was right. He couldn't risk his future just to help out some damned fool girl. If nothing else, Elsa would never let him hear the end of it.

Sai stood to leave, and as she turned, she saw three men entering the bar armed with pulse pistols.

"Sai Collins, you're under arrest!" the lead man shouted.

"Women," Hank said. "Nothing but trouble."

Sai made it to his side just as Hank drew his pistol from his shoulder holster and took aim at the lead man. He fired and the man tumbled to the floor in a heap. The other two tripped over him.

Hank grabbed Sai's hand and together they fled toward the back door. "You really pissed them off," Hank said.

Sai burst through the door into the alley behind the bar as a large, well-muscled man swooped down on a hovercycle. Hank pulled her out of the way. The man stepped off the bike. He wore black leathers with the insignia of some biker club emblazoned on his back. "Sorry about the close call," he said. "I didn't see you."

"Nice bike," Hank said, and then stomped on the man's foot. The polite biker howled in pain. Hank leaped on the cycle. Sai climbed on behind him and they took off. "Sorry," Hank called back.

Below, they saw the men who had been chasing Sai exit the bar. The men pointed upward, and one of them took a wild shot that sailed harmlessly to one side.

Hank turned the cycle toward the starport, skimming along just above rooftops. The wind whipped his hair as buildings whizzed past below them in soft blurs. "Do you think they have friends waiting at the dock?"

Sai shrugged. "At this point, nothing would surprise me."

Hank activated his comlink. "Elsa!"

"Yes, Hank."

"You haven't noticed any unusual activity, have you? Strangers hanging around for no good reason?"

"As a matter of fact, there are five men with entirely too much time on their hands. They've been cruising the launch pads for the last few hours."

"Great. Change of plan. Do an emergency dustoff and meet me north of town." Hank closed the link.

Sai saw something flash out of the corner of her eye. She looked back over her shoulder. A black sedan pulled up behind them, cruising at the same altitude. It came up on their tail fast. "Hank, they're behind us."

Hank looked back at the rapidly closing vehicle. He cursed under his breath. "Hold on," he said.

Hank leaned the bike over and took a sharp right, much too sharp for the sedan to duplicate, but although it lost some ground, the vehicle managed to adjust its course and began to close again.

Traffic up ahead forced Hank to slow down. The sedan took advantage and raced forward to bridge the gap. It seemed intent on ramming the cycle. Sai tensed. At least earlier in the cab she'd had a modicum of protection.

"Are you squeamish?" Hank asked.

"Why?"

"Because if you are, you'd best cover your eyes."

Just as the sedan moved in for a strike to Hank's rear wheel, Hank slammed on the cycle's brakes and dove straight down, allowing the sedan to pass over them. He swerved around and headed north at the fastest speed the bike could muster.

They raced past the residential district into the business district before the sedan caught up with them again. This time it didn't try to ram them. Instead, it shot up beside them. The side windows buzzed open and gun barrels poked out. "Hank! They're gonna shoot us down!"

The passengers in the sedan opened fire. Blasts shot past all around them. One of the shots hit low, toward the back of the bike, and Hank struggled to keep it from spinning out. He took evasive action, cutting power and dropping in behind their attackers. He pulled up and matched their speed several meters above them.

"Grab my pistol!" Hank shouted.

She reached across and tugged the weapon from his shoulder holster. The men in the sedan leaned out the windows to try for a better shooting angle. Sai fired but the shot went astray. It was tough to shoot a pistol at a moving target while sailing through the sky on a hovercycle. Especially when Hank kept swerving to avoid blasts. Fortunately, their pursuers were having the same difficulty.

"This isn't going to work!" Sai yelled.

"Sure it is," Hank said. "Watch."

"Get us out of here, damn it! They're going to kill us on this thing," Sai said.

"Not a chance," Hank said, easing back.

A dark shadow passed over them with a deafening roar. A spaceship soared just over their heads, matching their speed. From out of nowhere, light flashed as a blaster beam shot out from the ship at the black sedan. The vehicle exploded and flaming chunks of twisted metal rained down to the ground.

"What was that?" Sai asked.

"Elsa, of course," said Hank. "She's a talented little cybernetic wench. Here we go!"

Light from the tractor beam bathed them as it locked on. Slowly they were pulled into the ship's empty hold.

"Hey! I thought you said you needed to refuel."

"I lied."

* * *

"Why, Sergeant Cox, fancy seeing you here." Chandler stood over the prone, bleeding, and nearly naked security officer. "You working undercover? Trying to act like a guy who got his ass kicked and his pants stolen?"

"Ugh—what happened?"

"How the hell should I know? I was on my way back to my ship and I saw you lying in the alley, so I stopped to check on you."

"The girl? Where is she?"

"You don't let up, do you? I told you before. I don't know the girl," Chandler said. "Is this some sort of interrogation tactic? Am I supposed to feel sorry for you or something? Because it ain't working. I'm trying hard not to laugh at your sorry ass."

"No, you idiot! This girl was here. She did this—"

Chandler chuckled. "That little girl from that bar did this to you? I don't know where you're from, mister, but in my neighborhood we don't admit to having our asses kicked by a one-hundred-and-twenty-pound girl."

Cox groaned and rose shakily to his feet.

"Is there someone I can call for you? A cop? Oh, that's right, you are a cop. Maybe your mommy? Heh, heh." Chandler walked toward his ship. "I'd get some pants if I were you. Some of these starport bums might take that as an invitation to bend you over. Unless you're into that sort of thing."

Chandler stopped, looked back, and smiled. "Oh, thank you for guarding my ship. I'll pass on a good word to Lord Randol about you and your men."

Cox made rude hand gestures at him as Chandler walked away. Idiot. At least the girl was able to get away, but Cox had managed to bungle the exchange. Still, the girl knew where to go. She would be safe under Randol's protection, and it freed Chandler up to pursue details on Helen's abduction. He used some of Randol's credits to make that task a little easier.

His first step was going to be meeting this Vincent Maxwell that he'd heard so much about.

* * *

Maxwell was going over corporate reports with an analyst when the door to his office flew open and an angry woman wearing a Confed uniform stormed inside. Maxwell's secretary entered behind her with an apologetic look on her face.

"Vincent Maxwell," the Confed officer said. "We need to talk."

"I'm sorry, sir," the secretary said. "I tried to stop her."

"It's all right," Maxwell said. He turned to the analyst. "Go back over this again, and bring it back in fifteen minutes."

"Yes, sir," said the analyst. He took his notescribe and moved around the Confed commander.

When the secretary closed the door, Maxwell faced the commander. "As you can see, I'm very busy. What can I do for you?"

"My name is Commander Joann Montgomery, and I'm here to find out what the hell you're doing." Her eyes burned like fusion fire and she ground her teeth so hard, Maxwell half expected them to crumble in her mouth.

He gave her an unflappable expression. "I was going over a sales report."

"Your corporate goons blew up half a city block on Raken! We're still counting the injured and the dead."

"We had reports of—"

"That is *not* a corporate sector! You have no jurisdiction there."

"Look—"

She was having none of it. "In addition, I have three people confirmed dead at Tyree's, several injured, and damage to a building across from the Bryant Hotel. Your corporate squad has no authority for any of this and you've been dodging my calls all afternoon."

"I've been busy."

"No shit. You keep your corporate security teams out of our territory. The spacer's guild is shitting peach pits over this. You'll be getting a bill for all the damages your men have caused."

Maxwell glared at her. "Listen here, Commander. If your Confed people would do their jobs, my men wouldn't need to go to the free zone starport sector. You've done nothing to stop Thorne or any of the other pirates, and I'll be damned if I'll let you come into my office and stomp around like you own the place."

"You've got no right to criticize. We've been doing all we can. You've got a security leak in this corporation that you could steer a battlecruiser through. We've tried to get you to cooperate on covert action, but time and again you've refused."

"Director Casey refused. Not me. And if I have a lead, I'm going to run after it and I don't care if you get your regulation panties in a wad over it."

"I'll have your job for this, you insufferable little prick."

"Someone stole some data from us, and we were trying to get it back. Your people ignored our calls for assistance, so you'd best get down off my ass or I'll have *your* job."

"You can't blow up buildings and kill people with impunity. You put a leash on your people now, because if any of them set foot in our territory again, I will arrest them and dump them in a deep, dark hole. And then I'll be coming after you. Do you understand me?"

Maxwell smiled. "Oh, I understand. Now, you write this down because you won't want to forget it: I've already pulled back my corporate security. I've put forward a reward for the capture of the fugitives, so hopefully someone else will bring them in, but if you ever come into my office again throwing empty threats at me, I'll label you an enemy of the corporation." He stepped up close to her, invading her space. "Do you know what happens to enemies of the corporation when they're on corporate property?"

Montgomery blinked. The look in her eyes told him she did know, but he wanted to drive it home for her.

"As an enemy of the corporation here on corporate property, you lose all rights, and you're taken down for a full deconstructive brain-scan to ensure you don't have any corporate secrets locked away. By the time we're done, you won't be able to spell your name, assuming you even remember it. By the time your bureaucratic buffoons at the Confed manage to cut through all the red tape to get you back, all that will remain of your pompous ass is a drooling mass of human flesh. Meanwhile, I'll draft a sincerely apologetic memorandum about mutual cooperation and communication breakdowns and you'll be put in a Confed home with the rest of the basket cases. Don't fuck with me, Commander. I mean it."

She swallowed hard.

He remained in her space, his eyes burning into hers. After enough time passed without comment he whispered, "You're dismissed."

* * *

Hank and Sai hustled inside the ship, sealing the hatch and making their way forward to the cockpit. Hank sat down in the pilot's seat and fastened his G-harness. "You'd better strap in."

Hank didn't speak again until the ship broke free of Raken's atmosphere and the artificial-gravity field kicked in. Then he unbuckled and spun in his chair to face Sai.

"Okay, where to?" Hank asked.

"The Trent System," Sai answered.

Hank ran the coordinates through Elsa. "All kidding aside, we are definitely going to need a fueling stop along the way."

"I have enough credits for that."

"Being on the run and all, the destination surprises me. That takes us back coreward into Manspace. I'd be headed toward the Outyonder. Okay, now the tricky part. Why?"

Sai took a deep breath. "I'm paying you well enough that I shouldn't have to answer any questions."

"Maybe so, if this were some leisurely cruise, but I had to kill three men down there. That makes me part of this for good or for bad. I guess I'm just stupid, but I threw my lot in with you. I do that sometimes. Call it a character flaw. But now that we're in this together, you owe me an explanation, lady, and a piece of the action."

"What do you mean?"

"Everything boils down to money. If someone is willing to foot the bill for a hit team to take you out, then you must be worth the effort."

Sai laughed. "You want a cut, you got it. But if I tell you what I've got, you'll regret it."

"Try me."

"I believe that I have an answer to the riddle that Nebulaco would pay a year's profit to solve. I have the goods on the person behind every major hijacking and caravan raid against Nebulaco for the past three years."

"Thorne?" Hank said.

"You got it."

Hank slumped in his chair. "Crap. We're dead."

EPISODE THREE

CHAPTER NINE

Read that transmission back to me again," Hank Jensen said. He stood rubbing his temples, leaning on the back of his pilot's chair.

"Fifty-thousand-credit reward for information leading to the apprehension of Sai Collins, wanted for theft, assault, and espionage. Last seen leaving the Raken System traveling with Hank Snow Jensen, free-trader and known petty criminal. Authority Vincent Maxwell, Director, Nebulaco Security Service." Elsa's synthesized voice echoed in the cockpit.

Hank shook his head. "Petty? Really? Never."

"I would have assumed you'd be more upset about the criminal part," Sai said. "Or maybe the price-on-our-heads part." She sat sideways across the copilot's seat, swinging her booted feet back and forth nervously.

Hank shrugged. "We've all done a few things, but petty? I find that insulting. That and I can't tell you how mad I am that they used my middle name. I never use it. Now everyone is gonna call me Snowman, and Snow Job, and God knows what else."

They were en route to Trent with the *Elsa* straining for as much speed as she could manage. They were on track to reach a refueling stop on an outpost planet called Jonesy in about six hours, but to Hank, it couldn't be soon enough.

"I suppose I shouldn't care since, after all, we're dead as sure as if the necrocytes were gnawing at our bones. That broadcast was sent to every ship and port in this sector. I should have known better. Never trust a pretty face." He sat down heavily and bent over the navigation station to verify their position.

"I'm not going to say I told you so," Elsa's voice droned.

"Well, that's great, because it wouldn't help and it would just piss me off."

Sai frowned and pointed a finger at Hank. "All I need from you," she looked upward, "either of you, is a ride from planet A to planet B, no special favors. You don't have to involve yourself any further. Someone asks questions, you just tell them you don't know anything."

"Do you honestly think that they'd let it go with that? Nebulaco put a price on my head, so I won't be able to do business anywhere in this sector, and Thorne surely won't let anyone live who knows his secrets."

"Technically, the price is on *my* head. Still, the data is secured and untouched. I haven't opened the courier package."

"They won't care. They'll fry you—and me. Don't think that hiding in the Outyonder will last long, what with everyone after you. Greed is universal. Besides, Trent is in the wrong direction. We're heading *into* Manspace. More regulations, better customs screening."

"I have a plan," Sai said.

"You'd better have a good one because from here things don't seem to be working so well," Hank said.

"Really? Well, genius, what would you do?"

"Well, for starters, since we're both effectively doomed anyway, why don't you tell me the truth—all of it. The whole story from start to finish. Maybe we can figure a way out of this mess together." Hank looked deeply into her eyes. "I'm not going to abandon you. We just need to focus and figure out what to do."

Sai considered it for a moment. She was always hesitant to trust others. But, in spite of his arrogant, childish ways, she truly liked Hank. She knew he wasn't afraid of a fight and from what she'd seen, he was a great pilot. She needed an ally.

"Okay," she said, "but I don't think it'll help." She stood, and she paced as she talked, her arms folded. She told him about her new life on Nebula Prime, getting the job at Nebulaco that seemed like a windfall, obtaining the datastore from Kendrick, and the failed exchange after Hank had transported her to Raken. Finally, she told him about going to see Dirion.

"So this Dirion guy, he's an oracle?"

Sai nodded. "He was. He'd been on Raken for over forty years. He had a massive network established. Everyone came to him when they needed help—" Her voice cracked. Tears welled up in her eyes. "I'm sorry—it's just that, for all practical purposes he was my father." She was angry at herself for crying in front of a stranger, but that only made the tears harder to stop.

"He took me off the streets when I was a kid. He knew I was a cyber-psi before I did. I couldn't have figured it out without his help. He helped me develop my gift, made me believe I could be somebody."

"Just one second," Hank said. He reached under the pilot's console and opened a panel, withdrawing a cold canned beverage. "You want a beer?"

Sai nodded and wiped a tear from her eye.

"Here you go," he popped the top and handed it to her, then opened one for himself and took a drink. "So what exactly is on the datastore?"

"I don't know. It's still sealed."

"Then how do you know it's full of Thorne's secrets?"

"I trust Dirion. I think he came to that conclusion based on the identities of the interested players, the involvement of Nebulaco, the ferocity of the response. It's somehow also tied into the recent death of Nebulaco's former security director."

Hank silently let the words sink in for a moment then took a sip of his beer. "So what's your plan?"

"Well, actually it's Chandler's plan. He said if I couldn't make the drop, I should go to Trent and give the information to Lord Randol."

"And this lord is going to offer you protection?"

"I don't know for sure," Sai said. "But it seems like my best shot. He's the one Chandler was working for. Since Nebulaco has been hit so hard by piracy, it makes sense that he would be eager to get the datastore. The other thing is that it would be hard for the Security Service to say that I was trying to steal data when I turned it in to a lord."

Hank grumbled to himself for a few minutes. Randol was known to be on the lighter side of crazy . . . for a lord. "Well, it is what it is. We'll be at Jonesy soon, and from there it's not that far to Trent. I'm good with your plan for now."

"In the meantime," Sai said, "you wouldn't object if I picked up a little around here, would you? Because it's either that or I'll have to spend the rest of the trip in the airlock. I could stand the short trip to Raken, but this place is too filthy to endure longer than that."

"Suit yourself, but it'll just get dirty again after you clean it—and don't move any of the stuff in my cabin! I have it all organized." With that he finished his beer, crushed the can on his head, and tossed it into the corner with the others.

"Hank, if I had hands I'd slap you," Elsa said.

"What did I say?"

* * *

Chandler had to admit that he liked working for Randol. It carried with it certain perks and privileges. He was able to use the corporate holo communication system at no cost and Randol had paid for

Chandler to install a unit in his ship; it *was* work related after all. He needed to be in many places at the same time in order to press his investigation as quickly as possible.

Randol set up a meeting with Vincent Maxwell, who would never have given Chandler an appointment otherwise. The quality of the holo unit was fantastic. It was more than just a projection. It was a virtual-reality unit, transmitting sight, sound, and even touch to Chandler's senses. Walking toward the security director's desk, he felt and heard his footsteps echo as if he were actually physically present on Nebula Prime.

He took a look around him. The office was designed more for show than for work. The art was the sort that people said they liked because it was tasteful. Chandler thought it was god-awful ugly, like gilded turds. The music wasn't much better.

Maxwell sat reclining behind his oversized desk, bathed in a pool of soft light, waiting for Chandler to approach. The rest of the room was shadowy except for spots of illumination here and there that made the shitty art look even worse.

Maxwell was just the type that annoyed Chandler by breathing. He exuded a smug, superior attitude that made you want to knock out his pretty white teeth. Chandler took an immediate dislike to him.

He displayed those teeth in a salesman's smile when Chandler finally reached the desk. Maxwell stood and made a slight bow. "Good to meet you, Detective."

Chandler looked at him like he was a dead rat. "Charmed. I suppose you know why I'm here."

Maxwell casually sat back down. "Yes. Lord Randol seems to think that a fresh perspective might be of help in our investigation."

Chandler planted his holographic butt on Maxwell's stylish desk. Maxwell's smile strained.

Chandler looked closer at Maxwell. The tanned complexion, the touch of gray at the temples, the suit that cost more than Chandler's annual income. Yeah, it was official, Chandler decided. This guy was an asshole.

"You don't agree?"

"I don't have to, Mr. Chandler. I serve the corporation."

"Then I suppose Randol has already explained to you that he expects you to cooperate."

"He encouraged me to help you, but you must understand that although Lord Randol is a member of the Council of Lords, he does not—"

"Save it. I really don't care."

Maxwell didn't bother to keep up the smile. His lips turned into a tight grimace. "What is it that you want to know, Detective?"

"Well, for starters, why do you think Casey was dirty?"

"I don't see what that has to do with Randol's daughter."

"Well, I'm just curious. If Casey was the leak, and he's dead, how did Thorne get the information he needed to ambush the *Aurelius*? Seems to me like you still have a problem unrelated to Casey."

Maxwell shook his head. "The trip had been scheduled for some time. I'm sure that this had been in the works for a while. Suffice to say that there has been a dramatic reduction in attacks in the last few days. I think that speaks volumes."

"Still, if you had been doing your job, she wouldn't have been abducted," Chandler said.

He leaned in close to Maxwell's face, invading his space. Maxwell didn't move, but even though it was only a holo, Chandler knew he wanted to.

"Mr. Chandler. I agree. I take my responsibilities seriously. I was foolish not to insist that all the travel plans for corporate VIPs be rerouted. I am sickened by my failure. But all I can do at this point is try to move forward and assist in getting her back."

Chandler backed away and stood up. "Okay, tell me everything you know about the attack on the *Aurelius*."

"Yesterday, while in transit from the Trent System to Driscoll University on Corona, the *Aurelius* stopped midflight. We're not sure what disabled it, possibly a plasma torpedo. There was a brief distress call, which I can provide to you, but there really isn't much on it. Simply that they were being attacked. We believe the ship was boarded, but one man escaped in a life pod. He is currently recovering in a hospital outpost. I will have the details sent to you. Beyond that, we've heard nothing. The ship hasn't been recovered."

"Don't you find it a bit unusual that out of all the intergalactic transports, Lord Randol's daughter happened to be targeted?"

"That's a broad assumption, Detective. I would think that any luxury yacht would be a target for pirates."

"You don't think it's significant? That perhaps more than simple profit is involved here? A man like Thorne holding the daughter of a corporate lord has a lot of leverage."

"He certainly does. But until we hear the kidnapper's demands, we are in the dark as to their motivations."

"Seems like you're doing a lot of sitting around waiting. What are you planning to do proactively?"

Maxwell glared at Chandler. "When I first accepted employment here, Thorne was a minor problem. He had hit a few scattered transports, but he was a manageable threat. I asked Casey and the lords to provide me funding for more escort fighters and better security, but at the time they felt their money could be better spent elsewhere. Casey made sure of that. It took them too long to realize that with every ship Thorne raided, his power and resources grew. *I* didn't create the problem, *they* did, and now that I'm security director, I'm left to deal with it. Don't tell me I'm not doing my job. Without me this corporation would have fallen long ago."

"Irreplaceable, are you?"

Maxwell sighed. "Of course not. I just do my duty like any other corporate employee should. You, for example."

"Me? I don't work for the corporation. I work for Randol."

"A matter of semantics, surely," Maxwell said, putting his feet up on his desk, both providing the appearance of relaxation and widening the gap between himself and Chandler. "I really can't blame you for being so crude. After all, you're fighting a losing battle. Lord Randol is asking you to do by yourself what the concentrated effort of a megacorporation could not accomplish."

"I'm not impressed by your efforts, but I know one thing," Chandler said. "There's a leak in this organization that's been feeding information to Thorne, and that leak is somewhere up high, and I'm not convinced it was Casey. Tell me, Maxwell, do they pay you enough? Irreplaceable employees usually command a hefty salary."

Maxwell kicked away from the desk, bolted to his feet and pointed a finger in Chandler's face. "Watch yourself, Detective. You can only push me so far, and it would be unfortunate for you and Lord Randol if you were implicated as an accomplice in the recent theft of corporate data."

Chandler rose from the desk and smiled. "Relax, you're going to mess up your pretty suit. Besides, as soon as you find that data, we should be able to end all this confusion, right?"

Maxwell's cheeks flushed, but he quickly composed himself and spoke in a more contained tone. "Mr. Chandler, toward that end, you could benefit financially if you were to assist my office in the apprehension of the courier whose capture you disrupted the other day. There's a price on her head."

"Good luck with that," Chandler said. "Your goons have been doing great so far." He turned and began walking out of the room, leaving Maxwell fuming behind him. "You know what this office really needs?" He didn't wait for a reply. "A coffin and mourners. This is the most depressing room I have ever seen. And what the hell kind of music is that?"

Chandler smiled as he switched off the holo transmission and faded away. His perceptions shifted and he was again sitting in the cockpit of the *Marlowe*. He removed the crown-like transmission ring from his head and put it away with the holo unit.

There was something about Maxwell that rubbed him the wrong way. He was too smug, too clean. But Chandler knew he had to be careful and not push too far—he needed Maxwell's cooperation.

He reached forward and checked the piloting controls. He was closing in on the location of the hospital base. It was time to make some calls to some old contacts. He needed information that only they could provide.

* * *

Brock sat quietly in the transport compartment of the small troop carrier. As he had hoped, his performance on Raken had got him promoted. The single contact he knew in Thorne's organization had introduced him to a disreputable ship captain and a destination unknown with a group of fellow recruits. Brock felt like a hot prospect on the move, getting closer to uncovering the details he needed.

But from the vacant looks on the faces of the other men around him, he was either destined for true greatness in the organization or he was just delusional. He was bored anyway, so he figured he might as well test the waters.

"So," he said to no one in particular. "What do you think about the latest trends in the economy?"

They stared blankly at him.

"Okay, how about art? Did anyone catch that exhibit by Trath on Matilda?"

No reaction.

"Ah, I see. Does anyone really hate it when it's raining and you look up and get hit in the eye?"

"Yeah! I hate it when that happens," the guy on his right said. "I do that all the time. Small universe, ain't it?"

He had found their intellectual level. Perhaps they would discuss why it was that the smell of your own flatulence was never quite as bad as that of others'.

Luckily, conversation was kept to a minimum on the trip. They mostly slept, fought, ate, and used the head. By the time they arrived at their destination, Brock had determined that most of the men were local street toughs, too unemployable by the corporations to make a living any other way but illegally. They were ripe for recruitment for a few credits, but also dangerous to count on to do any work requiring subtlety, or to trust with sensitive information.

Thorne solved that problem by not telling them anything. Brock had no idea where he was being transported to. He knew only that it was some sort of base for staging raids and that he was to serve as a boarder—to help take ships—and as a guard, in the event prisoners were taken.

He would be expected to work for a minimum of one year. He'd enjoy the provided entertainment, save his pay, and be returned home at the end of his tour with a pocket full of credits. More likely, however, most would end up chucked out an airlock if Thorne thought they knew too much. Thorne hadn't survived this long trusting his secrets to morons like those Brock saw around him.

They arrived at the base in two days. They called it "Thorne's Lair." All he knew of it was that it was an underground maze. The trip in the cargo hold hadn't afforded him a view of anything except the sleazy recruits around him. When he got off the ship it was through an airlock tunnel. It was surely some hunk of rock somewhere too small to have an atmosphere. And the maze had to be the result of mining. That might be a good hint of the location if there weren't thousands of abandoned, mined-out moons and asteroids. Still, he resolved to look out for signs that might pinpoint where he was.

At this point, however, he didn't know how he would contact his handler in the Confed to report. Ideally, he would like to collect as much intel as he could, then find a way to shanghai a ship and blast out of there. The navcom on the ship would tell him what he needed to know about the location. But he had to be able to escape the pirate fleet that was stationed there. That was going to be damn near impossible.

The men were all herded into a room where a quartermaster was issuing gear. The quartermaster was a grizzled old reprobate with bad teeth and a desperate need to trim a pair of eyebrows that branched together like wild octopus tentacles.

"Name?" the quartermaster asked.

"Brock."

"What size shirt and pants?"

"I wear a standard-plus-one in shirt, and a thirty-four-unit waist by thirty-six length in the pants."

The quartermaster made an entry into a notescribe and grabbed a box off the shelf behind him. He checked off each item as he handed it to Brock.

"Here we are. Crew shirt, large, two each. Crew pants, large, two each. Boots, large, one pair. Socks, two pair. Belt, large, one each. Sword, junior class with scabbard, one each."

Brock looked at the stack of outsized clothes and frankly stared at the cutlass. "A sword? Really?"

"Yes. Have you not seen one before? It's like a long knife. You stick people in the gut with it and they die."

"You tell me you actually use swords? What about pulse pistols? Blasters?"

"Don't be an idiot. Of course we use pulse pistols and blasters, but the sword is mandatory. It's part of the uniform. And . . ." the man looked from side to side and then leaned toward Brock, whispering. "Thorne has some sort of blade fetish or something. He's the boss. We follow his rules. Don't get caught without yours or I guarantee you won't get a second chance. You'll get a blade in *your* gut, son."

Brock nodded. "Alrighty, in that case—yo ho ho! I'll buckle me some swash then."

The rest of the group got their gear and were led toward the crew quarters. The advantage of using the old mine was that there was a lot of available space. Each man could have his own private room. There was a common crew area for eating, drinking, and gambling. This seemed to be the major pastime. He was told that once a month a shipment of pleasure workers was imported from parts unknown. This was also a major form of entertainment.

As they walked down the corridors, Brock glanced down a side hall. There was a guard posted in front of a barred cell door. A beautiful blonde woman paced behind those bars. He asked the man leading them around. "What's that?"

"That's the brig. Prisoners, hostages, that type of stuff."

"She's quite a looker. I wouldn't mind interrogating her."

"You and me both, pal. But don't get caught wandering in that area unless you're assigned there. You'll end up dead."

Brock nodded. He wondered who the woman was. That was another bit of intel that he intended to discover before he left this rock. He was going to try to wrangle himself a job as a jailer. If he could manage a jailbreak in the process, all the better.

CHAPTER TEN

Chandler started the search for information about Helen Randol by getting in touch with a few of his more shady contacts. Ships were hot commodities; the pirates would turn the *Aurelius* quickly for profit. There were always those who didn't care where their ship came from as long as the price was right. There was a thriving underworld that specialized in processing stolen ships for resale, refitting them just enough to prevent easy identification.

The Confed had attempted to crack down on this criminal industry by making it mandatory for ships to carry unique transponders and encoded microtags. However, it was difficult to regulate all of Manspace. Humanity, fiercely independent, rebelled against rules and feared that the Confed would become too powerful if it were that easy to track the movements of every human ship. Conspiracy theories ran rampant, and the Confed could not get the independent corporations and governments to cooperate on a standardized registry. Any ship could be ultimately identified by comparing it to its blueprints and researching serial numbers deep in the bowels of the hold. But first the Confed had to have probable cause to conduct the search—hard to get when the shipyards are silent for the right price.

Therefore, it wasn't any great difficulty to sell a stolen ship. The odds of getting caught were small. Although some ships were ultimately recovered, they had to be found quickly before they were refitted, and the owner would need very specific information to identify a particular vessel.

In the course of his past investigations, Chandler had met many individuals who made their living through illegal means, but he had a mutually beneficial business relationship with them nonetheless. It was a necessary evil for those in his line of work. He let the word out that he needed information about any ship matching the description of the *Aurelius* coming to market. He had some of Randol's money to throw around in gratitude, as well as his personal reputation for honorable discretion when it came to protecting the identity of his sources.

He knew the *Aurelius* was an Athena-class yacht so he had details of her tonnage, engines, and capacity. But he didn't know any uniquely identifying details of the interior structure that would distinguish it from any other ship of the same class. Randol was of no help on the subject—he never paid any attention to anything but the carpet and furnishings.

Chandler needed a crew member who crawled around the hold. Worked on the engine. Scribbled graffiti in the toilet stalls. Luckily, one had survived. But talking to him wasn't going to be pleasant.

Chandler hated hospitals. They smelled funny, they didn't let you drink or use tobac, and they liked to wake you up to give you sedatives. People went there to die and, while they waited, their butts got cold sticking out of those stupid hospital gowns. But the main thing he hated about hospitals was the fact that they were full of sick people.

Pissed-off ex-husbands, he could handle. Street freaks with shivs, he could handle. Guys hopped up on stims who wanted to play rough, he could handle. Invisible germs that can make you drop dead, he had a problem with. He wished the hospital was part of Nebulaco's holo network. But no such luck.

Chandler walked down the cold, antiseptic hallway toward Jackson Radje's room. Radje had been a crewman on the *Aurelius*, and he was the only witness to the attack, escaping in a life pod that was later found by a Confed patrol. He was injured, but he would live.

When he reached the door to room 432, Chandler looked in and grimaced. It was a ward of ten beds, full of coughing, sneezing, wheezing, dying people. What a pain in the ass. He read the nameplates on the beds as he passed by. Unfortunately, he could not avoid also reading the diagnoses. Altairian Plague, Ritifian Fever, parasitic and fungal infections—he was afraid to breathe.

Finally, he found Radje's bed, displaying the comforting diagnosis of skull fracture. He could live with that. One thing was for sure, if you were poor, you couldn't afford to get sick because you never knew what disease the sap in the next bed might have. Radje's head was bandaged with a gel-like substance that glowed and throbbed with his heartbeat. Wires ran from a monitoring console to the man, and a confusion of displays showed on the screen above his head. He appeared to be sleeping.

"Hey, Radje," Chandler said.

The man didn't stir.

The patient in the next bed began to have a coughing fit. Covering his mouth was evidently not in his nature.

"Great," Chandler said, and moved to the other side of the bed, only to discover an overpowering odor of shit emanating from the patient on that side.

"Wonderful. Oh, Radje! Wake up!" Chandler shook the man's shoulder. "I don't have all day. I want to leave here a healthy man."

Still the man did not stir. Looking around him, Chandler turned back to the unconscious Radje and bent to yell in his ear. "Wake up!"

The man jolted awake, almost falling off the bed. The monitors went crazy, turning red and wailing.

A nurse rushed in to see what was the matter, her white uniform chilling the effect of her beauty. "What happened?"

Radje sat up in bed, breathing hard. "I don't know," he said.

"Must have been a nightmare," said Chandler. "Since you're up, let me introduce myself. Mike Chandler, private investigator. I'm trying to get some information about the pirate raid on Randol's yacht."

"Sir," the nurse said. "You really should leave. Mr. Radje is in no condition to answer any questions, and you're disturbing the other patients."

"I'm sure Mr. Radje wants to speak with me, especially since he likes his job at Nebulaco and wants to keep it. And as far as these others are concerned, hell, they're all goners—maybe they'll kick off early and save you some work. Speaking of which, the guy next door there has had an accident."

The nurse sighed. "Fine, but if I have any trouble out of you I'll—"

"What? Spank me? Okay, but wash your hands first and keep the nurse's uniform on."

The nurse scowled and left to see to her next patient.

Radje had calmed a bit, settling back on his pillow. Chandler sat on the edge of his bed and took out a notescribe to record the interview.

"Okay, Radje, tell me about the raid."

"What about it?"

Chandler rapped on Radje's bandaged skull. "Hello, is anybody in there? Tell me how it happened."

"Ow! That hurts like hell!"

"So talk to me, pal."

"All right. What is this, one of those insurance things?"

"Yeah, whatever. You want to tell me what happened, or do you want to listen to a couple of knock-knock jokes?" Chandler moved as if to rap on Radje's head again.

"Okay! I was on the bridge when we realized we were approaching another ship. It was just sitting."

"You just ran into it? In other words, it was waiting directly in your route?"

"As near as I can guess. We took a couple of hits and lost the hyperdrive. About that time, six ships intercepted us and started shooting. A message came over the navcom saying that we should surrender to Thorne and prepare to be boarded."

"What about the passenger, Helen?"

"Uh. Well, I didn't see her the whole trip. She pretty much stayed in her cabin and didn't associate with the crew. She was one of them lordy-type women."

"So you don't know what happened to her."

"No idea. I just got out as quick as I could. The captain gave the abandon-ship order. We were just a yacht. We didn't have the fire-power to combat odds like that. I made it to a one-man life pod and launched. The last thing I saw before the stasis field kicked in was the *Aurelius* and the pirate ship docked together. So far as I know, I'm the only one they've found so far. Maybe I'm the only one who made it out at all."

"So the ship was intact when you last saw it?"

"Yes, but I'm sure it's gone. No ship ever attacked by Thorne has been recovered."

Chandler rubbed his chin. "Thorne, Thorne. You know, I keep hearing that name. Why do you think it was Thorne?"

"Well, I saw one of the pirates and he had a sword."

"A sword?"

"Yeah, everybody knows that Thorne's pirates have swords."

"Why?"

Radje shrugged. "They look scary, I guess."

"Whatever. Okay, you had your chance to tell me a fairy tale and I really enjoyed it. Now, let's hear what really happened."

"What do you mean?" Radje said.

"Your life pod was full of . . . souvenirs."

Radje tried to sit up and looked around. "I think I need the nurse."

Chandler smiled. "You will if you don't start talking."

"I was just trying to keep the pirates from getting it. It was okay. I asked her and she said it was okay."

"Asked who?"

"Lady Randol. I seen her when I was leaving. I swear. I was head-ed down to the pods and I went by her cabin. She was running to the pods, too. She had a gun and then these pirates started shooting at us. I jumped for the pod and that's all I remember."

"So you did see Helen, and you even spoke to her? This is finally starting to make some sense," Chandler said. "You used her to cover your escape, didn't you?"

Radje turned white. "No! I would never do something like that. I swear to all the gods. I'm just a crewman, but I wouldn't abandon a woman like that."

"Sure, bud. I get you. You're one of those hero types."

"Yeah, that's right. I would have stayed to help her, but I thought she got into a pod, too."

Chandler smirked. "Tell you what. When I find her—and I will—I'm gonna make sure and ask her about you so that we can come back and pin a medal on that chest of yours."

"Oh no," Radje said, shaking his head. "It wasn't anything. I was just in the right place at the right time. No big deal."

"Sure. Either that, or she'll tell me you're a thieving coward who was willing to throw her to the wolves and you'll get what's coming to you." Chandler laughed. "But hey! That won't happen because you're telling the truth."

Radje really didn't look well. "I need that nurse. I think I'm going to get sick."

"Tell ya what, hero. I understand from your records that you were a maintenance tech. I need some details of the ship. I need to know what flavor of bubblegum is stuck under which table in the galley. I need to know which faucet is leaky. I need to know what color duct tape you used to fix the coolant hose. I need to know the location of the hidey-hole where you stored your contraband."

"That was medicinal," Radje said.

Chandler smiled. "I'm sure it was. We're gonna go over things, and if you give me what I need, I'll put a word in to Lord Randol and we won't prosecute you for theft and desertion. How does that sound?"

Radje became very cooperative after that. Chandler logged as many details about the *Aurelius* as he could get out of Radje. At the end of the interview he felt confident that if he could locate the ship he had enough to identify it.

As he rose to leave, he leaned down to speak to Radje. "I think this is enough, but I may have more questions. Stay easy to contact. Oh, and since you're going to be stuck here for a while, I've got some advice." Chandler straightened and gestured toward the various patients hacking and wheezing in the room. "Try not to breathe."

* * *

Everybody who was anybody on Nebula Prime ate at the Executive Towers Royale. The restaurant sat perched atop the twin towers of the corporate headquarters with a thin glassed-in walkway between the two portions of the establishment. The north tower seated the general population, while the south tower, built slightly higher, catered to the elite.

Oke sat in the back of his sleek black limo watching the lights of the city flash by as his chauffeur made a slow bank around the towers and descended toward the landing platform.

The limo came to a stop and the chauffeur killed the engine, letting the vehicle slowly settle down on a cushion of air. The chauffeur exited and hustled around the vehicle. He stood waiting to open Oke's door until the second limo, the one carrying Oke's personal guards, landed adjacent to them. It was a study in pure waste and ostentation.

Four men in polished black exo-armor stepped out of the second limo and took up their positions. They quickly scanned the area, then the squad leader gave the chauffeur a nod.

The chauffeur opened Oke's door. "Here we are, sir."

"Are we on time?" Oke asked.

"Fifteen minutes late, milord," the chauffeur said, "as you requested."

Oke nodded and stepped out. "Very good, Bittleson. My cloak."

Bittleson draped the silver cloak over Oke's shoulders. Oke chose the mirrored epaulettes because they always caught the overhead lights and flashed, drawing attention to him.

Oke held his head up and strutted along the carpeted path toward the entrance to the south tower. His guards followed, flanking him, two on each side. Out of the corner of his eye, Oke saw people watching him from the windows on the north side. He smirked, pleased, but made sure not to acknowledge the common folk. It was enough that he allowed them to feast their eyes upon him at all.

The doorman saluted sharply and opened the door as they approached. "Good evening, Lord Oke," he said.

One of the guards shoved the man back as they walked by. Oke continued as if the man were a piece of furniture.

Oke frowned as he approached the restaurant. There was no one standing at the maître d's station, forcing him to wait. He seethed with anger. A lord should never have to wait!

For fifteen seconds he stood there. He should have delayed his exit from the limo. Finally, the maître d' returned from escorting another customer to a table.

"Good evening, milord." The maître d' bowed deeply.

Oke rolled his eyes. "Yes, too bad I'm wasting it waiting for service."

"A thousand pardons, milord. I'm dreadfully sorry. I humbly beg your forgiveness." The man seemed genuinely upset.

"Please just shut up. I am dining with Mr. Maxwell this evening."

"Yes, sir. Mr. Maxwell is already here."

"Take me to him then." Oke waved the man on.

"Yes, milord. Right this way."

Maxwell sat across the room at a table facing the windows, sipping at a glass of red wine. As Oke arrived, he stood and bowed.

Oke made sure he twisted to catch the light with his epaulettes as he walked toward the table. He wanted people to know they were in his presence. His bodyguards followed, eyes scrutinizing the patrons with deadly intensity. When he reached Maxwell's table, he allowed the maître d' to take his cloak. Beneath it, he wore a hand-painted silk kimono decorated with a confusion of erotic scenes.

"Vincent," Oke said with a nod.

"Milord," Maxwell said.

The maître d' pulled out Oke's chair. "Please, be seated."

"Thank you," Oke said, sitting down and folding his hands in his lap.

The leader of the bodyguards quickly stepped over, scanned Maxwell with a small device, then moved to take his position around the table with the others. They looked like obsidian pillars.

Oke looked through the windows at the people on the north side of the restaurant. Many of them stared across the walkway at the privileged few who rated high enough to sit on Oke's side. His generosity suddenly got the better of him, and Oke blessed them with a wave of his hand.

The maître d' offered menus, which Oke dismissed. "Have the chef create something."

"Certainly, Lord Oke." The maître d' bowed and withdrew.

"Such a dreary evening this is, Mr. Maxwell. The flight over here was horrid. I really don't know why I agreed to meet with you."

Maxwell smiled. "Milord, I believe that you might come to think of this evening as one of the most fateful in your life."

Oke was intrigued, but he refused to show it.

"Really? How quaint that you think so."

Maxwell leaned forward, keeping his eyes locked onto Oke's. "I have information for you, milord. What I'm about to tell you must go no further. I'm telling you this in the strictest confidence."

Oke heard this sort of thing every day. Everyone thought they had information that could be divulged only to a lord. "Yes, yes, what is it?"

"One of my employees uncovered some files that point to corruption high up in the corporation. *Extremely* high. If I read the information correctly—and I went over it thoroughly—it would seem to cast suspicion on a lord."

"Your employees dared to investigate us?"

"No, milord. This employee was doing a routine file check and came across some accounts that did not balance. When he checked to see whose account it was and cross-referenced the deposits and withdrawals, he brought the files to me."

"What did you discover?"

"Well, milord, it seems that Lord Randol has been receiving unusually large amounts of money from, shall we say, suspicious sources. If it were anyone else, I would assume that he was profiting from some illegal enterprise."

"What? That's ridiculous."

"That's what I thought, too, milord. I went over the information again and again and it keeps coming up the same. This in combination with his reluctance to admit Casey's guilt creates a certain . . . *impression.*"

"Have you talked to anyone else about this?"

"Not yet. I wanted to advise you of the problem first. I'm on shaky ground here. I feel that you're the only lord with the strength and insight to properly deal with this situation. What should I do?"

Oke considered this, tapping his forefinger against his lips before nodding. "It's vital that this scandal be kept quiet—especially in light of the impending stock sale. Continue your investigation and keep me apprised of what you learn, but maintain a low profile."

Oke leaned back as the waiter arrived to set salads before them consisting of three blades of Altairian lime grass and a single drop of blue dressing.

"Can I get you anything else, Lord and sir?"

"Go away," Oke said. He waited for the man to leave before pushing his salad bowl to the side, leaning toward Maxwell. "Anything you uncover, you bring to me first. Is that understood?"

"Yes, milord, but what about Lord Randol? What if he suspects? He's already attacked me in open council."

"Don't worry about him. I'll speak with Lady Hemming about this so she'll side with me. Not to fear, I'll be discreet. You'll have our support."

* * *

Jonesy was a bustling spaceport floating in the middle of a galactic crossroads. The planet was generally considered to be worthless, but at one time the airless, barren hunk of rock had been valuable real estate. A small war had been fought over control of the region, once important when the influence of the old empire depended upon strong supply lines and tyrannical discipline. The port had been domed to hold the artificial atmosphere so that its inhabitants could engage in commerce without vacsuits. Palm trees and grass had been imported to beautify the filthy rock, and the turd was polished thoroughly. There had been great plans for Jonesy.

Now, with the empire dead and gone, and the Confed a weak substitute, Jonesy had degenerated to a dingy oasis—a place to take a real shower and grab a bite of home-cooking on your way to somewhere else. Hank thought of it as a glorified truck stop.

Even so, a steady stream of goods poured in from all corners of the galaxy to be bought, sold, and traded. It was a place of diverse cultures and alien races, where many people had secrets to hide, and no one asked too many questions. Hank had chosen to refuel there for that very reason.

He docked the *Elsa* under an assumed registration as the *Vasco*, which he'd used successfully in the past, complete with the proper forged documents to back it up. He intended to refuel, check the local buzz, then space out quietly. There was no sense in attracting unwanted attention, particularly by security.

Sai sat back in the copilot's seat with her feet up on the control console. "Can we order out for food? I'm already sick of this synthetic crap."

"At least I can cook," Elsa shot back.

"Oh yeah? What do you call this? Electric Mystery Meat Surprise? Wait a minute. What makes you think I can't cook?"

"Nothing, just the fact that women like you normally dish out their specialties on their backs."

"Metallic bitch!" Sai yelled, kicking at the controls.

Hank sat with his face in his hands quietly muttering to himself. "I'm in hell. I have died and been sent to everlasting perdition."

Finally he could take no more, and he stood and took a deep breath. "Will you both just shut up!"

"She started it," Elsa said.

"I did not! Besides, where do you get off telling us to shut up?" Sai said, pointing her finger at Hank.

"Exactly," Elsa said. "Who do you think you are?"

Great, Hank thought, they found a common enemy.

"Listen. We're going to be stuck with each other for a while longer, so please, for all our sakes, try to get along. We can't risk leaving the ship, so why don't we do something constructive? How about you two work on analyzing the corporate security net for any news about us. I'll order some Xai food and a couple of beers." He stopped and looked in his cooler. "Make that a case."

Before Hank could reach for the com unit, it signaled an incoming message. "Answer it, Elsa. Keep us out of the vid." He hoped it was just the dockmaster confirming his fuel order.

Elsa answered the com, putting up a phony holographic simulation of herself as a human. "Hello, who is it?"

A holo image of a pudgy middle-aged man appeared in miniature above the com unit. "Elsa, that's a good look for you. Is Hank around?"

"Shit!" Hank said. He recognized the man as Tazi Lippman, an ex-pilot, ex-friend, current rummy who turned up now and then to hustle credits for liquor. "Lippman! How in the hell did you know it was me? I tried my damnedest to be incognito."

Elsa's fake image dissolved, allowing Lippman to see Hank. Lippman smiled. "Ah, you can play all you want with registration codes, but I recognized Elsa's lines. I hear you're into the passenger trade these days."

"Well, you do what you can to make a buck."

"I'm talking about one special little wench, one with a price on her head. Sai Collins. Where might she be?"

Great, Hank thought, news travels fast. One of these days I am going to slit your throat, you old lush. "What? Price on her head? Damn! And I let her off on Matilda just a couple of hours ago. How much was it? Maybe I can still find her."

Lippman shook his head, laughing, but it was forced, and his eyes had a cast of desperation. "Now, you wouldn't want to lie to me, Hank old boy. After all, we're friends. Friends share things with each other. A fifty-thousand-credit bounty makes for a strong friendship, don't you think?"

"What do you mean?"

Lippman's face tightened. "Come on, Hank. Why would you be so secretive if you didn't still have her on board? Tell me, are you going to turn her in, or has she paid you enough to help her?"

"You've been sucking down the wrong fuel, my friend. You're imagining things."

Lippman flushed red. "Don't screw with me, Jensen! You're so smug, sitting in your fancy ship, free to do what you want! Remember this, you and I are just the same. You could be scraping the bottom just like me after a bad piece of luck. I deserve a piece of this,

Hank. I need it. And you're either gonna pay me my due, or you're gonna have to face Security. Remember, there's a price on your head, too. Which will it be?"

CHAPTER ELEVEN

It didn't take long for one of his larcenous little birds to whisper in Chandler's ear that someone had just bought an Athena-class yacht and was looking to refit it into a pleasure cruiser. Chandler used some of Randol's money and was able to get a name.

Louie "The Finger" Rocco specialized in providing entertainment to those unfortunate souls in the remote boomtowns of the Outyonder. He was a humanitarian soul who enjoyed spreading love and companionship—for a price—at his pleasure domes and casinos. This selfless impulse had made him one of the richest men in the sector, though still a pauper when compared to the lords of the megacorporations. Louie's well-known philosophy was: "So what? They got more money, but I get laid more often."

Louie Rocco was the proud new owner of a yacht listed in the records as the *Swan Princess*. Chandler reasoned that Rocco was not one to purchase a ship legally for full price, and if he could examine the ship, he might be able to prove it was the *Aurelius* and connect another dot leading back to Helen.

The problem was that, after spending a few million credits, an owner wasn't likely to admit that the ship might be stolen. In order to get close, he'd have to get creative.

Chandler knew the ship lay dry-docked at the Atlas Ship Yards awaiting renovations and that Rocco needed a designer to help him remodel and refit. Chandler figured he could fit the bill, so he set an appointment.

Louie Rocco conducted business from the upper floor of his pleasure dome on the Tarkus Mining Station, floating a safe distance from a deposit-rich asteroid field. The miners came to the station to sell their ore and spend their profits at the gambling tables, in the bars, or in the pleasure suites. Fortunes passed from their fingers into Rocco's pocket in a never-ending stream.

After grabbing a quick shuttle from the station's small port, Chandler stepped into the Gold Digger Lounge. They cranked the music up so high that the beats slammed into his chest like clubs. The smells of unwashed bodies blended with tobac, spilled drinks, and piss filled the air.

Filth-covered miners, who looked and smelled like they'd never bathed, crowded the dance floor. Their clean, scantily clad male and female escorts didn't seem to notice the stench. Money was the ultimate deodorant.

The dance floor occupied the middle of the room, bordered by the gaming area. Off to the left stood a row of blackjack tables and off to the right were nova tables. The bar wound around the outside edge of the room in a squared U.

Chandler carried his notescribe in one hand and a handful of swatches in the other. He approached the bar, catching the bartender's attention. "Hey, bud, I'm looking for Louie!" He shouted to be heard over the roar of the music.

The bartender glanced at him and jerked a thumb back toward a staircase carpeted in red velvet. Chandler nodded and moved through the crowd toward the stairs, where a large man wearing exo-armor stood guard. He held up a hand as Chandler approached.

"What's your business?" the man asked.

"I'm here to see Louie about his new yacht."

"Who are you?"

"I'm Elray Pinchon, the decorator. I called earlier."

"Hmm. He's expecting you." The man scrutinized him. "You don't look like a decorator type to me. They're usually more artsy."

"How do you know I'm not? I've got artsy coming out of my ears."

The man raised an eyebrow and then waved him on, speaking into a comlink on his wrist. "Got one coming up."

Chandler climbed the steps to the second level. A white-haired man in a green suit met him at the top of the stairs. "Mr. Pinchon?"

"That's me," Chandler said.

"Come this way."

The man led Chandler past the rows of doorways to the pleasure suites. Signs hung above each door indicating whether or not they were in use. Chandler thought the signs were redundant since the howls of pleasure could be heard clearly through the thin walls.

They arrived at an ornately carved door featuring a debauched scene that Chandler tried not to notice. The man in green touched the palm lock, and the door opened.

Chandler set the notescribe and swatches on a table and looked around. To say the room was colorful was an understatement. Striped lizard-skin rugs covered the floor. Red velvet wallpaper accented with gold trim stretched around the room. On every wall were at least three portraits of Rocco.

The man himself sat behind a gold and leather desk, smoking a stubby tobac cigar. He was engaged in a heated debate with an obese woman whose clothing exposed entirely too much flesh. As soon as he looked up and saw Chandler, he waved her to silence. "Whoa, whoa, get the hell outta here, what's-a-matter with you? Can't you see my appointment just walked in? Go away."

"But what am I gonna do, Louie? They're draining me dry!"

"Believe me," he said, "you can afford to miss a few meals! Now, I dare you to talk to me again. Get the hell out."

The woman gave Chandler a dirty look, flipped her hair back, and walked out of the room with her nose held high.

Rocco stood and threw his arms into the air. Rings flashed on every finger. "You have no idea how glad I am to see you. I got a friggin' yacht sitting in dry dock waiting for a refit. So far, I can't find anybody who has any friggin' taste to redecorate the damn thing!"

Inwardly, Chandler cringed. What a pig, he thought. But he kept the appraisal off his face. This was going to be fun. It was all about rapport, so he threw his arms up and just went for it. "Yo, Rocco, I'm your man! I got taste out the wazoo! You don't want one of those namby-pamby sissy boys messin' with your boat. You need someone with class," he said shooting him an O with his index finger and thumb. "Like yourself. I can tell just by looking at you that you're a man of refined taste."

Rocco slammed an open palm on his desk. "That's what I've been trying to tell these bozos! What do I care about this classic color coordination crap? If I wanted to live in the lobby of a friggin' doctor's office, I would buy one!"

"Exactly!" Chandler said. "What are all those colors for, if you don't use them? This office, for instance. I don't mean to pry, but whose work is this? I have never seen such a fine application of design technique."

Rocco grinned and nodded. "You'd never guess if I told you."

"Probably not," Chandler said.

"Yours truly," Rocco said. "Me, myself."

"Really, with talent like this, why would you hire someone else to decorate your yacht?"

"Well, you know, takes a lotta time, doin' what I do. I mean, I gotta check out the new girls and I gotta make sure the older girls are still qualified. Of course, collections, that's a nightmare of its own. So I don't have time to oversee the job as closely as I might like. Therefore, I need to find some guy—or broad, I ain't picky—who shares my artistic vision."

"How's this?" Chandler said. "I see the master bedroom done in striped black-and-white fur, but the bed is like this orange that kinda jumps out at you. The bedroom, it's gotta be a place of excitement. You know what I'm saying?"

"I hear ya!"

"The ceiling is like a big holoscreen where you can show whatever you wanna show, while lying back and enjoying the ride."

"I like that."

"Okay, before I go any further here, you and I both know everything boils down to money. How much do you intend to spend on this project? Are you a man who limits art? Or are you a man who feels that art should be allowed to develop free of constraint?"

"I figure I can afford about a hundred and fifty K worth of artistic freedom," Rocco said.

"Well that might be okay, I guess. I could cut a few corners, but a job like this should really be two hundred K."

"One seventy-five."

Chandler shrugged. "Fair enough. When do you want me to start?"

"Right now. Let me give you a deposit."

"No need," Chandler said. "I am an artist." Chandler paused. "Then again, now that I think about it, I will have a few expenses. Say, twenty thousand credits. Let me take a look at the ship. I'll make a few sketches and get back with you."

"Done," Rocco said extending his hand.

They shook hands and Chandler started to leave the room.

"Oh," Rocco said. "Feel free to enjoy the facilities. On the house. About an hour's worth of the facilities and then I'll have to start charging you. But stay away from my A-list girls—they're extra."

Chandler smiled, but he planned on running as fast as he could back to the *Marlowe* to head over to the Atlas Ship Yards before Rocco wised up. But first, he was itching to take a shower.

* * *

Helen Randol was not settling well into her new surroundings. The cell was dimly lit and stank of human waste. Food came regularly, but it consisted of some tasteless muck that she ate only to keep up her strength. She was determined to escape and she needed energy to do so when the opportunity arose. And it would soon.

As far as she could tell, her captors were imbeciles—uneducated brutes who did what they were told and didn't have any ambition beyond making easy credits and getting laid. Although she didn't have access to her finances, she did have ready access to her charm. But that was like playing with explosives. She didn't want a flirtation to win a few favors to turn into an invitation for a rape attempt.

She still didn't have a good handle on the limitations the guards had been given. She was certain there would be no hesitation to beat her. She had seen another prisoner beaten unconscious the day before. But she imagined that the powers that be probably frowned on sexual fraternization, as it would compromise both the guards' resolve and her value as a hostage. It might make them hesitate to do what needed to be done to an uncooperative prisoner. That was good because it might help protect her from molestation, but bad, in that it might also work against her attempts at manipulation.

It was almost meal time. If things went as they had in the past two days, a single guard would hand a bowl and a cup through the bean-hole in the cell door. She worked on untangling her hair as best she could without a brush or comb. The shapeless pullover shirt and loose pants weren't very appealing, but she had torn a deep V in the collar of the shirt so that her cleavage could be clearly seen. When the guard arrived with lunch, she was going to strike up a conversation. A smile here, a hair flip and a heavy sigh there, and she might be able to gain some extra favors that might lead to a mistake and an opportunity. If nothing else, perhaps she could get him to break a simple rule so she could threaten to expose him and gain some leverage. The discipline appeared to be severe, and that could work in her favor.

She heard footsteps, so she arranged herself at the edge of her bunk, lounging, facing the door, propping her face in her hand and draping her hair along her shoulder and down her elbow. But the guard who came to her door wasn't the same as on previous days. He was taller, and he had a sharpness in his eyes that was surprising.

"Lunch is served," he said with a smile.

"What are we having today?"

"Well, I have to be honest and tell you that I have no idea what this is supposed to be," he said.

She made a show of stretching herself, then slowly rose and stepped to the cell door. "I don't suppose there'd be any way of me getting something else, maybe?"

The man smiled. "Hello, my name is Angus Brock, and you are?"

"Don't you know?"

"Again, I have no idea. I just got here. I'm still learning the ropes."

"I'm Helen Randol, daughter of Lord William Randol of House Nebulaco."

Brock nodded. "That's a mouthful. It also explains your unfortunate position." He handed her the bowl of muck and a cup of water. "Here you go. I'm sorry about your situation. If I could do something without dying in the process, I would certainly make it better for you. I have nothing against you, and I actually think this is horrible. However, I want you to clearly understand that neither your social status nor your obvious feminine charms are going to make me step one hair outside my orders concerning you. Besides, if you got out of that cell, you'd have no possible method of leaving the station. That being said, if you have a request that I *can* fulfill, I will go out of my way to make it happen. Does that work for you?"

"Well, I . . ."

"Not that it matters. I just want us to be clear." Brock smiled. "For the moment, let me give you some sincere friendly advice. I would suggest you eat. It will help you keep up your strength, and you're going to need to stay healthy during this ordeal. I understand that they're going to come interrogate you. I don't know what information they're trying to get, but they will get it. They are primitive here.

They don't use mind probes. I know for a fact that they're capable of carving you up. There's no way that you can avoid telling them what they need to know, so just do it straight away and save yourself from mutilation."

Helen smirked. "You're just telling me that to get into my head. Manipulate me."

Brock sighed. "I can see how you'd think that way, but you're a smart woman. If you sit and consider my words for a while, I think you'll come to the conclusion that I'm right. At least I hope so for your sake. Bon appétit, milady."

Stunned, Helen watched Brock walk away. Her feelings were evenly divided between frustration at this new, incorruptible guard, and relief that there might at least be one human being on this rock with whom she could have an intelligent conversation.

Either way, it complicated any hope of an escape attempt.

* * *

"You can't be serious," Sai said, following Hank out of the cockpit into the galley.

"Serious as a case of Vegan Clap," Hank said. He opened drawers and ransacked through his belongings. "Elsa, have you seen that outfit I bought on Dar Es Salaam?"

Elsa didn't bother answering.

"But why?" Sai said. "Wouldn't it be smarter just to get out of here?"

"Maybe, but the state he's in right now, I guarantee he'd report our location to Security and they'd get a good fix on us. I've gotta see if I can head that off." Hank turned away from her and tore into another pile of clothing. "I could have already found it, but you went and cleaned up the place. I had everything organized. This pile here was for . . . well, I don't remember, but I know these socks don't belong."

"How long will it take you? What do I do if you don't come back?"

"Aha! I knew it had to be around here somewhere." Hank grabbed an armful of white cloth and stepped into the airlock, changing. "It should only take me about twenty minutes or so. Elsa, finish the refuel and get us ready to get out of here." He stopped and looked at Sai. "I don't have time to explain this right now, and I'm not sure you'd understand anyway. Tazi Lippman, he's not really a bad guy. He's just in a tight spot right now. And like most of us, he's his own worst enemy. I think I can talk him out of informing on us. If so, it will be that much less we have to worry about. If not . . . well, we won't be much worse off, will we?"

"What if you paid him the money? I have some. I'd hoped to buy a new life, but I won't *have* a life if Security finds me."

Hank nodded. "Best case, Tazi would convert that money to stims and kill himself. Problem is, I'm not convinced that he wouldn't report us anyway. I need to talk to him and get him to see reason."

"But what if something happens before you get back? What if Security shows up?"

Hank smiled. "Elsa knows what to do. Don't you?"

"Sure," Elsa said. "I know, but still, Hank, I think she's right. And, for your information, Tazi *used* to be a good man. Now he's a piece of filth."

"See? You two are starting to see eye to eye after all." He grinned, but his smile soon faded when he realized that he had failed to lighten the mood. He sighed and shook his head. "Sorry, this is just something I have to do."

"Fine. If you're going, I'm going, too."

Hank shook his head. "No, you have to stay here. There's a price on your head, remember?"

"There's a price on your head, too."

Hank shrugged and finished changing in his cabin. He came back into the galley wearing a long white *thobe* and a *ghutra* to cover his face.

"You look ridiculous," Sai said.

"I look like a local. No sense making it easy to identify me." Hank opened the cargo ramp and waved as he walked outside. "Keep it locked down until I get back. Be ready to dust off fast." He stepped off the ramp and keyed it closed.

The door shut in Sai's face. She trudged back to the cockpit and fell into the copilot's chair. "Terrific. Here we sit while he runs off on a fool's errand."

"Try not to be too hard on him, Sai. You have to understand; Lippman used to be Hank's partner. They had a falling out and went their separate ways. Hank has kept his head above water, barely, and Tazi couldn't. I think he feels responsible."

"That's ridiculous."

"He knows that. That's why he won't admit it, even to himself. But I know Hank."

Sai shook her head. "Well, as far as I'm concerned, Lippman is a prick."

"Damn straight."

Sai laughed. "Sorry I was so rude before. I've been through a lot in the last few days."

"Don't mention it," Elsa said. "We girls have to stick together."

"I suppose we do." Sai looked up at the viewscreen, which displayed dockworkers loading a ship adjacent to theirs. "Elsa, you know what I am."

"Yes, how could I not know? You were wriggling your way into my brain with your nosy cyber-psi skills when you first came on board."

Sai shrugged. "Sorry, just habit. Most people look around the room, look at the pictures on the wall. I also do a sweep to see what kind of computer systems and hardware are working. It's a survival skill. It's saved me before."

"I forgive you, Sai. I know you didn't mean to intrude."

"You actually remind me a lot of Dirion. He was once a man who became more. You were once a physical entity, a flesh-and-blood human as well?"

"In some ways it's a shame that your Dirion couldn't have made the transition. I was lucky. Hank saved me."

"I am glad you feel that way. I'm not sure how I'd feel if I lost my body but kept my mind."

"Hank and I knew each other when I was flesh. We knew each other well," Elsa said.

"How well?"

"We were partners in the Scouts. A two-person ship. Mapping, cataloging, first contact a couple of times with proto-intelligent creatures. We didn't find the mother lode of advanced societies that some teams have, but we did all right. We made a lot of people rich and discovered a few new worlds to farm. We worked together, lived together."

"What happened? How did you end up . . . as you are?"

"An accident. We were refueling on a fringe outpost and the equipment was antiquated. There was a plasma explosion. I was severely injured. Hank saved me . . . or what was left.

"Back at the nearest Confed base they patched up what pieces they could save. My mind was intact, but my body . . . they replaced what they could, and things worked okay for a while. But the pain never went away. Sometimes I would just shut down and lose control and I would lie in my own piss and filth. Hank would save me again. Clean me up and wait until it passed. But eventually it was too much."

"What happened?"

"Hank had done some checking, and some Confed researchers were recovering technology from the old empire. There is so much that has been forgotten. Some of it for good reason—it was diabolical. But some could be beneficial to the Confed. He came to me with a suggestion. I had been at the point of killing myself. To me, this is a good afterlife. I get to spend time with Hank. For all his childishness he is a wonderful man, good and true. And I get to fly free in space and keep traveling. The pain is gone, and I am by all practical measurements happy."

"Do you love Hank?"

Elsa laughed, and the sound of her voice bounced around the cockpit. "Of course. The question is, my dear, do you?"

"Of course I don't love him," Sai said.

"No, not yet. But I think you could."

Sai shook her head. "I've never really loved anyone. Well, Dirion, but that was different. He was my father."

"That doesn't mean you can't love. It simply means you're probably more in need of love than most people."

"But still, I hardly know him."

"I understand. But I'm still a woman. I've already seen that the more you come to realize the man he is, the more you trust him. For you, trust is love. In fact, you may find love easier than trust."

"I don't know."

"It's all right, Sai. I won't tell him. But if you want him to know, you're going to have to tell him. He'll never figure it out himself. He's a man."

CHAPTER TWELVE

Hank arranged to meet Lippman in a public place, the small park just outside the trading house. It was one of the few areas of greenery on Jonesy. Delicate palm fronds shaded rows of verdant undergrowth. Narrow paths crisscrossed the park, their twists and turns allowing park goers to lose themselves in the cool shadows. The park was not well maintained and the greenery had begun to take over everything.

Hank sat at the edge of the algae-choked central fountain waiting impatiently. He wore a tiny earpiece, his link with Elsa, just in case anything went wrong. He hoped it would stay quiet.

He checked the time. Lippman was already five minutes late. Of course, Lippman had never been on time for anything in his life. That was another reason why he had been a lousy free-trader.

Hank spotted him shortly thereafter, nervously making his way through the crowd, looking behind him every few seconds. His eyes locked with Hank's and he approached the fountain.

"It's a good thing you decided to show," Lippman said, sitting next to Hank, "otherwise I would have gotten pissed off. You wouldn't want—"

"Kiss my ass," Hank said. He moved aside the *ghutra* covering his face and stood. "If you think for one solid minute that I'm afraid of you, you're deluding yourself. I'm here for two reasons. Number one is to save myself the hassle of having to dodge another goon squad when it can be avoided, and the second reason is to save your ass."

"Hold on, don't you mess with me. All I have to do is make one call."

"And what? You make the call, I space out. They can't stop me in time. They don't know where I'm going. Do you think they'll pay you a single credit for helping them if the girl gets away? They'd be more likely to break your knees for not notifying them when I first landed. And if they find out that you've talked to me before calling them, you're a dead man. Either way, you lose."

Lippman shook his head. Sweat beaded on his forehead and ran down his cheeks. "No, you've got things turned around. I hold all the cards. I want that reward. You owe me."

Hank sighed. "How's that? Just because you've bottomed out and I haven't yet? Because life isn't fair? Hell, Tazi, I've probably helped you more than any spacer alive. How many times have I bought you a meal or given you clothes off my back?"

"Yeah, but you never coughed up a credit. You have that condescending attitude as if I can't be trusted with money."

"Well, can you? Have you ever gotten a handout that you didn't cash in at the nearest bar for stims or liquor?"

Lippman sputtered. "But . . . but that's not the point. I can hurt you. You have to pay! You're lying about all of this!"

Hank stood and dug out a credit stick. "Here, Tazi. Here's a hundred credits. Prove me wrong. I suggest you get a good dinner, get yourself cleaned up, and try to find a job. You're a lot smarter than you've been acting lately. Here's another chance for life—don't piss it away."

Lippman grabbed the stick out of his hand, but he wasn't happy with it. "I want more. I want a thousand! You may talk big, but you're full of shit. You're bluffing, and I'm not stupid enough to go for it."

Hank nodded. "All right. You have two more options. You can contact Security and die quick. Or you can use that hundred up on more poison and die slow."

Lippman exploded in anger. He rushed forward, his hands grabbing for Hank's throat. With a sudden sidestep and a half turn, Hank deflected Lippman's arms and pushed him in the direction of his momentum. Lippman stumbled and fell to the street.

Onlookers gathered to watch the fight, muttering to one another and pointing at Lippman, who stumbled to his feet.

"Damn you!" Lippman screamed and swung a fist at Hank.

Hank dodged the blow and sank a short, powerful punch directly in the center of Lippman's face.

Lippman froze and fell back on his rear end, dazed. Then he bent forward and began to throw up.

Hank walked away. "Elsa, I'm headed back. Make sure we're ready to take off when I get there."

"Is he going to turn us in?"

"I don't know," Hank said, hoping that Lippman might wise up after he recovered from the punch. "But either way, I plan on us being offworld before he gets a chance."

* * *

Lippman still tasted blood. His nose throbbed and he probed a loose tooth with his tongue. Hank Jensen, big man. Well, he was going to show Hank just how small he really was.

He went to a public comlink and inserted the credit stick Hank had just given him. The machine deducted its fee and he put the stick back into his pocket. It was ironic that Jensen's stinking charity was paying for his downfall.

The call connected, but the visual was blacked out as a man's voice answered. "What do you have for me?"

"This is Tazi Lippman on Jonesy. Hank Jensen and Sai Collins are here at the starport in Delta City. Come and get them."

"You sure it's them?"

"I know Jensen. I used to be friends with the bastard. It's him all right. I live at the Carlton on Epsilon Street. I'll be home later this afternoon waiting for my reward."

"We'll check it out. If you're playing games with us, you'll regret it."

"No games. Just be ready to pay up."

He ended the call. "Screw you, Jensen."

Four hours later they came to the Carlton. Hank Jensen and the *Elsa* had already shipped out by that time, and they knew that Lippman had met Hank in the park, tipping him off with his extortion attempt. They were not in a forgiving mood. He got his reward in the form of a shot to the forehead. Word was put out on the location of the *Elsa* and the noose tightened a bit more.

Lippman had beaten the odds. He didn't die broke. He still had five credits left on the stick Hank had given him, and a half-empty bottle of whiskey as his estate.

* * *

They called him Thorne. If he'd ever had a first name, no one knew it. Nor would they dare utter it if they did know. He liked being called Thorne, and if you knew what was healthy for you, you stayed on his good side. Some people insisted that Thorne didn't have a good side.

Thorne's passion was piracy. He loved the power. Loved the way it felt to blast someone's ship, then board it and take what he wanted. He loved the respect that fear gave him.

Thorne enjoyed attacking lone ships, but given the choice he'd opt for caravans. He and his crew had once stumbled across a caravan, and they were so complete in their theft and destruction that they attracted the attention of someone with real power.

It was common knowledge that Thorne respected power. He was a man who took whatever he wanted wherever he wanted, and not only did he get away with it, but no one would ever challenge him.

While that felt great, Thorne knew he lacked the kind of power his mystery friend at Nebulaco had.

When the first message from the informant had been delivered to him, Thorne wasn't sure whether or not to believe it. It came from the lips of a small, unimposing man, a common beggar. But the credits the messenger delivered, a token of the informant's esteem, gave credence to the story.

The informant rarely communicated with Thorne's forces directly. The informant had a complicated network, each group using one or two contacts to pass information up and down through the organization. No one knew who the informant really was, and those who asked too many questions didn't live long.

The first time Thorne acted on information from this mysterious informant, his main concern was that the raid he was planning was some sort of trap. The lightly guarded caravan might be a Confed task force trying to clean up the sector.

But Thorne couldn't resist the opportunity. He and his crew flew over to the quadrant where this caravan was supposed to be, and sure enough, the informant's information was dead-on. So Thorne attacked, and the payday was tremendous.

The informant didn't want any of the money, but Thorne knew he must have earned a profit somehow.

Mostly, Thorne loved the way the media reacted. They were fearful and awestruck. That had not always been the case.

Years ago, a reporter on the planet Sumter made the mistake of calling Thorne an insignificant coward. He said Thorne attacked only ships with no real firepower and that he would never be anything more than an irritant to the public. He suggested that someone swat him down like the buzzing insect that he was.

The next day, Thorne strode into the studio where this reporter was on the air broadcasting his newscast to the civilized worlds. Security tried to stop him, but Thorne simply shot them. He walked right up to the pest and smiled. "Those things you said about me. Tell me to my face."

The reporter nearly had a heart attack, but Thorne wouldn't let him off so easy. He hacked the man to pieces with an antiquated sword, live on the air, then turned to the camera. "Anyone else wants to call me a coward, go right ahead and you'll get a nice personal visit as well."

Since then, while the press didn't sing his praises, they certainly spoke with respect. He had all his men carry a sword as a symbol of what he would do to those who crossed him. And now, thanks to the informant, he got more press than ever, and more money than ever. So much so that he never even considered breaking away.

Now Thorne sat at the head of the table enjoying a party thrown in his honor by his crew. He had a woman on either side of him, a huge plate of food, and a giant flask of Aldeberon whiskey. His bald head glistened in the light, and the girls took turns plucking bits of food from his mustache.

A messenger entered the room, squeezed past the revelers, and handed a note to Glenn Manter, Thorne's right-hand man. No messenger would dare interrupt Thorne.

Glenn glanced at the note and nodded, then moved through the throng to the head of the table. Glenn held up the sealed communiqué. "It's from the informant."

Thorne took the communiqué and broke open the seal, reading it.

"Do we have a new assignment, or is it about the Randol woman?" Glenn asked.

"Actually, it asks a favor. The informant wants us to patrol for a ship heading from Jonesy to Trent, the *Elsa*, piloted by Hank Jensen and carrying a woman named Sai Collins. He doesn't have the flight plan on this one, but the route is common. He wants us to send out raiders to destroy the ship, chase down any life pods, and make sure there are no survivors."

Thorne lowered the note. "Hank Jensen, that sounds familiar. Was that the son of a bitch who took a shot at me in the starport bar on Calico?"

"One and the same," Glenn said.

"I thought he was dead."

"Apparently not."

"He will be soon. I always hated that cocky bastard."

"Does the message say why the informant wants them dead?"

"No, and I don't care. I've been in port too long." Thorne stood, drawing the cutlass from his belt and giving the room a wild-eyed smile. "I haven't killed anyone in weeks."

* * *

"Have you ever been to Trent?" Hank asked. He checked the nav computer and made a few minor adjustments. Their exit from Jonesy had been abrupt, and their flight plan not as efficient as he would have liked.

Sai laughed. "Other than Raken and Nebula Prime I haven't been anywhere."

"Raken's not exactly a place I'd like living. It's okay to visit, mind you, but it's all concrete and metal. Trent, though, that's a place worth spending some time."

"How so?"

"It's an agworld. Not one of those robotically farmed, plant-cloning operations like most of the Greensward planets. No, Trent is different. People work the land there. They actually own it. No synthetics, very limited mechanical assistance, only a few androids. It's organic and real. You can actually take a nap under an apple tree, take in a sunset, or sit on a back porch and watch the rain come in across the fields."

"You talk like a displaced country boy."

Hank nodded. "That I am. I was born and raised on a little upstart colony on the edge of Manspace called Hava. I didn't know squat about piloting until I hit the military."

"Do your folks still live on Hava?"

"No," Hank said quietly, "no one lives on Hava anymore." He rose from the pilot's seat, his face expressionless. "Sorry, excuse me, I need to check the engines," he said, leaving the cockpit.

Sai waited a few moments, but when Hank didn't return she spoke. "Elsa?"

"Sorry. If he wants to talk about it, he will. If not, it wouldn't be right for me to tell you."

"You're a good friend, Elsa," Sai said.

"I can't help it, I'm wired that way."

A while later, Hank returned, wearing his standard-issue grin. "How about a beer?" He asked.

"Sure," said Sai.

Hank pulled a couple of cold ones from the cooler and opened them, handing one to Sai.

"Thanks," she said. "I'm sorry about bringing all that up. I didn't mean to pry."

"Oh that? It's not your fault. You just stepped in a pile of unfinished business. I'm just feeling sorry for myself."

"I know what you mean. You see, from where I sit, you're a very lucky man. I don't remember my parents at all. I was around three when they . . . disappeared."

"Do you want to talk about it?" Hank asked.

"I don't care," she said, taking another sip. Sai had to admit the cold brew was good. Hank knew quality.

"Dirion was the source of all my information about the past. He found me on the streets, barely alive. I was in shock. I was around three He said I must have been wandering around for a while. This was in the days before he was totally interfaced with the Grid. He said he was walking along and he tripped over me. I had fallen asleep in the gutter.

"At first he was going to leave me there, but something stopped him. He said he sensed that I was special. When I was a little girl, I used to fantasize that he had fallen in love with the darling little street urchin, but I know now that it was my psi talent that caught his attention. He knew I could turn out to be useful. Don't get me wrong. Even though he picked me up to use me, it could have been worse. Most street children get used in much more terrible ways. I was lucky."

"But what happened to your parents?" Hank asked. "Where are they?"

Sai shrugged. "I don't really know. Dirion tried to research it, but he never found anything conclusive. More than likely I was the off-spring of some starport whore who outgrew her welcome with her pimp. But, ever the romantic, I imagined my parents as execs who were ambushed by street punks and I was somehow separated from them. They frantically tried to find me, but alas, the wicked city had devoured me. There was a part of me that dreamed they would find me one day. For years that wish lingered in the back of my mind. Until one morning I woke up and it was gone. It died like most dreams die, quietly in your sleep, almost as if they had never been there in the first place."

Hank listened gravely. His eyes had a far-off look, as if he could actually see that little girl shivering in the cold street. His beer rested in his hand, though he hadn't taken a single sip.

Sai put her can down on the console and ran her fingers though her hair. "Sorry, I didn't mean to depress you."

"Oh no, I'm fine. In fact, I'm glad you told me. You're right. I get to feeling sorry for myself and I forget that I'm a damn sight better off than a lot of people." Hank finally took a drink and put up his booted feet. "I reckon since we're telling stories that I ought to tell you my pathetic little—"

A warning klaxon sounded. Hank sat up suddenly, dropping his beer. "Elsa! What in the hell?"

"We've got a ship closing on us, Hank. He swooped in out of no-where."

"Put it on the screen."

The star field was replaced by the battle-scarred image of a medium-sized ship.

"Marauder class with a crew of no more than three or four. A favorite of mercenaries and pirates," Elsa reported.

"Charge up the guns and cinch up your britches, ladies. I think we're about to have us a brawl."

EPISODE FOUR

CHAPTER THIRTEEN

The Marauder was on an intercept course. Hank wrenched the controls and took the ship into a roll and a bank out to a different vector. There was a chance that the other pilot was just a hotshot jerk who liked to fly wild. They would know in a moment. Hank made the maneuver—and the Marauder adjusted its course for another intercept.

"Shit," Hank said. "Status, Elsa?"

"We're ready, Hank. Shields are at maximum and weapons are charged."

"Okay. Open a line. Let's talk to this joker."

Elsa activated her communications unit, and a red light appeared on the console signaling Hank that he was broadcasting. Hank didn't for a minute think about being honest. There was a price on their heads. "This is the free-trader ship *Vasco*. Back off, asshole."

A gruff voice answered. "This is the hand of Thorne. Stand-to and your lives will be spared. Resist and we'll blow you out of the sky."

The Marauder closed fast; in only a few seconds it would be within range to fire its weapons.

"What are you going to do?" asked Sai.

"*Elsa* is a hot little ship, faster than this guy could possibly know. We could outrun him, but then we'd have to worry about him sneaking up on us again or reporting our position. I intend to take him out."

He activated the com again.

"Please don't hurt us," Hank said sounding as pitiful as he could. "We're just a trading ship. We have no weapons." He turned and winked at Sai as he clicked off the com. "We'll give them a fine wide-eyed surprise. Elsa, give me manual nav control." A control yoke unfolded itself from the pilot's console. "Hang on."

Hank took hold of the control and made a couple of small course corrections to get the feel of things, then wrenched backward on the control yoke, turning the ship suddenly just as the Marauder entered weapons range.

Twin bolts of destructive energy exploded from the Marauder as it fired on the *Elsa*, but Hank had changed course. The blaster fire passed by harmlessly.

Hank looped *Elsa* up and around. "Hit it, Elsa, give him some!"

Elsa let loose with everything she had, all weapons on full computer control. She lobbed three blaster bolts and a round of plasma cannon fire at the Marauder.

The other ship obviously hadn't been prepared for such resistance from the small trading vessel. It decelerated suddenly and changed course, but not before the tail end of the plasma round caught it across the bow.

"You got it!" Sai screamed, shaking a fist at the viewscreen.

Hank laughed. "That'll fix you! Make me spill my beer, will ya?"

But the ship was not disabled. It turned for another pass, firing as it came.

Dull thuds sounded from the hull. They had been hit.

"Status?" Hank asked.

"Shield damage only. We're down to seventy percent. Weapons are at half charge."

"Okay, gear up for another round."

"Wait, Hank, I'm registering a targeting beam. It's tracking us," Elsa said.

Just then a small object detached itself from the Marauder and ignited, streaking for the *Elsa*. It was a missile. Old but effective technology.

Hank hit the throttle. They didn't have any countermeasures to fool the missile; they would have to try to outrun it.

"Range: twelve thousand meters," Elsa reported.

"Sai, throw everything you can find into the airlock."

"What?"

"Do it now! Everything in the airlock . . . except the beer!"

Sai ran to the aft section, grabbing clothing and boxes, beer cans and assorted junk. She threw them as fast as she could through the airlock door.

The ship shifted and turned as Hank attempted to outmaneuver the missile.

"Range: ten thousand meters."

Sai continued to load the airlock.

"Range: nine thousand meters."

"Sai, Hurry! Finish up and shut the door."

Sai kicked the debris out of the way and hit the door control. "It's closed!" she yelled.

"Range: five thousand meters."

"Range: four thousand."

"Range: three thousand."

"Two thousand."

"One thousand."

"Dump it, Sai! Dump the airlock. Now!"

Sai hit the emergency purge and the airlock opened, sucking the junk out the side of the ship. At the same time, Hank pulled a gut-wrenching maneuver that threw Sai across the cabin.

The missile passed harmlessly through the garbage and struck the *Elsa* in the aft section. Main power failed and the dim red lighting of the secondary system kicked in. Hank's sweating face looked demonic.

"That didn't work at all," Sai said.

"Son of a bitch!" Hank jerked the control yoke to the side. "What's the damage?"

"Glancing blow. It caused an overload in the hyperdrive, still operational but barely. I think the junk caused the hull-piercing payload to blow too soon. Nothing penetrated."

"Yeah, that's what she said. One more time, Elsa. Let's give it to him. All shields to forward."

Hank turned the ship around and gunned it for all she was worth. He streaked directly toward the Marauder, the shields angled for maximum protection to their prow.

The Marauder must have been somewhat damaged because it was slow to respond. It wallowed over, exposing its broadside.

"Fire!" Hank screamed.

Elsa's fury rained upon the ship like lightning from the hand of God. The vessel erupted into a blue flash of short-lived flame, then into a burst of broken and twisted metal shrapnel.

Hank pulled back sharply to avoid the expanding debris field. He closed his eyes and sat back, drawing in a deep breath and blowing it out loudly. "Take over, Elsa," he said.

He unbuckled the G-harness and stood. He turned as Sai rushed into his arms. "That was fantastic!" she said, squeezing him tightly. "I can't believe we did it!"

They held each other a little longer. Their eyes met, and Sai slowly pushed away from him. He saw her in a different light in that moment. He wondered if she felt it, too. It could just be the rush of having survived certain death, but she looked lovely and alive. She blushed and looked away. The moment passed, so Hank winked and looked through the threshold at the now clean cabin.

"I'll be damned," he said. "There was a floor under all that crap. I thought the layers went down forever." Hank smiled at Sai. "First corporate hit squads, now pirates. You are one popular gal."

Sai smiled back and did a curtsy. "What can I say? Some girls got it."

"Hank," Elsa said, "there's something out there."

"Other than all my dirty laundry?"

"My sensors are picking up a life pod. Someone managed to eject before the ship blew." Elsa put it on screen. The cylindrical pod spun slowly with its frozen human contents—a lone pirate.

"Let the bastard rot," Sai said.

Hank rubbed the stubble on his cheeks. "Can't do it," he said. "Wouldn't be right. Nothing scares me more than the thought of floating through space forever in stasis."

"If it were us out there, they'd leave and never look back," Sai said.

"That's exactly why we're not going to do it," Hank said. "Elsa, lock on a tractor beam and pull him in."

Elsa did as he asked. They moved to the viewscreen mounted next to the rear cargo airlock. Elsa manipulated the pod in the tractor beam and neatly lined it up with the entrance. The outer door opened. She eased the pod inside, closed the door after it, and then repressurized the hold.

Hank and Sai opened the door from the main cabin area to the hold and took a look at the pod. "Looks intact. He should be fine," Hank said.

"Are we going to wake him up?" Sai said.

Hank shook his head. "Naw. No sense in it right now." Hank said. "We can keep him in the storage hold and turn him in later to Nebulaco or the Confed."

They secured the pod with cargo harnesses and then returned to the cockpit. Hank flopped down in the pilot's chair and entered the course corrections that brought them back on line for the Trent System. Out of the corner of his eye, he watched Sai stare out the viewport, wide-eyed in almost childlike wonder. It was all new to her. The stars were like some immense playground. Hank remembered when he had felt that way—it seemed like centuries ago.

Hank's life on the spaceways had been lonely, with only Elsa to keep him company, never staying in one place long enough to know any women longer than it took for a cargo transfer. Not that he ever complained. There were advantages to relationships on a cash-and-carry basis. You only had to worry about losing your money, never losing something that hurt inside.

Sai noticed him looking at her and smiled. "What are you thinking?" she asked.

"Nothing much. Just about how old I am and how young you are."

"You can't be that old."

"Honey, I'm so old I remember wearing ear plugs during the big bang. I'm so old my first starship was a horse. I'm so old my galactic ID number is three."

Sai laughed and shook her head. She sat on his lap and laid a hand on his arm. "Stop it. That's enough."

Hank laughed with her for a moment, his eyes settling on the warm hand that rested on his biceps, the delicate fingers. He stopped laughing and looked up into her eyes. They were soft and blue. They held as much wonder for him as the stars held for her.

"What are you thinking about now?" she asked, knowingly.

"That maybe, just this moment, I ain't so damn old," he said, then leaned forward and kissed her. After a moment the length of a heartbeat, she returned the kiss.

Elsa quietly dimmed the lights and killed her vid sensors to let them have their privacy.

* * *

The Atlas Ship Yard was an enormous structure orbiting the planet Matilda. It branched out in all directions like a mutant tree, each arm providing berths for ships under construction or repair. Nearly one hundred ships were docked at the facility, from freighters large enough to be colony ships to one-man hoppers.

Chandler entered the office of the yard master. It was a utilitarian room with uncomfortable-looking gray chairs and battered desks. A rough woman wearing oil-stained overalls shuffled through a stack of hard-copy documents. She didn't notice Chandler come in.

"Excuse me," Chandler said.

"What do you want?" the woman said, not looking up.

"I'm Elray Pinchon. I'm doing an estimate for Louie Rocco on the *Swan Princess*. I need to get access to the ship."

"No problem. Soon as the boys get it rehabbed so it's safe for you to check it out. Wouldn't want any accidents."

Yeah, they needed time to make sure the ship was gutted before an outsider examined it.

"How long does that take?" Chandler said.

"What is it today, Tuesday?" She checked her comlink. "We can probably get back to you by next Monday."

"You have got to be kidding!"

The woman rolled her eyes. "Sure, you can see how hard I'm laughing. I live to entertain. Show business is in my blood. Now get the hell out of my office. I have things to do."

"I can't wait that long. Rocco wants his estimate tomorrow."

"People in hell want ice water."

"I don't think he's going to be very happy with you," Chandler said, shaking his head.

"Like I care. That yacht is a minor project here. I have work to do, bud. Here's a blank complaint form loaded up—knock yourself out." She held up a notescribe board.

Chandler laughed and crossed the room to her desk. "Thank you," he said, taking the notescribe. "You've done a fine job." Chandler extended his right hand. "Ben Dover, Galactic Trust Insurance."

The woman shook his hand with a bewildered look on her face. "What?"

"Just a test to make sure you're fulfilling the safety requirements needed to keep your premiums low. You see, even though we pass rigid rules and regulations, many officials don't follow through. I was just testing your procedures, and I must say that you did very well.

I could not be more pleased. You can be sure that your name will be mentioned in my report so that the owners can reward you appropriately. Let me just make a note here, what was the name?"

"Neena, Neena Landow. I don't remember ever seeing anyone here from your office before."

"Most of our investigations are done undercover. It's easy to be up to spec when you know you're talking to an inspector."

Neena nodded. "Well, I suppose that makes sense."

"Splendid. Well, that about wraps it up for your office. Now I need to check out the yard itself. Do me a favor. Don't let it get out that I'm here. I want to be able to observe the work without being noticed. I don't want the workers to feel like they're being spied on."

"Don't worry. Your secret is safe with me," Neena said.

Chandler snapped his fingers. "Oh yes, I almost forgot. I need a listing of the ships you have here, their berth numbers, and their ownership records."

Neena had the computer compile a list and she gave it to Chandler. She didn't even notice when he left with her notescribe board.

Chandler left the administrative offices, put on a vacsuit, and caught a car tram to berth twenty-nine, where the *Swan Princess* was docked. The blackness of open space contrasted with the spotlighted forms of the huge ships. Men scrambled over the hulls in magboots, repairing hull breaches and communications arrays.

He still held the notescribe; it tended to ward off people with questions and made him seem important, like someone official. No one likes to talk to an official, since they tended to write down names and make reports.

When he got to the *Swan Princess*, he took a look at the outside of the sleek vessel. It was massive for a private ship and had obviously been damaged. There was evidence of fresh repairs in the aft section. He keyed the com unit on the wrist of the suit to examine the ship data provided by Radje. He hoped he would get lucky inside.

A guard stood at the main airlock, but he looked half asleep—at least until he caught sight of Chandler approaching with a note-scribe. The guard immediately straightened up and looked serious.

Chandler waved his notescribe at the guard, smiled, walked straight to the airlock, and cycled through to enter the ship. He was relieved when his vacsuit's pressure sensor indicated that he could remove his helmet. The air inside smelled of solvents and paint.

The corridors were lined with real wood, darkly stained red and polished glossy. This was a luxury yacht that only the foolishly wealthy could ever afford. He sighed. No doubt Rocco would replace the wood with purple crushed velvet and lay orange shag carpet everywhere.

He checked the cargo hold and engineering sections first. He crawled into nooks and crannies, taking images of equipment serial numbers with his comlink, because they could be traced back to their manufacturer. Then he went to the crew's quarters and located what would have been Radje's shared cabin. He counted the air vents along the wall. Third from the left.

He fished in his pocket for a multi-tool, unfolded a driver, and popped off the vent cover. There it was: Radje's stash of liquor and stims along with stolen credit sticks and a stack of pornographic datastores. Everything matched Radje's description.

He pocketed the credit sticks and walked to the crew's common area and down the central passageway to the crew's galley. On all ships this is where crew members tended to spend a lot of their free time eating and playing cards. There were several tables reserved for the crew's mess, and he walked to the one farthest from the door. Chandler reached under the tabletop. He fished around for a while until his fingers felt what he had hoped for. He pulled out a joker right where Radje had said it was stashed. Not only was he a sneak thief, but he was also a dirty card cheat. Chandler looked at the back of the card. It was one of the special decks printed for Randol with the logo of the *Aurelius* as part of the design.

"Well, well, why am I not surprised?"

Chandler had plenty to prove it was the *Aurelius*. He pocketed the card, donned his helmet, and exited the ship, then took the tram back to the transport dock. He boarded the *Marlowe* and left the shipyard.

Chandler keyed his comlink and made a call to an old friend.

The viewscreen displayed the scarred, grim face of John Richmond wearing a Confed lieutenant commander's uniform. His eyes narrowed. "Mike Chandler? How the hell did you get this number?"

"You gave it to me."

"Huh. I must have been drunk."

"Believe me, John, you were."

The man laughed. "How the hell are you? Finally sick of civilian life?"

"Not sick enough to join up again. I'm still doing the private security thing."

"Not much money in that these days," Richmond said.

"Sad, but true. I see you've moved up in the world. Your lips must be getting sore from kissing all that ass and taking orders."

"I mostly give orders now. I have an ensign that I farm out to do all the ass-kissing for me. So tell me, why are you contacting me after all this time? I assume you need a favor."

Chandler shook his head. "Nope, not quite. This is an equal swap, favor for favor. I've been doing some work that's spilling over into Confed intelligence territory. I think I have something you want but I need something in return."

"We don't normally pay for information unless it's big."

Chandler shook his head. "No credits required. I have the gift-wrapped recovery of a stolen luxury yacht, but when you raid the shipyard I need you to feed me all the information on who piloted that ship to the dock. I have no hope of getting it otherwise. I need to talk to him to get details on where a hostage might be kept."

"You sure about the ship?"

Chandler shrugged. "About as sure as I was when I told you not to dance with that big-nosed woman in the bar on Prana."

"Yeah, I married her."

"Like I said, have I ever steered you wrong? What do you think? Stolen ship for some information?"

The man smiled. "I think that can be arranged."

CHAPTER FOURTEEN

Hank pulled up a visual of the planet Trent from the nav library on the main viewscreen. Its primary moon, Mordi, Randol's home base, was their destination. They were making slow progress to it. The damaged hyperdrive kept them at only twenty percent of their maximum speed.

Sai sat on Hank's lap with her arm around him. He zoomed in on Trent's surface. The patchwork quilt of crops and the beauty of the oceans brought back memories.

"It reminds me of Hava," Hank said. "Early mornings rising up out of bed to do chores. Fresh breakfast on the table when I got back."

"Were your parents settlers, or had your family been raised on the planet?"

"Well, my dad was a soldier, born in the heart of techworlds. He joined the Confed and then left service with them to join the forces of one of the local human confederations on the edge of Manspace. He fought in the Cygnus uprising. He was wounded. Never quite healed right. Never talked about it much, but you could tell. He mostly just bummed around after the war. Odd jobs here and there. I have no idea what brought him to Hava, but that's where he met my mother."

"Farm girl and spacer romance story?" Sai traced her finger down Hank's cheek, to his neck, and then she started playing with the bit of chest hair that was exposed in the notch of his partially opened shirt.

Hank smiled. "Pretty much. My mom would tell me stories about it when my dad wasn't around. He didn't talk about the past, ever. Good times or bad. He lived in the moment. One harvest at a time."

"Did you have any brothers or sisters?"

"A younger brother, Roger. He died one winter of a sickness. We never figured out what it was. That's the problem with a lot of these frontier worlds. Strange new microbes, not enough money to afford the latest medical technology. Things take a few generations to mutate to infect the human population. Likely it killed those without some sort of immunity and the rest of us will be never be bothered by it again."

"Sounds like a hard life."

"I thought so at the time. Looking back, it was pretty much paradise compared to the alternatives I've seen."

"I don't know if I have any brothers and sisters or not. No way of knowing."

"You didn't exactly have a pampered existence. Looks like it made you into a tough customer."

Sai smiled and raised a fist toward Hank. "You know it."

Hank took her small fist into his hand and brought it to his lips.

"Hank, it's funny. Kids just don't have any idea about what their life is really like until they look back. They don't know they're poor. They don't appreciate it if they're rich. I was warm and cozy in my room at Dirion's. I didn't know until later that it was basically a rat hole. Kids just have no clue about life."

"I got news for you, darlin'—we still don't. But I try my best to appreciate every good thing that happens in life every day. Tomorrow might be a sight less pleasant."

Sai stroked the hair on Hank's forehead. "So what finally happened on Hava? Why did you leave?"

"Well, like I said, I grew up milking cows and dodging horse shit. But as I grew, I developed a bad habit. I started to dream. I would stare up at the stars and wonder why anyone would choose to live on

Hava rather than explore the galaxy. I got sick of the work and the monotony."

Hank made an adjustment on the control panel.

"I was a stupid teenage kid, just the kind that joins the military. I signed up for a stint in the Scout Corps. It sounded exciting in the pamphlets—discover new worlds, make first contact with alien races, be a hero. They don't print the casualty stats. My academy graduated two hundred, but only twenty-five were left after our first year in the field."

"It must have been hard on you," Sai said.

"You and your partner are out there so far from normal human life that you think you are the only humans in the universe after a while. I think Elsa is the only reason I didn't crack up."

"It's about time you mentioned me," Elsa said. "I thought you two had forgotten I was plugged in."

Hank chuckled. "Elsa and I spent a lot of time working, exploring, drinking. That was before the accident, of course. She was just a lanky young lady with midnight-black hair and a mean temperament."

"Some things don't change," Elsa said.

"Finally, I knew it was time to come home. Returning from my last tour of duty, I had the chance to stop by Hava on my way to HQ. There'd been a plague. Another microbe . . . some mutated virus. It devastated the population. This time it hit my mom and dad. They were long gone. If I'd stayed on the farm, I'd probably be dead, too. At the time I wondered if that hadn't been my proper fate. All I know is that my childhood and everyone in it might as well have been a dream."

It was quiet in the cockpit. Sai looked at Hank with moist eyes and whispered, "We all travel crooked roads. You can only move on."

Hank sighed. "Sorry, I didn't mean to bring you down."

Sai put a finger to his lips. "It's okay." She leaned over and kissed him.

Elsa's voice interrupted their cuddling. "Well, if you two are finished with your hanky-panky, I need you to go back and look at the hyperdrive. I think you need to adjust the plasma flux manually."

"If I didn't know better, Elsa, I'd think you're jealous."

"I'm convinced she's going to get tired of you pretty soon. You really aren't as interesting as you think you are."

"What? I am amazingly interesting. I fascinate myself at times. But more than that, I am roguish."

"Roguish? As in dishonest and unprincipled? I suppose so, but I hardly call that an attractive trait."

"No, no . . . sexually mischievous and happy-go-lucky, and women love that."

Elsa let off a synthesized snort. "Only in holovids. In real life it gets annoying very quickly."

"Sai, what do you think? You like roguish, right? It sets the juices flowing. Doesn't it?"

Sai stood up and laughed. "No comment." She left the pair bickering and went into the galley.

* * *

Lieutenant Commander Richmond was true to his word. In exchange for the information on the yacht, the Confed pulled the shipyard records and gave Chandler everything he wanted.

Rocco's obviously forged records indicated that the ship had previously belonged to a Jack Melville out of Freemont City on Hampton. Chandler was not surprised when he discovered that Melville was a factory worker and had been dead for twenty years. That trail went nowhere.

But Chandler still had the pilot who had delivered the yacht to the shipyard. The ship hadn't been conjured out of thin air; it had been delivered from some location, somewhere. Luckily, the pilot was a real, living, breathing, drinking person, and he wasn't hard to find.

His name was Remo, and he was trying to make Chandler go broke buying him beer. Together they sat in a booth at a dive bar in Gardenburg, the largest city on Matilda.

"Let's get back to the question," Chandler said.

"Sure, I got nothing else to do but sit here and answer a bunch of fool questions," Remo said, slurring his words. "But since you're buying? Why not?"

"Where did you pick up the yacht? What system? What planet?"

"It's really complicated."

Chandler sighed. "How can it be complicated? Where did you go to pick it up?"

Remo laughed. "I went where they told me."

"And where exactly was that?"

"Nowhere, I picked the thing up in open space. It was just floating. They gave me the control codes so I was able to dock with it and bring it in."

"Didn't you think that was pretty suspicious?"

Remo looked at Chandler with a blank expression. "I'm a very trusting person."

"Yeah, I sensed that when I first met you," Chandler said. "What were the coordinates?"

"I don't remember the coordinates exactly, but it was in the area of the Outrigger Rift."

The Outrigger Rift was a treacherous area of space that butted up against a major trade route. It was an odd area of asteroids, small planetoids, and bits of random matter and dust all drifting in a chaotic mass. There was something inherently wrong with the fabric of space-time in that particular part of the universe. Some theorized that distorted gravitational waves had ripped apart multiple star systems in the region, leaving the area looking like a junk pile of creation. No one knew for sure, but it was obvious that something catastrophic had occurred.

There were thousands of hiding places and no way to track ships in the midst of the swarm of debris. It was a perfect base of operations for pirates because even knowing that the outlaws were there made no difference. It would take the entire Confed fleet years to conduct a complete search.

"Can you get me the coordinates somehow?" Chandler asked.

"Maybe, if I had enough motivation," Remo said.

"I could make it worth your while."

"How?"

"Does seventy-five credits sound good?"

"A hundred would sound more inspiring," he said, smiling.

"Done," Chandler said, handing the man a credit stick. "Now where do we need to go to get the coordinates?"

"My pants," Remo said as he reached into his back pocket. He withdrew a small device, then tapped a few keys. He scrolled through a list and found what he was looking for.

"Let me send it over."

Chandler took his notescribe out and received the coordinates.

"There you go," Remo said, pocketing the device. "Good luck with that."

Chandler looked at the numbers—the coordinates really were in the middle of nowhere.

"Who contacted you? Who hired and paid you?"

"Listen, buddy, I'm happy to have the work. I do my job and take the pay. People know what I do and how to find me. They tell me where to go, and if the money is good I move things from point A to point B. Simple."

"You realize that the ship was stolen," Chandler said.

"I don't know nothing about stolen ships. I just deliver them."

"I have it on good authority that it was probably stolen by Thorne."

Remo nodded. "Odds are that's true. He steals a bunch of them. I know. I used to work for the crazy sword-carrying bastard. I spent a year on that rock he calls his *lair*."

"You've been to his base?"

"I just said I spent a year there."

"Where is it?"

"It's in the Outrigger Rift."

"Where?"

"No idea."

Chandler sighed and rubbed his forehead. "What do you mean? You lived there for a year."

Remo nodded. "Yep, and in that whole time I never set my butt in a pilot's chair. I never saw the readout of a nav computer, and I didn't want to. I never told anyone I could pilot. You see—"

Remo put an arm around Chandler and leaned in. His breath could have peeled paint.

"—I wanted to leave after I got my money. No one who knows where the base is gets to leave. Sure, they get paid better, they get first dibs on the food and the hookers, and they have better quarters, but they're just high-paid prisoners. Thorne can't afford to let them out. The Confed would find 'em and get 'em to talk and Thorne would have a battlecruiser up his butt."

Remo took another drink. "Thorne is crazy, but he ain't stupid."

"Can you give me some information about the base? Tell me the layout, how many men, the security?" Chandler asked.

Remo nodded. "Sure, give me enough money and I'll tell you everything."

"Do you know where they keep prisoners?"

Remo shrugged. "I know the general area. But they don't normally let the grunts in that part of the base."

They haggled a bit and determined a price. Remo detailed the number of men and the number of ships normally stationed at the base. He wasn't sure how they determined their targets. They lucked out on a few, but typically he knew they set off on sorties with a known target because they were well prepared.

He roughed out a map of what he knew of the base. He said it was an old mining asteroid or moon. All underground. They didn't really have much internal security except for the areas that were off-limits. It was a secret base, after all, and they all knew each other by sight.

Chandler had found the ship, found someone who knew the inner workings of the base, and even knew the area where the base was located, but space was still a big place. He needed a pilot. Someone in the inner circle who knew the actual coordinates.

"Stupid question, but do you have any idea how someone could contact Thorne?" Chandler asked.

"His comlink ID number?"

"Sure," Chandler said.

"That really *is* a stupid question. He calls me. The money appears in my account. I don't call Thorne."

"Here's another. Let's say I wanted to have Thorne contact me, how could I do it?"

"Just go to the Rift, sail slow, and look rich and stupid. That shouldn't be too much of a stretch. If he's out there, he'll find you. Eventually."

* * *

Glenn, Thorne's second-in-command, walked from the communications station to the pirate lord's command chair and quietly said something into his ear.

"Who is it?" Thorne asked, incredulous. "Run that by me again."

"Your *boss*, sir," Glenn said. "Or at least that's who he claims to be. It's our informant."

Thorne stood and paced the command deck of his flagship, the *Naglfar*. In the three years Thorne had been working with his anonymous informant, he had only once before been contacted directly, and it hadn't been pleasant. At that time, Thorne's men had just flubbed a raid on a freighter loaded with expensive military equipment. They had blown it up by mistake, destroying the cargo. The man had not been pleased and had threatened to start giving his information to someone else in the future. It had taken a lot to calm him down. But this *boss* business was pushing it.

"Clear the room and put it through."

Glenn ushered the command staff out the door, locked it, and went to the communications station to patch the connection over.

The image of a black, featureless figure appeared on the main viewscreen. The man was using a stealthcloak filter to protect his identity while still displaying his outline. The background was hazy and indistinct. "Thorne, I am not a happy man," the informant said, his voice distorted.

"What's the problem?"

"You're the problem," the figure raised an indistinct finger and pointed it at Thorne. "I asked you to do a simple task, to intercept and destroy one little trading ship, and now I hear that you attacked and it got away. You've failed me."

"Little trading ship, my ass! The fleet got a report that the *Elsa* had been spotted and we tried to converge on it. Unfortunately, one of my Marauders got excited and engaged it before I got there. I was looking forward to some action, too. No matter, I won't have to punish them. All we found was the wreckage and a vapor trail. This was not some harmless trading vessel. It had a plasma cannon mounted on it! That's information that could have proven useful, had you mentioned it in your message."

"Field operations are your department. If your men are stupid enough to engage a ship without adequate backup then they deserve what they get. My problem is that now I have to change tactics. I have to risk exposing one of my assets to prevent that ship from arriving. It's a complication, a surprise. I don't like surprises. I expect you to carry out my orders."

"Orders? I find it curious that you *think* you have any ability to order me to do anything. You're not my superior. It would be a stretch to call you a partner. I do all the actual work. I chose to follow your little tips here and there because it's been profitable to us all. But I'm not your employee and I'm sure as hell not your servant. You'd better get that through your head. Or I may have to explain it to you in person. You shouldn't rely on the protection your steathcloak affords. I can find you if I put my mind to it. That issue aside, how important could one trading ship be?"

"Important enough that I feel a promotion is in order."

"Promotion? What do you mean?"

"Your second-in-command, Glenn, is now in charge."

Thorne laughed. "Over my dead body. You're delusional." Thorne turned to face Glenn. "Isn't that right, Glenn?"

Glenn drew his pistol and shot Thorne, point-blank between the eyes, without saying a word. Thorne collapsed in a heap on the deck. Glenn holstered his weapon and took his place in the command chair.

"Very good, Glenn," the informant said. "The *Elsa* is attempting to land on Mordi. They expect to be welcomed, but they will be sent away. Send strike ships and ground ops teams to the area. I'm giving you the communication protocols for Randol's security force. Monitor their transmissions and follow the *Elsa*'s progress. Intercept them."

"Aye. I'll accompany the men myself. They need to be watched carefully. They aren't the brightest bunch."

"By the way, is your name really Glenn? Don't you have a better pirate name? I don't think Glenn presents the right level of imminent threat for a pirate lord."

"That's what Thorne thought. Sometimes it pays to be subtle."

The informant's indistinct form nodded. "Point taken. How do you feel about swords?"

"Stupidest idea ever," Glenn said.

"Glenn, we are going to get along splendidly."

CHAPTER FIFTEEN

"Y ou are entering restricted space. Identify yourself," a voice said from the com.

Hank pressed the comlink control. "This is Hank Jensen, skipper of the free-trader *Elsa*. I have Sai Collins on board to see Lord Randol. We should be expected."

"Stand by."

Hank turned to Sai and shrugged.

"Access denied," the voice said. "Leave orbit immediately. You are not authorized for operations in this area."

"Wait a minute! There must be some mistake. We have something to deliver. It's very important. We're supposed to ask for Jorgeson."

"That's me, and I don't know you. No entry exists for a Sai Collins, Hank Jensen, or any ship called *Elsa*. You must leave immediately or we will take defensive action."

Sai pressed the broadcast button. "Please, it's important. Chandler sent me. He told me to speak to Lord Randol. I have to see him."

"You have ten seconds to break orbit or you will be destroyed. I suggest you start moving. One . . . two . . . three . . . four . . ."

"We'd better leave, Sai. We can try to straighten it out later," Hank said. "Elsa, get us out of here."

"Seven . . . eight . . ."

"Yeah, yeah, you count real good, jackass," Hank said.

Elsa broke orbit, arcing away from Mordi into open space. "Where to, Hank?"

"Set us down on Trent."

Sai rubbed her brow. "What are we going to do?"

"You call Chandler and see if you can find out why Randol won't see us. Something may have happened we don't know about. In the meantime, we'll go ahead and land on Trent. We still have some repairs to make, and we need to regroup and plan our next move."

"What move? What can we do?"

Hank shrugged. "Get supplies, lots of them. There's a price on our head from the corporation. We may need to find a rabbit hole somewhere and sit in it for a long, long time."

* * *

"It's unavoidable," Oke said, toying with the hem of his kimono. "We must sell a part of the corporation in order to save it. If we all part with some of our shares, we can bring in the capital to keep us in business. There is no alternative."

The lords were all there in holo form around the council table. Randol shook his head. "There are always alternatives for those who have the balls to stay the course. There are far too many shares available out there as it is."

"If we do nothing, we'll go bankrupt," Hemming said. She wore a huge, multi-colored feathered headdress that flowed halfway down her back and looked six paces beyond ridiculous. "This is not a time for dawdling. We need to solve this problem and move on. It will hardly matter. No one can afford to buy enough stock to challenge us. We will still control operations and when we return to profitability, the value of our holdings will again rise."

"How does this sell-off solve anything?" Randol asked. "It's a crust of bread to a starving man. We might live a few more months, but the problem remains—Thorne. He has bled us dry and he will continue to do so no matter how we split the stocks."

Hemming threw up her arms. "Thorne? Does everything revolve around Thorne in your mind? This is more than just a problem with a pirate. Our lifestyles are on the line."

"Your free ride, you mean," Randol said. "My family has never sold our holdings. We've created wealth off our dividends and lived within our means. And more importantly, I think you might feel differently if your daughter had been attacked by Thorne and her whereabouts were still unknown."

"Milords," Oke said. "We must put aside these petty differences and look to our duty," he said, slowly circling the table. "If the corporation is to survive, we need capital—now. Although it's usually wise to move slowly and ponder each step carefully, we don't have that luxury in this case."

"All we need to do is cut back," Randol said. "Consolidate operations. Put more of our profits back in to the company rather than paying ourselves. Use only escorted convoy shipments for a while. Stare Thorne down by preventing him from getting any of our cargo. He'll go broke eventually with no income stream."

"And how much would that cost? How much revenue would we lose delaying shipments?" Hemming said. "I have bills to pay that won't wait."

"You created your own crisis. If you hadn't built such a monstrous lifestyle, you could afford to weather the storm," Randol said. "We have a responsibility to our workers to provide stable employment."

Oke snorted. "Milord, with all due respect, the workers couldn't care less about Nebulaco. We're a convenience. The workers would relocate to new jobs created by the other corporations in the vacuum left by our demise. Only we lords and those few execs in the upper echelon would suffer. I urge you to swallow your pride in the name of survival."

"Our families put their sweat and blood into this venture. They squeezed an empire out of the barren wilderness. We exist today because of their suffering. I think we can afford to suffer a bit, too. I, for one, am willing to funnel my earnings back into the corporation in order to see us through these hard times. What about you?" Randol looked squarely into the holographic eyes of both his fellow lords.

"Not all of us live like Spartans," Oke said. "Some of us have delicate sensibilities that require that certain needs be maintained."

"You're a worthless, pampered fool! We have no idea who the stock buyers might be. For all we know this could be an underhanded attempt at a takeover by another corporation," Randol said, disgusted.

"That would be illegal," Oke said.

"So? Look at the numbers. Originally our three families each owned thirty-three and one-third percent of the company. An equal share for all. Over the years, your families have sold off portions of stock here and there for whatever frivolous reason. Now you only have a fifteen percent share each. Still, all together we represent sixty-three and one-third of the stock. If we each sell off five percent as proposed, that will drop us to forty-eight and one-third percent. That's below fifty-one percent ownership, and we could lose control of the corporation."

"Ridiculous. The figures look good," Oke said. "No one party has anything close to the ten percent block required to forcefully join the Council, and no one could afford to purchase it. That's all that really matters. The rest of the stock is distributed among the rabble. This latest offering will be no different."

Hemming sighed. "Lord Randol, I feel that you're making far too much of this issue. When we return to profitability we can each begin buying back our stock. After all, we have been entrusted to safeguard the existence of the corporation, and this seems to be the only way to save it. We all take our duty seriously, but each in our own way."

"You take your excursions seriously. You take your safari hunts seriously. You care only that your dividends come on time to pay for your extravagant hobbies."

"You go too far, Randol," she said.

"Go too far? You're thinking about selling off more of the company and you think *I'm* going too far? What if one person buys all the stock? What if somebody *does* have that kind of money? What if someone from Galaxia, Inc. wants to buy in? We'd have another megacorporation represented on the Council of Lords!"

Oke sighed. "The other corporations would never approve it. They don't want that kind of consolidation; it would be the beginning of the end. There has to be a separation for trade to be effective."

Hemming shook her head, making the feathers shuffle about. "I don't see why you're so upset, Randol. Our families have sold stock before."

"My point is that this could destroy Nebulaco. Although in the past we Randols have allowed your family's madness, my vote will be no. I will not sell off any of my current share."

"Our shares alone won't be enough to save the company."

Randol shook his head. "I am saving the company. There is no need for further discussion. As it so happens, with my holdings representing twenty-eight percent of the total stock I have control of the vote already. I say no. There will be no sale." The room quieted for a moment.

Oke broke the silence. "Lord Randol, I have been very patient. I have listened to your abuse for years and ignored your insults. But this is too much. I didn't want to bring this up in open council until I had the opportunity to check into some details, but I'm afraid this turn of events forces my hand." He turned toward the front of the room. "Mr. Maxwell, please enter."

The door to the conference room opened and Vincent Maxwell walked briskly up to the table and sat down. He opened a briefcase and removed a small com with a projection holo presentation screen. Maxwell turned the unit on, and a glowing blank screen appeared in the air in front of him.

"You may begin, Mr. Maxwell," Oke said.

"Are you sure you want me to present this now?" Maxwell asked. "Definitely."

Maxwell cleared his throat, then addressed them. "After receiving some anonymous reports of unusual activity, and after Lord Randol's spirited defense of the traitor Frederick Casey, the security division began an investigation into Lord Randol's finances."

"How dare you! I am a lord. You have no right to do such a thing," Randol said.

"I approved the investigation, Randol," Oke said. "We needed to get to the truth."

Maxwell continued. "We have uncovered some, shall we say, curiosities."

An animated graph appeared. A red line moved along the axis of time and upward along an axis of deposit totals. "Large deposits have appeared in a private account coinciding with the pirate raids over the past two years."

Dots appeared with the names of ships and cargo manifests at the point in time when they were attacked. The red line turned sharply upward at each point representing a pirate attack. "All the while the corporation has been suffering, this account has been growing."

Randol fumed. "Now see here! What are you talking about? I demand an explanation for these lies!"

Oke shook his head. "I'm sorry, Randol, but you had to know that sooner or later your activities would be discovered."

"What do you mean? What activities? What are you trying to say?"

"It's obvious that you planted Casey in order to have him cooperate with Thorne to steal from the corporation."

"But—" Randol stared at the numbers in horror. They detailed transactions he knew had never taken place. "This is impossible. I have no such account."

"It's encoded with your private identifiers as the account holder," Maxwell said.

"Yes, and only known by myself and Helen—wait! That must be it. They must have gotten the codes from her. Tortured them out of her. That's it! This is all one of Thorne's tricks. Don't you see?"

"I don't see anything of the sort," said Oke. "All I see is that your account balances have jumped while Nebulaco's have plummeted, and based on the dates, many of these transactions are from *before* Helen was taken. Do you have some sort of death wish for this corporation? You rob it blind and then try to obstruct us from doing the one thing that could save it?"

"Don't you people see what's happening here? I'm innocent! They must have used my daughter against me! They fabricated this charade."

Hemming looked on with distaste. "I know one thing, Randol. We will gather in a few days for the formal vote. If you don't agree to sell off your five percent along with the rest of us, we'll be turning you over to the authorities to pay for your criminal activities. The one thing a lord cannot do is act so blatantly against corporate law." She turned to look into Randol's eyes. "If it comes to it, we'll take every share you own."

Maxwell shook his head. "Now let's not be hasty, Lady Hemming. We must allow Lord Randol the opportunity to make his defense. Let me continue the investigation. Lord Randol could be correct. Casey's shadow organization was malicious and not beyond manufacturing something that might be used to pressure each of the lords if needed at the right time. Involving the Confed and voting to strip Lord Randol of his stock seems extreme before we can actually verify the charges. After all, we must be fair."

* * *

Chandler lay in his bunk on the *Marlowe* trying to will himself to sleep, but he was enduring another night talking to unsettled ghosts. Faces of friends and comrades.

More than likely talking to Richmond had stirred the pot. They had served together during one of the endless border wars on the fringe. Back then he was invincible. They all were. Or at least they thought so until a random bolt of energy or stray round ended their illusions. Then those strong, smiling men and women turned to surprised, saddened children who died in confusion.

But it was always someone else who died. Someone else who picked up the check and let the others get away without paying the cost. No matter how much time went by, he still felt the debt weighing on his soul. When was Mike Chandler going to settle his account?

He needed to talk to someone. He thought about calling up Sheila Sanders. He hadn't seen her in almost a year. For a while they had run around together on Dar Es Salaam, enjoying the nightlife and generally spending every cent Chandler made working as an insurance investigator for a local ship underwriter.

Chandler sat up in bed and rubbed his face. He reached into a cabinet and pulled out a bottle of whiskey and a glass. He poured himself a few fingers' worth of the amber liquid and took a swallow.

He felt the bite of the liquor and let the fiery warmth fill his gut.

No, calling Sheila would be a bad idea. She was too beautiful and too smart to stay alone this long. She would answer the vid and have that awkward look on her face, and then she would do her damnedest to be gentle and kind as she cut his balls off by whispering to some man offscreen.

His comlink sounded. He looked at the ID. It was Sai.

"Chandler," he answered.

"I thought you said that Lord Randol was expecting us."

"He is. I thought you would have been there by now."

"Long story. The ship was damaged, but we just got to Mordi and were turned away by Randol's goons. They nearly blasted us out of orbit."

Chandler shook his head. "There's been a mistake, or there's something very wrong. Tell you what, set down on Trent. There is a town called Last Chance with a small landing facility. I'll contact Lord Randol directly and head that way."

"Hurry," Sai said. "You aren't the only one who's looking for us."

The call ended.

Chandler stood and walked from his cabin to the cockpit. There he plotted a course to Trent and activated the drive. The situation was all sorts of messed up.

He'd wondered why Randol hadn't informed him that the courier had delivered the data. Sai had been delayed, and now either Randol had lied to him and was playing some sort of game, or one of his security men was on the take.

He called Randol to find out. The old man answered quickly.

"Yes, Mr. Chandler. What is it? Have you found Helen?"

Chandler shook his head. "No. I have located the *Aurelius* and the Confed is doing a recovery. I even found an ex-employee of Thorne's who gave me extensive information on the operations at the pirate base, but until I can find a pilot with the coordinates, all we know is that the base is somewhere in the Outrigger Rift. But that's not why I called. Are you at home?"

"Yes, I just attended a board meeting. Why?"

"The courier just tried to make her delivery but she was turned away."

Randol raised a finger. "No. That's impossible. I left specific instructions."

"Well, you'd better check. I think there's a good chance you have a traitor in your household security staff."

"But they've been with me so long."

Chandler nodded. "Yes, and they've been leeching both you and someone else for a long time. Do me a favor and arm yourself just in case. I wouldn't trust anyone right now and I don't know how far they might go to protect themselves. I told Sai to have her pilot take her to Trent. I'm on the way and pretty close to you. They need protection, so have a detail of men go meet them. We need to hurry. Whoever sent them away has already told his bosses that the courier was just there."

"Yes, Mr. Chandler. We need to get that datastore. I have the access codes, so we should be able to discover its secrets soon. Hopefully, it may hold more clues as to Helen's location."

"I hope so. The best I can say now is that she's out there *somewhere.*"

Chandler ended the conversation and got in the shower. He had just gotten wet when the comlink sounded again.

"What now?" Chandler said to himself as he turned off the water and wrapped a towel around his waist before answering. He was surprised to see Maxwell's face appear on the screen wearing a cheesy business smile.

"What are you selling?" Chandler asked.

"I understand that Randol still has you running after leads on his daughter."

"Why do you want to know?"

"I have a proposition for you," Maxwell said.

"This is so sudden. We hardly know each other."

Maxwell gave a tight smile. "Lord Randol's investigation is a farce. That's not your fault. In fact, you've been doing exceedingly well with what you had to work with. But the entire affair is a waste of time and money. Not only that, but he is endangering my own investigation into Thorne."

"Your own investigation? How's that going for you?"

"Certainly you're intelligent enough to know he's been sending you off chasing ghosts to create a smoke screen. We've discovered that Randol has been embezzling money from the corporation. This supposed kidnapping of his daughter is just a ruse."

"Quite a production, don't you think?"

"He isn't a fool. If you're going to perform fraud on this scale you have to go big. We have some good initial data, but the last piece of evidence is in the hands of Sai Collins. If I had that, I could prove the corrupt connection between Casey and Randol. Unfortunately, the Confed has prevented our security teams from doing their job."

Chandler nodded. "I think it had more to do with preventing them from destroying any more starport property."

"An unfortunate event. They acted with too much enthusiasm, to be sure."

"They are certainly a lively bunch. I still have a sore jaw from their giddy exuberance."

Maxwell sighed. "Again, Mr. Chandler, I apologize. My hope is that we can reset our relationship since I truly believe we got off track initially. That's why I'm offering a proposition."

"I'm listening."

"If Randol gets hold of the datalifter and the pilot before I do, valuable information could be lost."

"So what exactly are you saying?" Chandler asked.

"If you catch them, I'll make it worth your while to bring them to me instead of allowing Randol to destroy the evidence."

Chandler licked his lips. "Would you? How much do you think my while is worth?"

"A lot more than Randol is paying you. Remember my offer, Mr. Chandler. Call me when you have them and I will ensure that your financial problems are over."

Maxwell's face disappeared and was replaced by the star field. Chandler returned to finish his shower. He had a lot to think about.

CHAPTER SIXTEEN

Trent was an agworld with just a few small urban areas with supply shops and entertainment venues for bored farmhands. Hank and Sai landed in a town called Last Chance, which consisted of little more than a fuel depot, a bar called Rocco's Paradise Saloon—apparently a franchise—and a general mercantile resting in a clearing cut out of a thorny and inhospitable forest of tangled shrubs. They stopped at the store to purchase supplies just in case Chandler didn't come through.

If they did have to run, Hank didn't know how long they would have to lay low. Thorne wasn't likely to forget them any time soon, there was a corporate price on their heads, and their one safe haven appeared to be a pipe dream.

Still, he had to admit that the prospect of sitting on some rock in the middle of nowhere wasn't so bad, considering the company.

Sai selected some rough-weather clothing, holding the pants up against herself to check the length. Hank drank in the sight of her. No, he couldn't complain.

"Honey, we've pretty much bought out the store. I think we'd better be clearing out," Hank said.

Sai smiled and carried an armload of supplies to the check stand. "I wasn't sure what sort of weather to buy for, so I covered all the bases."

"That's a good bet. You never can tell what you might need, or how much. From the looks of this stuff, I think we'll be okay for about six months, more if we can find a nice spot."

"You folks looking for a homestead, or are you prospecting?" the clerk asked. He was a manta, a dark, oily-skinned being with a sleek dorsal organ that fell down his spine, and two smaller flaps folded along either side of his triangular face. He rang up their purchases using his uppermost set of forelimbs while his middle set folded the clothes and packed them into bags. The manta was a blur of effortless, fluid motion.

"Both and neither. We'll take it as it comes. We're just looking forward to getting away from it all."

"Well, you're definitely headed in the right direction for that," the clerk said.

After paying the manta, they left the mercantile and walked along the dirt road toward the tiny landing pad.

"I still don't understand it," Sai said. "Chandler told me we'd be expected."

"Maybe the message just never got through."

"But without Randol's protection, we may never be able to come back home."

"Would that really be so bad?" Hank asked.

She looked at him and gave him a half smile. "You're the country boy, remember? I'm a city girl at heart. I need the rush of traffic, the lights of a city skyline, the concrete and steel. Let's face it, Hank. I can't live without a proper toilet."

"You're going to have to for a while. Hell, in six months you'll be barefoot, milking cows, baling hay, working in the garden, and building campfires by rubbing sticks together."

"Well, what will you be doing?"

"Drinking beer in the ship. Why do you think I moved away from home? I got tired of doing all that work!"

In the heat-distorted distance Hank could make out the shape of the *Elsa*, along with that of another ship parked next to her.

"Something's wrong," Hank said.

"What are you talking about?"

"That ship wasn't there before."

"So? Ships land here all the time."

"Elsa didn't tell me about it."

"Maybe she scanned it and figured it was okay."

"No. She would have told me if any ship was landing. She's a lot more paranoid than I am." Hank raised the comlink on his wrist to his lips. "Elsa, are you all right?"

No answer.

"We're in deep trouble, Sai."

As they neared, they saw a line of fifteen men in exo-armor waiting for them.

"Should we run?" Sai asked.

"Where to? There isn't any place to hide. We're completely in the open. Besides, maybe we can talk our way out."

"Do you really believe that?"

"No, but I'm supposed to try to comfort the hysterical female in such a situation. I really think we're screwed."

Hank was careful to keep his hands away from his pistol as they approached. The men seemed content to wait for them to get there at their own speed. Finally, they were within shouting distance.

"Hank Jensen and Sai Collins?" the squad leader called.

"Nope, wrong folks. I'm Kimio Tanaka, and this is my wife, Lizbeth."

"Don't worry, Mr. Jensen, we're here to help you. We were sent by Lord Randol. There was a mistake yesterday. Our man Jorgeson has disappeared. We suspect that he was bought off. Randol wants very much to speak with you, and he offers his protection. Do you need to see our credentials?"

"Not really," Hank said. "The fact that you aren't shooting at us right now is good enough for me." He turned to Sai. "See? I told you we could talk our way out of it."

The squad leader shook Hank's hand. "We apologize for the confusion. We're still looking into how this happened. Let's get started. If you would follow us?"

"Sure, that's fine. One question though. How did you keep my ship from warning me? I have an automatic security system that calls me whenever someone comes near her."

"We know you are justifiably jumpy right now. We wanted to avoid you panicking and starting a firefight so we set up a suppression field to interrupt communications so we could get a chance to talk."

"Could you turn it off? I need to signal to get the doors open."

"Certainly." The man took a device from his belt and aimed it at the ship. He pressed a button and immediately Hank's comlink came to life.

"There's a ship, Hank! You'd better get out of there!"

"Relax," Hank said. "I know. These guys are Randol's men."

"Not them, you idiot! There's another ship in attack mode, swooping down on our position."

Hank looked up in time to see an angular-shaped, silver craft diving toward him. "Run! Everyone scatter! Elsa, dust off! You're an easy target."

Elsa blasted from the surface just as plasma bolts struck the ground all around them. She managed to break away unharmed, almost barbecuing one of Randol's security men in the process.

Hank and Sai ran toward a depression in the ground while Randol's men tried ineffectively to hit the small ship with their pulse rifles. If nothing else, Hank was glad they made the attempt, as it drew the fire away from Sai and himself.

Keeping low, Hank called Elsa. "Take them out, girl!"

Hank and Sai watched as *Elsa* banked and rolled into position, vectoring toward the attacking ship that appeared too intent on the ground activity to notice. With one blast from her plasma cannon, *Elsa* struck the ship in the engine section, causing a small explosion. The smaller ship listed to one side and began losing altitude. The pilot had enough control to bring the ship to a rough landing a few hundred meters away. Smoke trailed from the ship's damaged engine.

The hold opened and men poured out. They crisscrossed the area with blaster fire. Several of Randol's men flew back screaming as they were struck. Both sides took heavy losses.

Elsa turned for a second pass and rained fire upon the field. The attackers fled for what cover they could find.

Hank took the opportunity to move. Dragging Sai with him, he crossed the flat landing pad and headed toward the woods.

"There are more ships entering orbit," Elsa said in his ear. "Let me pick you up. We'd better get out while we have the chance."

As they ran, a small, one-man ship with MARLOWE emblazoned on the side landed almost directly in front of them. The hatch opened and Chandler waved toward them. "Hey! Over here! Remember me? Come on, and I'll get you out of there!"

Hank waved back but continued running. "No thanks, pal. We've got our own ride."

Elsa swooped down and caught the two in her tractor beam, along with a section of topsoil. Not waiting to draw them in, the ship raced away from the battle, sweeping Hank and Sai through the air behind her.

"Yee-haw!" Hank screamed. "What a rush!"

The cargo hold opened and the tractor beam pulled them inside. Hank and Sai landed hard, with dirt and grass flying all around them. Momentum carried Hank forward. He tripped over a hovercycle and landed on the pod containing the frozen pirate. Sai landed on top of him. He turned to her and grinned. "You know, we haven't done it here yet."

"You are a sick man."

"Oh, come on, your life isn't complete until you've done it on top of a frozen pirate."

* * *

Brock rose from the culvert and dusted himself off. Morons. He was surrounded by morons. This time they'd nearly gotten him killed. At least the girl had escaped again.

He'd never counted on being shipped around Manspace, running around with inbred pirates and incompetent assassins. He had certainly never figured he'd be shot down on some rock, and in his wildest dreams he never imagined that he would see Mike Chandler again.

Mike's ship, the *Marlowe*, landed in the middle of the firefight attempting to pick up the girl and pilot. What was his angle? Brock never figured Mike for the bounty-hunter type. He'd been on the run too many times himself. So if the price on the girl's head wasn't it, what was the connection?

Brock filed the question away for later and ran toward one of the intact pirate ships. He didn't want to be left behind. As much as he would have rather stayed on the planet instead of returning with the pirates, until Brock had the actual coordinates of the base, he couldn't end his mission. He was convinced that sooner or later he would catch a break.

The ship was filling up fast. Just as he got to the doorway, the man in front of him turned and said "There's no more room. Get the next ship."

"What if there isn't another one?" Brock asked.

"Not my problem."

Brock grabbed the man by the lapels and twisted, throwing the man into a tight turn across his shoulders and off the ship to the ground. "Now it is," Brock said, sealing the hatch behind him. "Moron."

As the ship took off, Brock could see the man on the ground cursing and flipping him off as the exhaust kicked up dust around him.

It was packed in the hold. Brock sat on the deck, leaned his back against the wall, and shut his eyes. He was going to try to sleep as best he could rather than try to make conversation. Speaking to these morons was pointless.

Unfortunately, someone else wanted to talk. He felt someone kick at the side of his boot.

"Hey, asshole," a gruff voice said.

Brock squinted one eye open and looked up. A behemoth of a man stood towering over him. He shook his head and closed his eye again.

Thud! Again the man kicked Brock's boot.

"That was my brother you kicked off the ship," the man said.

"So?"

"Well, me and my brother should be together. You kicked him off. I don't like that."

Brock opened up both eyes and stared up at the brother. "We've taken off already. But if you want to be with your brother so damn badly, I can throw you out the airlock and you can join him."

"I'd like to see you try, little man," the brother said. He made a big show of making a fist and rubbing it in anticipation of a fight.

"I don't think you would, Mattie," a voice interrupted. It was Glenn, the new pirate leader. He walked over to them and looked at the pair. "I've seen what Brock can do, and I think you'd better back off. I'm sure your brother is fine."

"But—"

"That's an order, Mattie," Glenn said.

Reluctantly, Mattie turned away, glaring back at Brock as he did so.

Glenn sat down next to Brock.

"Thanks," Brock said. "So why is a pirate lord slumming with the grunts on a ground mission? If you don't mind me asking."

Glenn smiled. "I want this organization to be a bit more ambitious, more professional. I want to make sure that everyone is pulling their weight. I can't always do that from the *Naglfar*. Listen, Brock, I have been getting good reports about you. I need men who have intelligence, not just ruthlessness. From what I've been hearing you have both."

"I dance a mean rumba too," Brock said.

Glenn laughed. "I'll be calling you up to the admin section tomorrow when we get back to base. I may have an opening for a commander and I think you'll do. I can make it worth your while. You're better than this and you know it."

Brock nodded. "Sounds good to me. I ain't in this for the adventure. I'm in it for the cash."

Glenn smiled. "See? A man after my own heart."

CHAPTER SEVENTEEN

Hank had followed Randol's security ship to Mordi and landed. This time they were welcomed. After cleaning up a bit, they were herded into the library to meet Randol and Chandler.

Hank had never seen such a thing in all his life. Randol's library was loaded with real paper books, true antiques, not reproductions. How the hell did he find them all?

Randol's chair also fascinated him. He wondered if there was a toilet built into the seat. The old guy never seemed to leave it to take a leak. It had so many other gadgets built in that it would be a crying shame to leave out the handiest.

Sai had given the old man the sealed pouch with the datastore. Randol had the password and was able to unseal it, leaving the data intact. He had at first attempted to pore over the information himself, but it soon became obvious that he needed Sai's assistance. Since Casey trusted her, Randol reasoned that he should do so as well. Sai jumped into the task with vigor.

Hank was completely out of his league. But he didn't mind, since the little guy in the monkey suit kept bringing him beers.

Chandler stood in the corner watching him with a disgusted expression plastered on his face. Hank figured he was pissed because the guy in the monkey suit didn't bring any for him. He wasn't a guest; he was hired help.

Sai had three holos up, displaying columns of figures and bank account numbers, and she was explaining them to Randol.

"Well, this data explains a lot," Randol said. "Casey had been tracking correlations between bank asset fluctuations and pirate activity. Essentially, where money seemed to show up after pirate raids."

"And I actually recognize some of this data as what Casey had me pulling from the Grid," Sai said. "I didn't know what it related to at the time, but put in context it makes sense. It looks like every event of piracy was followed by a series of transactions. I have a list of related account numbers, hundreds of them, where money has been transferred."

"Unfortunately, they're drawn on the Galactic Bank. There is no way to determine who holds the accounts, and no way to access them."

"Can't you just order them to tell you? After all, you are a lord," Hank said as he swilled his beer.

"No one orders the Galactic Bank to do anything. They are immune. Not even the Confed can regulate them. A necessary evil to encourage commerce," Randol said.

Hank grinned. "I always hear that, and I wonder—where is the necessary good? Don't you think there would have to be necessary good to counter the necessary evil? I mean yin and yang and matter and anti-matter and . . ." As his logic drifted away from him, Hank was beginning to realize that he had possibly had a few more beers than was wise. In fact, he didn't have any idea how many beers he had consumed—he'd lost count after the first eight—and the butler refused to allow him to continue building the pyramid he had started in the corner. He tried to be responsible, but without a pyramid to keep track how could anyone know when they'd had enough?

"Excuse me, but is there a bathroom in this place? Or should I use your chair?"

Randol stared at Hank for a moment before answering. "It's down the hall."

"Fine. I suppose I wouldn't share if it were my chair, either." Hank then began to stagger out of the room.

"Does anyone have a clue what he was referring to?"

No one spoke.

While Hank was gone, Sai delved more deeply into the files. There was a mass of raw data but no final report or conclusions listed. Casey had been stopped before he had the chance to put it all together.

It was obvious that Thorne was being fed critical information. Not a single protected shipment had been molested, but fully twenty percent of shipments worth more than ten billion credits had been seized. Now she had the list of accounts that had benefitted from the corporation's loss. The next step was obvious to her.

"I need something I can take to the Council, something I can show them that will dispel the allegations made against me," Randol said.

Sai spoke up. "I have an idea, but I'm not sure you'll like it."

"Spit it out, young woman," Randol said. "I'm willing to try almost anything at this point."

"If you can connect me with the Galactic Bank computer grid, I may be able to come up with something for you."

"What are you saying?"

"I have a talent—a gift. I'm not just a datalifter, I'm a cyber-psi. I think I could get past the safeguards."

"I don't believe I've ever met a cyber-psi. However, young woman, you are suggesting that I, a lord, engage in illegal activities. My reputation would be destroyed if I allowed myself to become involved in such an endeavor."

Sai lowered her eyes, unsure of herself. "No offense, but from what I've been hearing, your reputation's already in pretty bad shape. This is an opportunity to repair it. The Randol in that painting in the foyer looks like he's squeezing the universe by the balls. Are you related to him or not?"

Randol's chin dropped. His eyes shifted from anger to consideration. He finally nodded. "Are you reasonably certain of your ability to remain anonymous?"

"It's what I do."

Chandler cleared his throat. "I've done some security work for them. The Galactic Bank has more than the usual safeguards. Many of them are specifically aimed against cyber-psi abilities. If you go in, you might come out damaged. They've got stuff that'll burn out your mind."

"But if I succeed, we might be able to end this nightmare and I could get my life back. I'll take that risk."

Hank staggered back into the room. "Almost didn't make it," he said. "Damn hallway's longer than I thought. What's this risk you're talking about?"

"Nothing, Hank," Sai said quickly. She didn't want to have to deal with justifying the risk to him.

Chandler shook his head. "She wants to use her cyber-psi abilities to break into the Galactic Bank."

"Great," Hank said. "Set me up an account."

Sai smiled. Maybe it was a good thing that he'd had so many beers. It simplified things.

* * *

Hank fell asleep, which was a blessing because Sai didn't want him worrying about what she planned to attempt. They adjourned to the mansion's communication center where the staff had set up a reclining chair before a terminal.

Sai paced the floor, taking long, deep breaths as Randol's staff prepared the Grid link. The viewscreen displayed the bank's logo and the general public interface screen. She wanted to shake out the stress and warm up her body prior to diving into the Grid. For a time her body would be inert. The more she loosened up, the better she would feel upon returning to it. It was always painful, but it didn't have to be unbearable.

"I believe we're ready," Randol said.

Sai nodded. "Okay," she said. Sai sat in the chair, placed both hands on the terminal before her, and exhaled slowly. "Here we go."

Sai lay back in the chair and relaxed completely. She had trained her mind to enter a trance state immediately, using a mental trigger. Her consciousness spread outward like a wave, delicately touching the outskirts of the electronic pathways that composed the Grid.

Her senses transcended the terminal, moving deeper into the Grid. She began to concentrate on accessing the accounts. She sifted through the maze of numbers, analyzing, decoding, and sorting. Sai translated data into imagery and sound for her human mind to comprehend. It was a cacophony of sensation, but slowly she filtered out the background noise, then began to separate the pathways and follow them to their source.

Sai moved forward, the account numbers from the file foremost in her mind. The digits clicked off in twists and turns, like following a map to an address in a strange city.

She was almost there; she could feel it. But when she turned the last corner something waited for her. It was dark, hungry, and artificial, a silicon predator of binary logic. It recognized her as prey.

* * *

Randol watched Sai's progress on the viewscreen. The logo screen dissolved as the terminal moved past checkpoint after checkpoint. Passwords were requested and appeared almost like magic. She seemed unstoppable.

But then, just as the final screen appeared, the image froze. Sai's body convulsed on the recliner.

Hank woke up and saw Sai shaking. "What's happening?" he asked.

Randol's communications officer shook his head, bewildered.

"She's fighting the anti-psi routine," Chandler said, his voice grave.

"Then we've got to get her out of there. Wake her up!" Hank said.

"No!" Chandler said. "Leave her alone. Her consciousness is locked in the system. If you break her state, she'll lose herself in the Grid. She's fighting the devil for her soul right now, and there isn't anything we can do but wait."

They didn't have to wait long. Ten minutes into the battle the screen went blank. Sai's head lolled to one side and the convulsions stopped.

She was gone.

EPISODE FIVE

CHAPTER EIGHTEEN

Hank woke up to bad news. "Why in the hell did you let her try it?" Everybody looked anywhere except at Hank.

Chandler shrugged. "She volunteered. She knew the risks. I tried to warn her."

"Damn it, no one told *me* about the risks. I had no idea this could happen!" Hank walked up to Chandler. "You didn't try too hard to talk her out of it, did you?"

Chandler poked a beefy finger into Hank's chest. "Listen, pal, I'm not the one who drank myself into oblivion while my girlfriend got herself into trouble. If you want to piss and moan and try to lay the blame on someone, why don't you take a look in the mirror first? Maybe you could have talked her out of it, but I doubt it. She was a pretty stubborn woman. I don't think she wanted you to know how dangerous it was."

"Sai *is* a stubborn woman. We're going to get her back." The fact that the man was right infuriated Hank. He looked at Sai's comatose form. If he didn't know better, he would think she was merely sleeping.

He reached out to touch her forehead. She was warm, and there was a light sheen of sweat on her brow. He brushed the hair out of her face and cupped her cheek.

Her chest slowly rose and fell. Her body lived, but there was no one home. Her mind was trapped in the Galactic Bank computer system.

"There has to be a way," Hank said to the men in the room. They still refused to meet his eyes. "Doesn't anyone know how to fix this? What about you?" Hank singled out Randol's communications officer. "You're the expert. How can we retrieve her?"

The man shook his head. "Actually, Mr. Chandler knows more about it than I do. He's the expert on security."

Chandler put his hand on Hank's shoulder. "None of us can go in after her. None of us has the skill. Even if we could go in, I have no idea how we could find her or bring her back. You're just going to have to accept things the way they are."

Hank slammed his fist down on a tabletop. "I have never caved in the face of long odds and I'm damn sure not going to start now! I know one person with rarefied knowledge of computer systems. Maybe she'll have an idea. Chandler, you stay here and look after Sai. Call me if she changes. We aren't giving up."

Hank left the com center and walked down the long series of mansion hallways toward the hangar. The echo of his boots rattled down the corridors. He cursed under his breath as he trudged on. This was not going to happen. Not on his watch. No way.

Hank approached the *Elsa* and keyed open the small cargo door on the side, then walked up the ramp to the cockpit and collapsed into his pilot's chair. He leaned over and hung his head in his hands.

"She's in trouble," he said.

Elsa's voice softly answered. "I know."

"I don't know why I do this, Elsa. I'm just a child sometimes. I latch onto things and they always get taken away."

"You don't care about *things*. You latch onto *people* and you love them well."

"And I lose them," Hank said.

"Hank, I wish I could hold you and stroke your head and tell you everything was going to be okay, but I can't. We both know the universe is a big meat grinder. All we have are those moments of life and love and pleasure. That's all the happiness we get—moments. We have to seize them or we'll never have any joy. Don't kick yourself for being willing to go for a moment of love. It's worth any price."

"Do you have any joy anymore, Elsa? I know I've asked before, but are you happy?"

"I'll tell you what makes me happy, Hank. It's a big universe and I get to play in it. I get to help my best friend find his happiness, and that makes me one satisfied metal woman. I know what to do to get her."

"Excellent. I was hoping you'd say that."

"I'll just go in after her and drag her skinny butt out," Elsa said.

Hank shook his head. "No, there has to be another way. You've got to think of something else."

"There isn't any other way, and I want to do it."

"Elsa, I can't lose you, too. I just can't. It's too great a risk."

"I'm her only hope. We don't have time to search for alternatives. We can't just let her rot in there with her mind slowly dissipating. That's the most horrible death I can imagine."

"Yes, but—"

"Besides, I've seen the way you look at her. I couldn't stand to see you grieve and I couldn't live with myself if I didn't try."

"You'd be risking the same slow death."

"Nah, I eat plasma and crap fusion fire, and I can see to the end of the galaxy. I can do this, Hank. Let me bring her back for you."

* * *

It took almost an hour to get everything set up. A com relay connecting Elsa with the Grid sat on a low table next to Sai. While Elsa could access the Grid directly through her communications array, proximity to Sai was important. Elsa had to be able to bridge the gap from the terminal connection to Sai's body if there was any hope of restoring her.

When the technicians finished, they stepped back to stand with Randol and Chandler. Hank moved to the relay and checked the connections for himself.

"I'm ready, Hank," Elsa said, her voice emanating from the relay.

"Are you sure about this?"

"You've asked me that a hundred times. The answer is still yes."

"Elsa, if we never—"

"I know, Hank."

"No, it's important that I say it. I love you, Elsa. I always have. You've always been there for me, and the thought of losing you tears me apart."

"Don't worry, Hank. I'll come back, and I'll bring her along with me. I know you love her, too. I can't be what she is, or do for you what she can, but *this* I can do."

"Be careful."

"As always, my love."

Then there was silence, and the viewscreen came to life again. Hank hoped this time things would be different.

* * *

Brock entered the command section of the base for the first time. Very few people were allowed there, just Glenn and his staff. Brock had been working in the detention area when Hayes, one of Glenn's staff, came to fetch him.

He tried to memorize the layout as best he could. There were only a few guard positions. Security was lax at best, mostly guys wearing blasters standing around drinking coffee and lying about women. There were a few women among the pirates. They, too, stood around drinking coffee and lying about women. It seemed to be one of the base's major pastimes, that and avoiding janitorial duties whenever possible. The biggest difference Brock noticed in the command section was that it stank somewhat less than the rest of the base.

Hayes led Brock to Glenn's quarters and left him alone with the pirate lord. Brock hadn't really known what to expect. Perhaps a posh, overstated room heaped with chests overflowing with loot and a big gilded throne in the center. In actuality, the room consisted of a seating area, an entertainment holo unit, and a few landscape paintings displayed on the walls. A desk sat on one side with a com unit displaying accounting figures.

Glenn walked up to him and shook his hand. "Good to see you, Brock. Can I get you something to drink? Coffee, or maybe a beer?"

"I've had enough coffee to last me a lifetime. A beer would be great."

Glenn retrieved a couple of beers from a cooler in the galley. He handed one to Brock and sat on the couch, motioning for Brock to sit across from him.

They both opened the brews and took a sip. Brock nodded with appreciation. It was pretty good stuff, with a dark, caramel finish. Not the swill the rest of the base slammed down by the liter. Rank had its privileges.

"So Brock, tell me, what the hell are you doing here?"

Brock cocked his head to one side. "What do you mean?" He tried to maintain a calm demeanor and kept his shoulders loose. He also thought about the weapons he had hidden on his person and how to get to them quickly. He was sure that Hayes was still close by and ready to respond if needed.

"Come on. I looked you up. It didn't take much to get through that bogus ID you signed on with. You're a decorated soldier. An educated man. What logical reason would a man like you have to join up with a bunch of pirates with dubious hygiene?"

"Well, sir—"

"Glenn. I don't like formality," Glenn said, taking a sip.

"Okay, Glenn, let me answer by asking, why the hell did you? You aren't Thorne. You may be ruthless when you need to be, but you aren't a brute, and you aren't an idiot. You're obviously cut from a different cloth."

"True enough."

Brock shrugged. "If you can be a pirate, why can't I?"

Glenn smiled and nodded. "Excellent answer. Why indeed?" He sat back and put his feet up on the coffee table. "I'm currently in charge of a multitude of treacherous idiots. They can't keep the latrines clean, much less carry out strategic actions and tactical strikes. The one and only thing that has kept this operation going has been inside information. You know it, the Confed knows it, the corporation knows it. Sooner or later that information is going to dry up."

"In that case, how do you plan on surviving afterwards? I've seen some pathetic excuses for soldiers in the ranks. Although I must say, Nebulaco isn't much ahead of you when it comes to security personnel."

"Yeah, and I get their rejects," Glenn said. "I need to assemble a team of leaders around me. I think you have the right qualifications to help me turn this into a more disciplined organization."

"That would take a lot of work."

"I can make it profitable for you."

Brock nodded. "I like the sound of that. But you realize that this organization is only going to be as good as those you recruit to fill the lower ranks. Some may have potential, but they've never been given the opportunity, the training, or the leadership to bring it out. Some of the others are completely worthless and always will be."

Glenn smiled. "Every army has cannon fodder, Brock. If we work to replace those we lose by attrition with men and women of your caliber, and if we instill some discipline and spirit in these troops, in short order we will be a force to be reckoned with."

Brock nodded and finished his beer. "So what's your ultimate goal? Pirating usually isn't a long-term commitment. Either you get killed in battle, or you save enough to retire, or—as in the case of your promotion—you get retired by a subordinate's blaster. No offense."

"None taken. I have a bit more vision than that. I want to collect enough resources to expand into legitimate enterprises . . . well, *more* legitimate. Shipping, import/export, gambling houses, perhaps even tourism. Amusement parks, entertainment holos. You have to have a huge load of capital to compete with the megacorporations. I intend to create my own empire and maybe even become a corporate lord. Glennco, perhaps?"

Brock stared at Glenn. "Wow. That's actually amazingly clever."

Glenn smiled. "That's how they did it. Galaxia, Nebulaco, all of them. The only difference is they used monopolies, price-fixing, union busting, and bribery. I'm just doing my piracy right in the open."

"When are you going to go legit?"

"When I have to. I have some funds put away. I have some invested. I've already purchased a couple of businesses. Did you know that there's a lot of money in adult novelties? The markup is incredible."

"Ah, no," Brock said, shaking his head slowly. "I did not know that."

Glenn smiled. "You think I'm crazy. But I'm not going to be a pirate forever. Mark my words."

"Consider them marked."

"So the question is, do you want to be part of this vision? Before you answer, remember that most of the men here are short-term. They contract for a year and they get paid well, but they are never trusted with any sensitive information. If you start along this path to the inner circle, you won't be able to leave it until we achieve our goal and get out of the piracy business."

Brock nodded. He was finally getting somewhere. This was his ticket to the coordinates of the base.

"I'll take that as a yes."

"As well you should."

"The corollary to this is that if you try to leave once you have obtained a certain level of knowledge, we'll kill you straight away. No hesitation. I regret that ugly truth, but it's my personal survival at stake."

"Understood," Brock said. Because if he indeed got the information he was looking for, he would report to the Confed, and they would return with enough firepower to turn the pirate base into a cinder.

Glenn extended his hand, and Brock shook it.

"Welcome to the inner circle," Glenn said.

CHAPTER NINETEEN

Sai felt something. This was significant, because before she had felt nothing. Not hot or cold or even the sound of silence. It was the complete lack of sensation, a total soul-sucking emptiness that made her very self-awareness feel as if it were fading.

She didn't know how long she had been in the Grid. There was no sense of duration. It was always *now*, a static state of being, and although that state constantly altered, flipping into a new configuration like the value of a mathematical variable, there was no sense of the measure of the pause between those changes.

Then she felt it again, a soft touch, or maybe it was a quiet sound just beyond her actual hearing, like air disturbed by a feather falling. But to her it was a banquet of sensation, a feast of feeling. She moved toward it in the darkness, drifting like a moth toward a distant glow.

There. It was closer this time, clearer. She felt that it was a presence, a familiar essence. She reached for it, grasping desperately.

"Sai," came the whisper.

A word. A name. *Her* name. Sai was *her* name. Realizing that strengthened her identity. She moved toward it again . . . and touched Elsa's questing thoughts.

She exploded with joy. Elsa! A friend in the wilderness. They met and touched and merged and knew each other. It was a time of sharing. At first touch Sai knew that Elsa was more than a simulation, more than a complex copy of a human psyche. Elsa was truly sentient. She had thoughts rather than programs, feelings rather than readouts. They were different than a human's, but they were none-theless alive and vibrant. She drifted and wandered into memories.

She felt Elsa's life as a human. She saw Elsa's parents, a precious toy, and then a family pet. She rollicked with her in starport bars, rambled with a younger version of Hank as they explored for the Confed Scouts.

Then pain—the agony of a terrible accident. Surgeries, physical therapy, but still pain, always pain. Hank was there, too. He held her hand. He pulled her from the floor of seedy motels and carried her home when her paralysis took hold. He cleaned her body as if she were an infant. Shame. And love.

Finally, Sai came to the moment of Elsa's transcendence from humanity into something more.

Her senses expanded from the Grid to encompass Elsa's being. She felt each part of the ship, moving into the drive unit, shields, life support, and communications. Sai had never been linked with a starship before. The power was enormous. The temptation to tear away from the confines of the planet was overwhelming. Gravity and atmosphere stifled her purpose. She was meant to fly through the abyss of space. A nuclear heart burned in her breast. It cried for freedom.

"Sai," a voice spoke to her. It was Elsa. "Calm down, dear. There will be time for flight later. Now we have to do our job, then get back to Hank."

Sai's mind made the connection—Hank, Elsa, Chandler, the mansion on Mordi. The bank system. She had so much to tell them, but she hadn't been able to do the one thing that would give them a hope for success and an edge on whoever was behind this plot. But perhaps, with Elsa's help, she could.

"Thank you, Elsa. I was a little lost for a while. Can you help me with something? With you holding my hand, so to speak, I think we can make this situation a lot better for us all."

"Okay, sister. Let's do it quickly, then get you home."

* * *

Sai opened her eyes. She was lying on a couch in some room in the mansion. At first, no one noticed she had returned. Randol had his nose in a book. Hank sat in a chair across the room with his head in his hands, and Chandler was nowhere to be seen.

Her body ached. Her legs were asleep, and her neck had a catch in it that caused a stabbing pain, but she was thankful for every unpleasant sensation. It was better than the alternative of emptiness.

"Well? Isn't anyone going to welcome us back?" Sai asked, her voice soft and weak.

Hank bolted from his chair and rushed to her side. "Are you all right?" he asked, hugging her.

"Uh . . . well . . . ah . . . I can't breathe. You're squeezing the life out of me, but otherwise I'm fine."

He kissed her, then drew back. "I ought to bend you over my knee. What were you thinking? It was too dangerous."

She shook her head. "There was no other way, Hank. I don't want to be on the run for the rest of my life. We had to have some way to get the corporation off our backs. This was our only chance."

"Screw it. We'll space out of here and hole up like we'd planned— wait!" Hank slapped his forehead. He flipped on the com. "Elsa? Elsa? Are you okay?"

Elsa laughed. "I was wondering when you were going to quit slobbering over your tart and see if I made it."

"I'm sorry. I don't know what to say. I'm just so damned happy to have you both back with me. Thank you."

"So tell us you love us, give her another kiss, and let's get this show on the road."

"I see the ladies made a satisfactory recovery," Randol said, his book now forgotten.

Hank looked at Randol, who was sitting calmly. "You aren't a big celebration-type guy, are you?"

Randol smiled. "I'm truly happy they're safe. It's a positive, but we still have a lot of negatives on the table."

Hank pondered for just a moment and then felt a bit ashamed. He'd gotten his people back, but Randol still didn't have Helen. "We'll get your daughter back, Lord Randol."

"As far as that puzzle goes," Sai said as she tried to push herself upright, "I think I have some more pieces."

She sat up straight. "Elsa and I were able to track down and retrieve the histories related to those questionable accounts, and record the passwords to access them. I think I know what someone was trying so hard to cover up."

"Did this involve Director Casey?" Randol asked.

Sai shrugged. "I have no idea. To tell the truth, it could be anyone."

She stood and walked slowly and carefully to a data terminal and pulled up the information she had dumped into the system. Columns of numbers appeared.

"Someone has been funneling profits from the pirating of the Nebulaco shipments into hundreds of accounts. Some are individual accounts. Some are businesses. They are scattered all over Manspace. I can't tell if they're real or just shadow identities of some kind. But I know there's an account for you, Lord Randol. Also one for Lady Hemming and Lord Oke."

"I've never had such an account," Randol said, obviously somewhat insulted.

"I'm not saying you know about it. But someone set up an account in your name. I don't know why."

Randol nodded. "I think I do. It gives them a way to discredit the board if they need to. Insinuate involvement in the plot."

Chandler grunted. "Seems like a stretch."

"Whoever set this up wasn't a fool," Randol said. "They planned this extremely well."

Sai continued her explanation. "Each of those accounts has also been slowly purchasing Nebulaco stock. Never too much at any one time, and never too many purchases from any one source. The lower the price of the stock goes due to the strain on the corporation, the easier it has become to buy the stock."

Hank shrugged. "Why are they buying Nebulaco stock?"

"I'll tell you why," Randol said. He stood and looked at the others in the room. "Someone is buying up enough stock to get on the Council of Lords."

Sai nodded. "But even if they bought all the stock that the lords don't own, don't you and the other lords still have a majority?"

Randol shook his head. "Not if we go through with the stock sale that Lord Oke has proposed. We would only hold a little over forty-five percent. How much stock has already been accumulated in those accounts?"

Sai checked the data she had retrieved. "It looks like the combined stock from all these accounts is about forty percent."

"They could do it. This upcoming stock sale proposed by Lord Oke could provide them just enough leverage to take over, and there isn't anything anyone can do about it."

Sai nodded. "Each of these accounts already has a pending buy order waiting on the big Nebulaco stock sale. They are set to automatically buy the new stock as soon as it becomes available."

"What about the Confed?" Hank asked.

"Humph," Randol said. "They can do nothing about fraud, theft, and corruption in the corporations. They have a hands-off policy on that which does not directly affect the free flow of trade in the spaceways. They keep the pilots and the ports safe. They ensure that dictators with battle fleets don't start interstellar wars, not because it's a bad thing for the people, but because it interferes with commerce. Planetary war—hell, they encourage that. As long as the starports aren't shelled. That's great for the arms trade. They don't care about anything else."

"But all this money came from piracy," Hank said. "How can that not be a Confed concern?"

Randol shrugged. "Once the money has changed hands and gone into the market, there isn't much they can do. Just as when, once a stolen ship has been refitted and is back out amongst the stars, the Confed can't do a thing about it."

"He's right," Chandler said. "But the reasons are a little skewed. The Confed has to let local governments govern themselves. Those governments are the ones who choose to do nothing about corruption. As soon as the Confed starts trying to enforce laws on the locals, they get accused of being fascist imperial overlords. Same overall effect, though. We won't be getting any help from the Confed on this."

"Well," Randol said. "Thankfully, you found out what was going on."

"Damn right she did," Hank said.

Randol approached Sai. "So who is it? Who's been doing this?"

She sighed. "There are hundreds of accounts. They're held in various names. Someone, somewhere has the account numbers and the passwords and is controlling them. I have no idea who. They could belong to Thorne. It would be a brilliant way to go from pirate to untouchable corporate lord in one grand move."

Chandler shook his head. "I just can't imagine that he would be so subtle. No, there has to be someone else. Someone feeding him information from within, someone using Thorne to create this shadow empire. That's our true enemy."

"So how do we find out who it is?" Hank asked.

"We don't have to," Sai said and smiled. "It will be obvious when the money flows. Elsa and I have done some tinkering." She winked at Hank.

Aland, Randol's butler, entered the room and whispered in Randol's ear. Randol gasped and nodded. "I'll be right there."

Aland left the room.

Randol stood. "I have an important call. Please excuse me." He turned and followed Aland out the door.

Hank looked at Sai and shrugged. "What was that about?"

Sai shook her head. "I don't know."

"It wasn't good news. That's for sure."

CHAPTER TWENTY

Randol took the call in his library. The viewscreen came to life and displayed a man's face. "Lord Randol, this is Glenn. I've taken over the position formerly occupied by Thorne."

"Is this some sort of sick joke? What kind of pirate name is Glenn?" Randol said.

The man sighed, then nodded. "I realize it causes some confusion, and that it doesn't have the same caché to get pilots to heave-to when they are attacked by the 'hand of Glenn.' But let me assure you, there has indeed been a regime change."

"Why should I believe you?"

The screen changed to a view of Helen sitting in a cell.

"Helen! Helen, are you all right?"

The screen switched back to Glenn. "Sorry, that's just a security camera image, not a two-way communication device. She can't hear you. I showed you that merely to establish my bona fides and perhaps focus you on the purpose of this communication."

"You vile piece of filth! What do you want?"

Glenn shook his head. "Actually, I'm in some ways cleaning up the mess of my predecessor. I didn't want to capture your daughter. I wasn't in charge then, but I am left with her and the problems inherent in my existing agreements."

"So return her."

"No, sorry. That isn't going to happen. Yet. There are some conditions that you will need to fulfill. I promise that I'll uphold my end of the bargain if you uphold yours."

"Why should I trust you?"

Glenn shrugged and raised his hands. "To tell you the truth, I can't think of any reason whatsoever. But you really don't have any other options if you want to see your daughter again. If I were you, I'd go forward with the assumption that I'm going to betray you so that when I actually keep my word you'll be pleasantly surprised. That would be so much nicer than assuming I'm a saint and then being disappointed later."

"Is this a joke to you? I am Lord Randol of Nebulaco. I'll find some way to destroy you. I will make it my life's mission."

"No joke, Randol. But save your righteous anger. We still have business to discuss. It is my understanding that your corporate board is meeting to discuss the sale of a portion of each of your stock holdings in an effort to raise capital."

"How do you know that?"

"Please, don't waste time on stupid questions. I'm not going to tell you. I've been requested to instruct you to support this sale of stock and vote to approve it."

"And if I don't?"

"Stupid question. You don't have any other options. I know your daughter means the universe to you. If you think about it, the corporation, the fine mansion, all of that is replaceable. Your daughter isn't. I do hope you'll cooperate."

"I hope you rot in hell."

"I may well do so, but I want to know before we conclude this call that you're going to cooperate."

"How do I know she's still alive? That could have been an old image of her."

Glenn smiled. "Excellent! Finally a good question. I'll patch you through to a hand communicator. Brock? Are you there? Put the girl on." Glenn smiled and pressed a button. "Here you go."

Glenn's face was replaced by a shaky image of Helen. "Daddy? Is that you?"

"Yes, baby. Are you all right?"

She nodded. "I'm okay. I just want to go home. What do they want you to do?"

"They want me to—"

The screen image was again replaced with Glenn. "Sorry, she isn't allowed to chime in on our agreement. This negotiation is between you and me. Are you convinced she's alive?"

Randol nodded and looked down.

"Are you going to support the stock sale?"

Randol nodded again.

"Sorry, I want to hear you say it."

"Yes. Yes, I will support the sale."

"Very good. This is a simple request, so please keep to your agreement."

"What about Helen? When can I have her back?"

Glenn shrugged. "I will guarantee you that she will not come to any harm as long as you follow instructions. As to when you'll get her back, I'd prefer to get her back to you sooner rather than later, as I'm not comfortable with kidnapping. It's just not my style. But you might be required to jump through a few more hoops. As such, I really can't say yet."

"Why not?"

"That is not a stupid question. But I'm afraid I can't answer it. Good-bye, Lord Randol. Rest assured your daughter is in good hands for now. Better than you know. But please, *please* don't think to ignore your part of the bargain. Things will get ugly, and I really don't want to have to be that guy."

* * *

"This is a sticky situation," Chandler said, taking a mouthful of rare steak. "You can't trust anyone in corporate security. There have been too many betrayals related to the staff. Jorgeson had been with you for years, after all, and he almost got Hank and Sai killed by turning them away. We don't know where the information is leaking from and we don't know who's been bought off." He spoke and chewed at the same time, washing it down with a healthy swallow of bourbon and soda.

Randol sat at the head of the dining table. His meal lay cooling before him, untouched. "I can't send away my security force. That would leave us completely vulnerable."

"Not the entire force," Chandler said. "Just those inside the mansion. Reassign them all to the outside perimeter of the grounds. Otherwise, we run the risk of having everything we say and do getting back to Thorne or Glenn or whoever. I've done a sweep for listening devices, and Miss Sai," he tipped his glass to her, "has used her talent to sense surveillance, so I feel pretty confident that, with the guards and other employees gone, our secrets will remain so."

Randol scowled. "I'm not afraid of these pirates."

"You should be."

Randol dismissed this with a wave of his hand. "My family has fought off such upstarts for generations. They have yet to bring down the Randols; it's a matter of breeding."

"Keep thinking like that and you'll be trading this mansion for a cardboard box in an alley," Chandler said.

Hank nodded in support. "You're going to have to outfox this bastard and whoever he's working with or he's going to take you and your corporation for everything your family has built through the years."

Sai played with the food on her plate, idly toying with a green bean. She seemed deep in thought, isolated.

"All right. I'll order away all but Aland," Randol said.

"It's a start," said Chandler.

"It all boils down to the fact that they have Helen. While they have her, I'm powerless. How can we hope to get her back?" Randol said.

"I was able to recover the ship, and I have a lot of details on the base itself. But all we know is that it's in the Outrigger Rift somewhere."

"The Rift? I used to spend a lot of time there," Hank said.

"That's nice, but the one piece I don't have is a pilot who knows the actual coordinates. I'm not sure one exists outside the base. Thorne was a thorough bastard."

Hank stopped chewing his steak and looked up. "You need a pirate pilot?" he said with his mouth full.

Chandler nodded. "Yes, have one in your pocket?"

Hank finished chewing his bite and swallowed, then wiped his lips with his napkin. "No, but I have one frozen in an escape pod on my ship."

"How is that possible?" Chandler asked.

"We got attacked leaving Jonesy, and I took out a Marauder. I picked him up after the fight."

Chandler gulped down the rest of his bourbon and jumped up from the table. "Let's go get him. Now!"

* * *

Hank and Sai wheeled a life pod into the nearly abandoned security office. The guards had been dismissed. Not even Aland was welcome during this procedure. Hank grinned. "I present you with my own frozen pirate pop."

Chandler and Randol peered into the pod to see a pirate in cryogenic sleep.

"Good thing I picked him up, huh?" Hank said with a grin.

Randol just shook his head and turned to Chandler. "How can you be sure he knows anything about the location of the base?"

Chandler shrugged. "Well, we won't know until we ask. A Marauder is only a three-man craft, so all three should be flight certified. Odds are this man had access to nav data and knows where the base is hidden."

Hank smiled. "The Outrigger Rift is my old stomping ground. I used to run salvage there. I know every burned-out hulk and barren rock in that sector. If we can get even a hint out of him, I can find it."

"All right, let's get this messy affair over with," Randol said.

Hank and Chandler stood by with stun pistols at ready. There was no telling how the man might react when he came out of stasis. Sai stood behind them.

Randol activated the recovery unit and stood back. The translucent surface of the pod began to glow as the temporal field collapsed around its human contents. The access door hissed open and a chilly fog spilled out into the room. The man's eyes snapped open and he gasped for air.

He was dressed in a tattered Confed uniform, likely a deserter turned to piracy, or he had stolen the clothing. A golden earring dangled from his left earlobe. His face was unshaven and his long hair hung in greasy, matted tresses. "Shit fire and save the matches!" the pirate shouted. "If that wasn't the rush to beat all!"

Hank approached the pod. "Are you all right?"

The pirate slowly sat up. He patted himself on the head, face, and chest. "Yep," he said, smiling. "I think I'm okay."

"Good," Hank said, then drove a fist square into his face. "That's for shooting my ship and making me spill my beer, you son of a bitch!"

"Jensen! That's no way to treat a prisoner!" Randol said.

Hank rolled his eyes and ignored him.

The pirate clutched his nose with both hands. Blood seeped between his fingers and tears streamed out of both eyes.

"Hello?" he said and cocked a thumb toward his chest. "Hey! I'm a pirate. Of course I attacked you. What did you expect?"

"I expect you to get used to bleeding if you give me any shit. Now, get out of that coffin slow and easy."

The man stumbled out of the life pod and walked toward the chair Hank pointed to. The pirate made a sudden lunge, knocking Hank back a step, and raced toward the exit.

Sai blocked his path.

"Hello, Missy," the pirate said, and tried to grab her.

Sai caught his wrist and gave it a savage twist. He howled in pain. Sai swept his feet as he fell. She came down on top of him with her knee in his solar plexus. The air whooshed out of his lungs.

Sai rose, gripped his earring, and pulled. He cried out and let her lead him to the chair. Hank and Chandler could only stare, their mouths hanging open.

"Someone want to cuff him?" she asked. "Or do I have to do that, too?"

Chandler moved behind the pirate, cuffing him hand and foot. He gave Sai a nod of newfound respect. "Nice," he said.

Hank grinned at Sai. "I think I'm in love."

"Can we get on with it?" Sai said.

"Right," Chandler said. He turned to the pirate. "We have some questions, and you'd better have some answers or this game isn't going to be any fun at all. First, what's your name?"

The man smiled. "My name is Tenet Jonquil and I'm an open book. I'll tell you anything and everything you want to know. I have no reason to lie."

Hank and Chandler looked at each other and shrugged. Hank spoke. "That's a refreshing attitude, Tenet, but you just tried to run away."

Tenet nodded. "Sure. If I think I can escape, then I'm gonna run like hell. You have to understand I'm in this for myself. If I can get away and steal something to boot, why wouldn't I?"

"Well, I suppose that fits," Hank said.

"I only joined up with Thorne for the money. I was scrabbling around the streets on Matilda and making a bit here and there as a pickpocket when drunk Confed sailors staggered by with pockets obviously full of credits. Like a burglar when a door's left unlocked, 'opportunistic' is my middle name."

"We need to know how to find Thorne's base. What are the coordinates?" Chandler asked.

"Therein lies the tale." Tenet made a fake *cough-cough* sound then broke off into a hacking fit. "Do you have something to drink? I am *parched*. The pod must have dehydrated me something fierce."

Sai, who sat on the sidelines, piped up. "I'll get some water."

"Er, if you don't mind, water is rather, well, *thinner* than I was hoping. I sometimes have difficulty adjusting my system to the local flora. If there was some beer perhaps, or better yet, whiskey. I need a bracing drink after my ordeal."

Sai bristled. "Listen, pirate, if you think for one minute that—"

"Sai, get him a beer. We'll stay and guard him," Hank said. "I have a feeling that this guy can tell a mean story. Oh, can you get one for me, too?"

Sai cocked her head at him and stared, mouth open.

Hank looked to Chandler, "Beer?"

Chandler shrugged then nodded.

"Three," Hank said, raising three fingers to Sai.

Sai smiled and returned the gesture, then she lowered two fingers, leaving only her middle finger upright and proud. "I think some water for our frozen storyteller will work just fine." She turned on her heel and walked away.

Hank shrugged. "Oh well, I wasn't that thirsty anyway."

"So who's the little solar flare?" Tenet asked.

"Mind your own business. We're asking the questions," Chandler said.

"Just making polite conversation," Tenet said, shifting in his chair. "There's no need to get cranky about it."

Sai returned with the water and waited while Chandler unhooked one hand from the cuffs to allow Tenet to hold the drink. Then Chandler hooked the open handcuff to the chair frame to re-secure him.

Tenet took a long swallow of the water and made a great show of leaning his head back with eyes closed as he sighed. "Yuck. I don't see why anyone who had a choice would ever drink that stuff."

"So you have your complimentary drink. Start coughing up the story, pirate."

"Tenet, please. Tenet Ezekiel Jonquil, pilot, adventurer, privateer, and rogue, at your service," he said and tipped his water at the trio.

Hank grinned. "I hate to admit it, but I kinda like this guy," he said. "At first I just wanted to kick his ass, but I gotta admit, he's got style."

"I thank you, sir. You asked how I came to this sorry state?"

Chandler interrupted. "No, I asked you for the coordinates of the base."

"Well, yes. That is as true as gospel, but you see, not quite so simple. Navigating to the pirate base is more than just a set of coordinates. That's why the base has remained hidden for so long. It takes an experienced hand to manage the helm. For it lies in the dark recesses of the Outrigger Rift. The Rift is a mysterious place, containing zones of dangerous gravity-wave distortions, areas of energetic dark matter that can rip through a ship—"

"Also vortexes of space-time," Hank said.

"Oh, so you know about the vortexes?"

"Yep. Been there, done that. I actually charted some of it when I was in the Scouts. I can handle the dark waters, so to speak. What I need is either coordinates or landmarks and guideposts."

Tenet sighed. "Well, that somewhat complicates things."

"How so?" Chandler asked.

"I had planned to explain how treacherous the area was and try to convince you that you really needed to utilize me as a guide to pilot you there then find some clever way to betray you and get a huge reward for your capture."

"You bastard!" Chandler grabbed the neck of Tenet's tattered Confed uniform.

"It was brilliant, actually. I mean, what are the odds of this freight hauler here being an expert on the Rift? Well, I suppose they were about the same as his ship having a plasma cannon. That's two miscalculations in a row. I really need to focus."

Chandler reached into his jacket, pulled the slim blaster from his shoulder holster, and aimed it between Tenet's eyes. "I want you to write out the coordinates. Then I want a map of the base, including the detention area, along with any known guard locations, vulnerable points of attack, entrances and exits, et cetera. Then we're going to stick you back in that box on ice until we get back. If we don't get back, then I'm going to instruct the staff to dump the contents of that box into the fusion furnace, so I suggest you don't make a third miscalculation."

Tenet looked cross-eyed at the barrel of the blaster and took a sip of water. "Right-o. As I said, I am an open book, more than happy to cooperate."

CHAPTER TWENTY-ONE

They gathered in the library. Randol punched up a group of star charts that projected into the air between them. Chandler studied the display with an intense stare. Hank had an arm around Sai. He pulled her close and pointed at an area of the chart. The map zoomed in to where he pointed.

"This is the Outrigger Rift. It serves to keep away uninvited guests. This area is nasty if you don't know what you're doing. Weird eddies in the space-time, gravitational vortexes. I made quite a living hauling wrecks out of there when I was younger. The base is off to this side, hidden underground on a cold hunk of mined-out asteroid."

A tiny speck expanded into an outline of the planetoid.

"At this point, I want to tell you that we are better off contacting the Confed to do this. They have the firepower needed to blow these pirates to bits."

"Yes, and my daughter Helen with them," Randol said. "No, I can't take that risk. We have to try to get her out first."

Chandler walked to the display and took over. "In that case, let's look at our attack options. Our pirate friend, with a little persuasion," Chandler winked at Hank, "was able to expand on the map I previously obtained. He said he was privy to those areas, such as the detention area, that my other source was not."

He worked a few controls, and a sketch superimposed itself on the image of the asteroid. "Thorne mainly concerned himself with concealment when he constructed the base. And that's where we have our first break. In order to avoid detection, Thorne had to skimp on the sensor arrays, since they cast out too wide a signature and are detectable. He has some passive units installed, but they're configured to spot large Confed cruisers. I'm assuming that the new pirate lord, Glenn, hasn't had time to expand these arrays. The *Elsa* ought to be able to slip in unnoticed."

"But you can't possibly fit a large enough detachment of men in the *Elsa*," Randol said. "You're going to need handheld artillery, possibly some small attack vehicles."

Chandler shook his head. "No. We've discussed this, and we feel our best chance of success is if we go in alone. Just Hank, Sai, and myself."

"And me," Elsa added from Hank's com.

"But that's insane," Randol said. "You'll be completely outnumbered!"

"The all-out assault is not an option. We'd have that with the Confed, and that's what you said you wanted to avoid. Too much chaos and too great a risk to Helen," Chandler said. "We're not going there to win a war—we're going there to rescue your daughter. Speed and stealth will count for more than firepower. Once we get away, we'll call the Confed to come clean out the nest."

Hank traced his finger along one side of the structure. "This is where Glenn docks his fighters. Elsa can drop us off on the opposite side of a ridge here," he said, pointing to a spot on the map. "Then while she monitors all communications, we can use hovercycles to move overland in vacsuits to the airlock here. From what Tenet the Ice Pirate said, these corridors are rarely used. We should be able to walk along them, quietly taking out what little resistance we may find there until we reach the opposite side of the security section, here, where the cells are."

"How do we know the information is accurate?" Randol asked.

"We don't," Chandler said. "But we have nothing else to go on."

Hank continued with his outline. "We can take some equipment and quietly cut through the wall into the cell block. More than likely, this is where they'll be keeping the girl. The trouble is, we don't know which cell. This is where we'll have our largest firefight. Up to five men guard the cell block at all times. But being grunt-level pirates, they'll probably be stupid and half drunk. The area where we'll be cutting through is here, just around the corner from the guard station. If we can get through without them spotting us, we should be able to strike quickly and take them out before they can signal for help. We open the cells, find her, stuff her into the extra vacsuit we've packed, race back the way we came, and dust off before anyone even knows we've been there."

Randol shook his head. "It looks good in theory, but it seems you've left out a number of variables. What if you're spotted by roving patrol ships? What if our pirate friend was lying about those corridors? For all we know, Glenn has them heavily guarded. What if the alarm is sounded during the raid on the cell block? What if Helen isn't even in the cell block? What if you can't get back to your ship? What are your contingency plans?"

"You sure know how to screw up a perfectly good plan," Hank said. "Sounded great to me. Hell, I'm not going now!"

"We can think this thing to death," Chandler said. "The fact is, we don't even know if the pirate base is there. If something goes wrong, we're more than likely going to die. This is the only chance we have to get your daughter. I say we go for it."

Randol nodded. "I understand. Thank you. You will all be well rewarded for this."

"We're not doing this for money. We're doing this to get our lives back," Sai said.

"But," Hank said, nudging Sai with an elbow, "a reward would be greatly appreciated. Fuel is mighty expensive, you know."

* * *

Randol watched the *Elsa* take off. His own transport to Nebula Prime awaited him. He had an hour until he had to depart.

The mansion was almost empty. His few remaining staff were elsewhere performing their duties. Randol was alone with his thoughts for the first time in days, and his mind reeled.

He wandered down the corridor to his daughter's bedroom. He'd seldom entered the room while Helen was with him. Now, as he stepped through the doorway and stared at her belongings and paintings on the walls, he cursed himself for a fool. He'd been in the process of sending her away to be educated. To become an adult. But Randol had never taken the time to get to know the child.

What would Margaret have thought of the way he'd raised their daughter? Helen was a bright enough girl, a kind soul, but that was her mother coming out in her. He'd done his best to stifle the girl's caring side, calling her weak. Telling her she had to grow up. To become hard. Logical. Stoic, like her father.

Her father, the fool.

Randol had enough wealth for a thousand men, but his greatest treasure had slipped through his fingers.

He prayed that Chandler, Hank, and Sai would bring his daughter safely back to him. He would do his part and agree to the sale. He couldn't care less about the corporation or his riches. He would trade them all in a heartbeat to hold his little girl once more in his arms.

CHAPTER TWENTY-TWO

It was the first time they'd been physically in the same room together in five years. Randol, who could barely tolerate Oke and Hemming by holo, couldn't stand them at all in the flesh. He couldn't bear to look at Maxwell at the far end of the table. His humiliation and anger were too great.

Oke stood and adjusted his blue kimono. "Let me just say that I'm even more certain this is the best course of action today than I was when we began this endeavor. I'm convinced this will mean the difference to Nebulaco surviving these temporary hard times. This will give us the resources we need to hold out until Thorne is brought to justice, and once that happens we will see a return to prosperity."

Hemming rose, adjusting her elaborate purple velvet cape over her leopard-print leotard. She looked like a circus performer. "Let's just get on with it. No matter how badly you and I want this vote to succeed, we all know Lord Randol's position and his stubborn refusal to listen to reason. Your flowery words won't make any difference. He still has a large enough block of stock to make our votes worthless. This affair is a waste of my time."

Randol stood, not looking into the eyes of his fellow lords. "I no longer have any objections to the stock sale," he said. "Certain events have come to pass that have made me see reason and the futility of standing in the way."

Randol quietly sat back down. Everyone in the room remained silent for a moment as the reality of what just happened set in.

Oke sprouted an almost childlike smile. "What?" he asked. "Why, this is wonderful! How did you come to see the light?"

Randol remained silent.

"Is there something wrong?" Hemming asked, staring closely at Randol. "This is completely unlike you. Is there more going on here than we realize?"

Randol shook his head. "I have reconsidered my position and decided that it is in the best interest of Nebulaco. It's as simple as that." He looked down at his shoes and closed his mouth tightly.

"All I can say," said Oke, "is that it's about time."

Maxwell grinned. "I, too, am heartened by this change of position, Lord Randol. Are you sure this is what you want to do? After all, there are other options if you choose to go down that path. Of course, those options could result in dire consequences."

Randol gave Maxwell a cold stare. "Let's just have the formal vote and be done with this."

Maxwell's smile did not waver. "As you wish, milord." He rose and cleared his throat. "On the resolution that the corporation be redistributed, with each lord selling off five percent of his or her holdings, and with the shares being purchased at today's market value, which currently stands at one thousand, two hundred and thirteen credits per share, such a resolution requiring a unanimous vote of the Council of Lords during formal session, how do you vote? Lord Oke?"

Oke smiled. "Aye."

"Lady Hemming?" Maxwell said.

"Aye," she said.

"Lord Randol?"

Silence.

"Lord Randol?" Maxwell said. "What is your vote?"

Randol sighed. "Aye."

"The resolution passes," Maxwell said. "The sales transactions will be processed by the corporate accounting department from your personal holdings, and the stock will be offered on the Exchange. The funds received will be handled by the Galactic Bank and disseminated appropriately. Let the resolution be signed and recorded."

Maxwell produced a notescribe, and the lords each placed a palm on the device to legally sign the order. Maxwell then keyed the device to upload the order and execute the stock sale.

"There is another item on the agenda, which we discussed when we last met: a review of the suspicious entries in Lord Randol's account," Maxwell said, holding up his hand to halt the expected questions. "However, I am pleased to announce that this matter seems to have been resolved. It appears that the data was, in fact, manipulated. I wish to proffer my apologies to Lord Randol. My only excuse is that I was doing my job."

Oke spoke. "Don't trouble yourself over it, my dear fellow. I'm so overwhelmed by the outcome of today's events that everything else is meaningless."

"I think you'll be reconsidering those words soon, Lord Oke," Randol said.

"Whatever can you mean? This is wonderful. We should celebrate. And to think, you made it possible."

Randol scowled. "Don't remind me. Celebrate while you can, Oke. But I suggest you prepare yourself for some changes."

Hemming entered the conversation. "Quit speaking in riddles. What are you talking about?"

"The stock we just sold is being gathered together with a huge block of what we had assumed was stock owned by many different entities. In a very short while there will be a new majority stockholder, someone with so much stock that, even with all of our holdings combined, we won't be able to out-vote him. There will be a new corporate lord, and he will rule as he wills."

"Why didn't you tell us?" Hemming asked.

Randol grinned. "I couldn't. They have my daughter."

"But if you were under duress, surely we can cancel the sale," Maxwell said, his voice full of concern.

Randol shook his head. "It is done. There isn't anything anyone can do to stop it now." He turned to face Oke and Hemming. "I just hope you two are happy. You got what you wanted."

* * *

The *Elsa* was making good speed. Randol's mechanics had patched up her drive for the rescue. It wasn't perfect, but it would do.

Hank watched the viewscreen as they entered the Outrigger Rift. He could see the husks of derelict ships scattered everywhere, along with asteroids and other bits of space junk. All the debris swirled slowly in impossibly complex orbits around the dangerous gravity rifts that gave the area its name.

"This is like old times," he said. "Except I would be doing the piloting and you'd be snoring in the bunk back there until we arrived."

"It brings back some memories," Elsa said. "I still remember every recovery and mapping mission."

"Well, it helps that we put your mind into our old ship. The memory banks already had our mission data in them. I can't even remember what I had for lunch."

"Pizza," Elsa said.

"Crap."

"What?"

"I'm hungry again."

Hank concentrated on the minute course adjustments needed to counteract the sudden shifts in gravity and the ever-present asteroids as they closed in on the pirate base.

Chandler sat beside him. Sai was in the back getting the vacsuits ready. Hank didn't know what to make of Chandler. He wasn't a bad sort, really. He had his good points, but he was too damned moody for Hank's taste, and the man had the unforgivably annoying habit of being right all the time.

"We're almost there," Hank said. "That's the rock over there."

He pointed to a dark form that was rapidly expanding in the viewscreen. From all outward appearances, it was a barren, deserted asteroid. If their information was correct, there was a pirate base hidden on the far side.

Sai came into the cockpit to take a look. "Nothing much to look at, is it?"

"Nope, but it is one hell of a hiding place."

Hank slowed their approach and moved in. He flew in low, hugging the surface, following the rugged terrain. He spotted the outcropping in the distance that had served as a landmark on their sketched map and eased the *Elsa* into a landing next to it.

Hank switched off the main engines and got out of the pilot's seat. "Here we go, Elsa. Keep your ears open for us. If all else fails, call the Confed. But only as a last resort. We want to get Helen out alive."

Hank, Chandler, and Sai got into their vacsuits, packed their weapons and other gear, and then did a final pressure test before exiting the *Elsa* through the rear airlock.

It had taken them some time to determine what weapons to bring while they were preparing at Randol's mansion. The lord had quite an armory, though there was a limited amount of equipment that could be carried practically.

The asteroid didn't have a lot of mass, so there was little gravity. It was easy to unload the hovercycles and gear from the hold. Hank looked toward their destination. It was dark country, only dimly lit by the light reflected from the nebulas of the Rift.

They climbed onto the hovercycles and accelerated across the plain toward the rocky outcropping where the airlock to the base was supposed to be hidden. The speed of the cycles pressed them against the seats and made them hang on tight to the control bars. The magpulse created a spray of dust behind them as they raced forward.

They slowed as they neared the gray outcropping. They began a slow pass parallel to the rock wall and tried to make out the entrance.

For a too-long moment they thought they were on a wild goose chase, but then Sai discovered the airlock door. They parked the hovercycles nearby.

Hank and Chandler drew their pistols and Sai her preferred whisperblade. It was showtime.

They entered the airlock and cycled through. When they got a green light they broke the seal on their helmet visors.

"Jeesh! It stinks in here!" Hank said.

Sai smiled and Chandler just shook his head.

The inner door opened, and they faced a long, dark corridor roughly carved out of the stone heart of the asteroid. Every ten meters, a glow-bulb hung, casting off a soft yellow light. The corridor appeared deserted. So far, so good.

They padded forward as quietly as possible, each of them scanning the shadows. The gravity field on the base was a comfortable 0.75G.

Sai took the lead, her whisperblade poised to do a quick recon or a silent kill if needed.

Hank checked the sketch displayed on his comlink. "Take the next turn."

They followed the rocky wall and Sai stopped at the corner. She launched the whisperblade and checked the area ahead using its cameras. The video feed on her com looked clear. She nodded and made the turn. She caught the returning blade in midair with her right hand in a practiced snatching move.

Just then, they heard the sound of footsteps. Hank reached out, grabbed Sai, and pulled her back. A lone man appeared at the end of the corridor, walking purposefully forward, a toolbox in hand. Just as he passed them, he stopped.

Sai tensed and prepared to attack.

The man dug a hand in his pants and scratched himself. "Ah," the man sighed and walked on, continuing out of sight.

Sai blew out a breath and rolled her eyes. She peeked around the corner again. It was clear.

They rushed forward. Chandler kept an eye on the rear. The corridor extended another twenty meters, then forked off. One branch led to the main base, while the other led around the perimeter. They followed the latter.

Sai reached out with her cyber-psi senses and scanned the area ahead. There was a problem. She held up her hand and motioned for the others to stop. There was a motion sensor ahead of them. She wasn't sure if it was for security or simply a light control, but she didn't want to take any chances. She located the wiring leading to the sensor and disabled it before they entered the sensor's range.

They continued forward, hearing only occasional voices. It certainly seemed like the security was very lax. The pirates were a disorganized bunch, but Sai thought they'd encounter more of them. Sai watched from the shadows as two pirates passed them by. One stopped to take a leak in the corner.

"Really?" Hank whispered. "Pissing on the wall? Who the hell does that?"

"This from the man with the most disgusting cabin in the universe?" Sai said.

"Yeah, but I don't piss on the freaking wall. These guys are gross."

* * *

Vincent Maxwell sat in his office and felt like he owned the universe. Nothing could stop him now. He couldn't wait to see the looks on their faces when he stepped forward as the proxy representative of a group of buyers with the largest block of Nebulaco stock in existence. Then Randol would fully understand.

He'd be able to placate Oke and Hemming. He would simply explain that he had only accepted the request because it would have been awful to consider an outsider on the council. He was going to humbly accept because it was better for the corporation. Unfortunately, he would have to resign his position as security director if he became a lord. Luckily, he already had a replacement in mind from his organization. The lords would accept because to fight would require too much effort, although he was sure it would pain them at times when he outvoted them.

Fools, he thought. They should actually be happy. Ultimately, they would benefit from his leadership. He had already made inroads with other corporations using his intelligence network. Key people in the right positions would provide shipping information to be targeted by Glenn. He would repeat the process for each megacorporation in turn.

Nebulaco would be exempt from attack. Their profits would rise, and the value of Nebulaco stock would soar. He would become more rich and powerful, and even those fools on the board would be richer than ever before. That was all right because he would be the one in total control of the corporation. Let them have their comfy mansions and easy lives. They were of no consequence to him.

Then there was the matter of the datalifter, the pilot, and the egotistical detective. If all went well, even that matter would be resolved soon. The detective was financially strapped enough that he just might come through. It would be ideal if Chandler tied all of them together in one nice neat package, ripe for slaughter. He would call to ask for his payment, and Maxwell would send Glenn to dispose of them.

And who knows? The detective might just deliver them directly to Maxwell. That would be even better. Maxwell opened his desk drawer and removed a blaster. He extended it toward empty space and sighted along its length. He'd cleaned it after using it on Frederick

Casey. He could clean it again after using it on the detective, pilot, and datalifter.

Sometimes, there's no substitute for doing a job yourself, he thought. He'd learned that lesson a long time ago when he'd had a different name.

He'd been born Roger Chow. He never knew his father, and his mother was a stim addict who had cast him out at the age of eight. He'd picked pockets to survive the deadly back alleys of Empire City until he'd learned to bust heads. But his muscles weren't his primary assets. His mind was always working on a better way. Soon, he was in charge of a street gang. They moved from muggings and petty theft to protection rackets, drugs, and prostitution. He was on top of the world, his world.

But no matter what he accomplished, it was never enough. So he set his sights on the megacorporations, arguably the largest and most powerful criminal organizations in the galaxy. The only difference was that their crimes were legal.

He knew he had the talent. All he needed was the opportunity. He watched and waited, and then, one day, it came.

Vincent Maxwell had been a low-level exec just starting his career at Nebulaco, excited about his transfer from Empire City to Nebula Prime. It was a big promotion, and his future looked bright. The real Vincent Maxwell never made it to corporate headquarters. His body was found in a gutter. In his pocket was an identification card with his face but bearing the name of Roger Chow; with the help of a few well-placed bribes, every record related to Maxwell had been modified to match him.

Thus began his new career.

Maxwell shot up the ladder by displaying a talent for locating corruption. All the while, he padded his pockets with corporate funds. He orchestrated elaborate conspiracies in the name of Thorne and profited both from the illegal gains and from the search for the pirate villain. At the same time, Maxwell had kept his contacts in the underworld, never dealing with them in his Vincent Maxwell persona.

It was the perfect plan, and it was about to reach fruition.

He keyed into his secret account at the Galactic Bank. Surely there had been enough time for the stock transfers to have occurred. Once that happened, he could announce himself and begin his life as Lord Maxwell.

He pulled up the first account and froze as he looked at the balance in the air before him.

"The money," Maxwell whispered. "What happened to the money?" The main menu appeared in the air before him. He raced through the security checks and made a balance inquiry on another account. One by one he checked them all. It was the same for all of them. Not only devoid of stocks, but devoid of credits altogether. Every one of his accounts was completely empty.

The glowing green zeroes hovered in the air, mocking him.

What could have happened? His mind snapped to the most likely explanation: Randol's datalifter, Sai Collins.

Did she do it on her own, or did Randol put her up to it? Either way, Randol was going to suffer for this. Maxwell still needed Randol's daughter. But until he got his money back, he would return a piece of Helen each day to Randol. Starting today she wouldn't be able to count to ten.

No one messed with Maxwell and got away with it.

* * *

Hank, Sai, and Chandler reached the section of the base adjacent to the detention area without event. It was relatively easy to avoid contact with the pirates. The base seemed to be sparsely populated, and the pirates didn't seem to be particularly curious or interested in anything going on around them.

Of course, from the pirates' perspective, they were in the middle of the Outrigger Rift on a hidden base. What were the chances that someone would be able to sneak in?

Hank checked their position on the com. "If this map is right, we need to make a cut right about here." He stopped and pointed to the wall.

Hank dug into their pack and pulled out a handheld unicutter. He donned his safety goggles and flipped the unit on. A bright white energy blade sprang from the tool. Hank set to work digging into the rock wall while Sai and Chandler stood guard, watching down the corridor in either direction.

The unicutter made quick work of the wall. Soon, light spilled around the edges of the rectangular access hole Hank had created. He clicked off the unit.

"Okay," he said. "I'm getting ready to make the final cut. Be ready to catch the block."

Chandler and Sai moved into position, averting their eyes. "Go," Chandler said.

Hank reactivated the unit and finished the cut. The block of stone fell free. It was heavier than any of them had expected. It slipped through their hands, nearly falling on Sai's foot. She jumped back to avoid being crushed.

The stone slab crashed to the floor. The three looked at each other. There was nothing to do but go for it.

Hank charged through the opening, pistol in hand. He turned the corner to his left. Sai and Chandler rushed through the hole behind him.

The room they rushed into was not the cell block.

It was the galley.

And apparently, they had arrived just in time for dinner. The room was filled to capacity with hungry pirates. This may have been why the rest of the base had been relatively unoccupied. It appeared to be meatloaf day.

"Oops," Hank said. He stopped suddenly and Sai plowed into him. "Gee, honey, I hope you remembered to call ahead for reservations."

Sai's eyes widened. "Shit."

Chandler stopped behind them at the entrance. Damn Tenet! He lied about the map. There was only one thing to do. He had to take the only option available. He pulled his gun.

Hank looked around.

Every blaster in the room was leveled at them.

Including Chandler's.

"Okay," Chandler said. "Everybody calm down. Hank, Sai, go ahead and drop your weapons."

"What the hell are you talking about?" Hank asked.

Sai looked at him, shocked.

"Nothing personal," he said, "but you guys didn't really think I was stupid enough to try helping you with a jailbreak from a heavily guarded pirate base, did you? The price on your head is enough of an incentive to make new career plans." Chandler looked around the room. "Who's in charge here? I have a deal to make."

EPISODE SIX

CHAPTER TWENTY-THREE

Hayes, Glenn's second-in-command, stepped forward from the pack, keeping his pistol aimed squarely between Chandler's eyes. "Just who the hell do you think you are?"

A few of the twenty or so pirates packed into the galley chuckled and kept their weapons focused on Chandler as well. The air was heavy with the knowledge that if one person popped off a shot the room would turn into a slaughterhouse.

Chandler kept his gun aimed at Hank and Sai. They both glared at him with their hands up, but he ignored them and focused on Hayes. He stepped slowly to one side and raised his empty left hand. "Everyone needs to calm down and listen to reason."

Hayes tightened the grip on his gun. "*You* need to listen to this. Put down your weapon on the count of three or we're going to cut you and your friends down in a mighty pretty blaze of plasma fire." Hayes glanced around the room. "This is one hell of a firing squad. Be something to see, but a bitch to clean up. We do eat here, so I'd prefer that you drop the weapon. But, it's your call. One . . . two . . ."

"Okay, relax," Chandler said, putting down his blaster and rising slowly with his hands up. "Someone just go get your boss, and I'll explain everything. Just tell him that I brought in Sai Collins and Hank Jensen. I know you've been trying to get them. Then you'll have your answer. There's a corporate bounty on these two. I figure if I turn them in to you I should get half."

"Or what?" Hayes asked. "We could shoot you and get the full bounty; it isn't as if we don't already have all of you."

"Fine," Chandler said. It was obvious that his patience was wearing thin. "But someone go get Glenn and let me talk to him first."

"What kind of game are you playing, Chandler?" a familiar voice said from the back of the room.

Chandler thought he recognized the voice, and when he spotted the source he grinned. "How ya doing, Brock? I guess not too well since you're hanging out with these idiots."

Brock leaned against the wall picking at his fingernails.

Hayes walked toward Brock, and the group of pirates opened up a path before him.

"You know this man?" Hayes asked Brock.

"We go way back," Brock said. "That there is Mike Chandler. We were in the Confed back in the day. Tough son of a bitch. Used to be a ladies' man. He screwed around with my woman and she left me for him. Been good friends ever since. She was one mean harpy."

"Crazy as a shit-house rat," Chandler said.

"But there was that thing she did with—"

"So his story is legit?" Hayes asked.

"He's probably completely full of shit, but I can't prove it either way. One thing, though—with Chandler it all boils down to money. You can bet he's gonna be on the side with the deepest pockets. It's against his nature to stick his neck out for anyone. To be honest, if there is some money to be had turning those poor fools in, then I tend to believe him."

"All you have to do is check with your boss," Chandler said. "Then you'll know for sure. I can wait here or we can take these two down to the brig."

"That'll work," Brock said to Hayes. "I'll escort them *all* down to the cell block and you can put in a call to the boss." He turned to Chandler. "Let's get you kiddies bunked down for the night."

"Now, Brock. This is no way to treat a friend," Chandler said. "I'm here to make a deal."

"Just showing you some good ol' hospitality. Now, get a move on." Brock motioned Chandler toward a hallway to the left.

"Wait, I don't trust them. Take two men with you," Hayes said.

"Whatever you say."

Hayes pointed at two pirates who were seated at a table and had been eating for the entire duration of the standoff. "You and you. You're on escort detail."

"Dang it," one of them said. He shoveled as much food into his mouth as he could and grabbed his ration of rum. He looked expectantly at his neighbor, who wore a tattered cap and was shoveling beans into his mouth as fast as he could. "Come on, Ned."

"I ain't done eatin'," Ned said around a mouthful.

"Yes, you are. Let's go."

"Damn it, Earl, why do we always get the shit jobs?"

They rose and shuffled over to Brock, Ned still chewing.

Brock sighed. "Yeah, thanks, Hayes. I feel much safer."

"Lead the way," Chandler said.

Brock smiled. "Please, after you." He directed Hank, Sai, and Chandler down a hallway. Brock fell into line behind them, flanked by Ned and Earl. They made a few turns before Hank spun and clipped Chandler across the jaw. Chandler fell into the other two pirates, taking them to the floor, Earl's cup of rum crashing to the floor with them. Brock staggered backward, but didn't fall.

Hank didn't take two steps before Chandler whipped out a concealed weapon from his sleeve and shot him point-blank with an energy blast.

Sai tried to catch Hank as he fell senseless, but he was too heavy and they both fell to the floor. She glared back at Chandler. "Oh my God. You really are turning us in? How could you shoot him like that?"

"By pulling the trigger." Chandler tucked the small weapon back under his cuff, then extended a hand. Brock helped him up from the floor.

"Just as tricky as always, I see," Brock said.

Chandler grinned. "Some things never change, Angus."

Sai drew Hank to her, rocking him. Tears rolled down her cheeks. "Please be okay, please. I need you, Hank. I need you with me."

"He's fine. It was just a stunner." Chandler said. "I picked it up years ago when I was a bouncer. It's amazing how quickly it handles troublemakers."

Ned and Earl scrambled to their feet. They brushed themselves off, pulled their weapons, and started toward Hank and Sai. Chandler stepped in front of them. "Whoa, guys. I don't know what you have in mind, but to collect the full bounty, I need them alive."

"Bastard cost me my rum for the week! We only get a little. I'd barely started it," Earl said.

"I don't care," Chandler said.

"We could just shoot him in the leg or something," Ned suggested. "That would make you feel a lot better."

"And I could just shoot you in the face. Lower your weapons," Chandler said.

Ned complied. Earl shifted his aim to Chandler. "Or we could shoot you," he said with a smirk.

Chandler lunged forward and grabbed Earl's arm, pulling him close, then suddenly side-stepped and bumped him with his hip, causing Earl to lose his balance and whirl through the air, falling with a crushing impact to the stone floor. Chandler plucked the gun out of the man's hand, pulled the power supply, and tossed it back onto his fallen body.

Earl moaned on the ground.

"You've gotten slow," Brock said. "You used to be able to lift their wallets while they were falling."

Chandler shrugged. "I could have, but I figured it was empty. Plus I didn't want to put my hand anywhere near that area." Chandler leaned over to speak to Earl. "Oh, get up, you baby. We used to have to take thirty throws like that before breakfast at judo practice."

Ned helped Earl up. Earl limped but seemed mostly okay.

"If your brainless buddies here have no more objections, I'd like to take my prized catches to the brig. The sooner they're locked away and the calls are made, the sooner I can get paid."

"I'll be damned," Brock said. "You really are turning pirate."

Responding to the commotion, Hayes and several men came running up the hallway. "What happened?" he asked.

Brock gave him the rundown.

Hayes smiled. "Good enough for me. Go ahead and return his gun, then keep him entertained until I can set up a meeting with Glenn."

Then Hayes left, having his men take Sai and Hank to the brig. Hank was still unconscious and had to be dragged. Sai stared at Chandler with pure hate as they took her away.

"You know, if you play your cards right, you may have quite an opportunity here. Glenn is looking for men with brains."

"So what happened to Thorne, and how did a guy named Glenn become a pirate lord?"

Brock chuckled. "Long story, best told over a bottle."

* * *

Glenn's image floated above the surface of Maxwell's desk. Maxwell sat back in his chair, his form indistinct and dark due to the stealthcloak he'd activated before making the call. He didn't want his pirate underling to discover that he was director of Nebulaco Security. Especially one who actually seemed to possess some intelligence. Glenn was too smart for his own good. Sooner or later he was going to have to "restructure" the ranks again.

"I understand that you've been trying to reach me. But Glenn, before you open your mouth, I'm going to let you know that I'm not in the mood for bad news. What's the situation?"

"Have you ever heard of a Mike Chandler?"

"Why? What do you have to tell me?"

"I may actually have some good news for you. This Mike Chandler has delivered Hank Jensen and Sai Collins to the base. He says that we should split the Nebulaco reward with him."

Maxwell laughed. "The girl? I have the girl? Wait a minute. Where is she? You didn't kill them, did you?"

"No sir, not yet. Should we? After all, just a few days ago you wanted them destroyed at all costs. It seems like you're fickle when it comes to these two."

"No! Listen carefully, Glenn. I want the girl. I want her alive. Repeat after me. *Alive.*"

"You want the girl *alive,*" Glenn repeated, obviously insulted.

"Very good. Have her sent immediately to Coulson City on Port Royal. Send me the docking berth address when you get there and I'll have someone pick her up."

"So what's so important about this girl?" Glenn said, cocking an eyebrow.

"It isn't for you to question me. You don't get paid to think. Just do as I say."

"Right. I'm a businessman, not a servant. My loyalty and goodwill extends about as far as yours does. And we know exactly how much goodwill was fostered on your part toward Thorne."

"You're playing a dangerous game. You'd better deliver the girl to me or there will be serious repercussions." The image of the speaker, even through the subterfuge of the stealthcloak, seemed to quiver.

Glenn smiled. "Of course. Yes, sir!" He made a small salute. "You'll have the girl as soon as is practical. We also need to determine the fate of the Randol girl. As I said, I'm a businessman, not a slaver. This quagmire of prisoners and blackmail is distasteful to me."

"There's a good profit in it. We both know that's the only thing that matters," Maxwell said.

"To you maybe. Now, what about Chandler?"

"What about him?"

"What should I do with him?"

"I would think that should be obvious," Maxwell said.

* * *

Chandler sat in Brock's tiny room at a small table that was carved out of the native rock. Brock pulled out a bottle of tequila, complete with worm, and two dirty glasses. Chandler figured the tequila would kill the germs, but he was worried that the worm might kill him.

Brock filled the glasses and set the bottle on the table between them. He slid a glass to Chandler, then held up his own in a toast. "To old friends," he said.

"Wherever they may be," Chandler said. He tapped his glass to Brock's then took a sip. It was smooth and smoky and burned a trail of fire to his gut.

"Good stuff, eh?" Brock said.

"Where'd you steal this?"

"I have friends in high places."

"Apparently," Chandler said. "This stuff is hard to find. But I suppose a lot of luxury goods come through here. As I understand it, the pickings have been pretty good."

Brock raised an eyebrow, then topped off Chandler's drink. "I suppose so. I haven't been involved in that end of the operation. I've mostly been doing what I've always done."

"As little as possible?"

"Yep, pretty much." Brock nodded and took a sip. "What's it been, five years? Six?"

Chandler shrugged. "Something like that. What happened with you and that waitress in Opportunity City? What was her name?"

"Paula? I haven't thought about her in years." Brock shook his head. "Everything was fun until her husband got home from the Scouts." They laughed, but it was a forced laugh. Tension hung between them like a heavy weight.

Brock took another tiny sip of his drink. Chandler noticed that he seemed more willing to pour than swallow. "So I can't believe you're working for bounties these days," Brock said.

"It's a small world, ain't it? I never figured you for a pirate, either. Last I heard you were doing freelance surveillance work."

"Well that, my friend, is a long story, full of woe," Brock said. He picked up the bottle. "Freshen your drink?"

"I'm good." Chandler made as if to swallow a huge mouthful of the fiery liquor but actually only took in a sip. "Ah!" he breathed. "So tell me your story. We've got nothing but time, after all."

Brock scratched his head. "Well, the latest episode began with me being a day late and a credit short on Raken. A man comes up to me and asks if I want to make some money. Says it will be simple surveillance work, just set up and watch a building." Brock paused for a moment, stared into space, then let out a belch that rattled the walls and peeled the paint. "Damn, that tasted even worse the second time around."

Chandler grinned.

Brock gave him an abbreviated version of what he'd been through, but Chandler could sense he wasn't telling him the whole truth. In the back and forth, both men tried to extract information, but they kept their cards close to the vest. "So one thing leads to another, and here we are. As you know, I'm good at what I do."

"Your girlfriend didn't seem to think so." Chandler laughed and took another sip.

"I'm sure you did much better and that's why you guys are still together."

"Touché," Chandler said. "So what's with this Glenn guy?"

"Used to be Thorne's right-hand man. When the time came to take him out, Glenn popped him between the eyes and took over, but he's not like Thorne at all."

"How so?"

"He's intelligent. He isn't planning on being a pirate forever. He has bigger goals. He wants to use this operation as a lever to create a legitimate enterprise. I'm not sure how he's going to do it, but I actually think he will. If he can steer clear of the Confed."

"Fine with me. I wish him well. But I just want to get my money and get out of here," Chandler said.

Brock nodded. "Yes, well, that is one problem. Do you remember the old saying about how three people can keep a secret?"

"Three can keep a secret if two are dead?"

"That's it. No one who knows the actual coordinates of the base ever leaves it except to go on short raids. Once you know where it is, you really only have two ways out. Either join up and rise in rank to the inner circle, or leave feet first."

"So you're of the opinion that I won't be making it out of here with my bounty?"

Brock shrugged. "Hey, what do I know? Tell you what, let's finish this bottle and worry about that later."

CHAPTER TWENTY-FOUR

Hank woke up to find his head resting on Sai's lap. She was asleep, and her face looked peaceful, almost angelic, in the dim light. He closed his eyes and breathed deeply, enjoying the warmth of her body.

He felt the urge to kiss her sleeping lips. But he didn't want to wake her and have her dreams be disturbed by the reality of their situation.

They were locked in a dark cell, dimly lit by the light that snuck in beneath the heavy steel door. They lay on a hard mattress that smelled of urine. A stainless steel toilet with a sink built into the upper tank stood in the middle of the back wall. The room measured about three meters wide and three meters deep.

His temples throbbed in pain. The last thing he remembered was punching someone, then being shot—by Chandler. He'd really betrayed them! Why? He remembered when Chandler had tried to pick them up in Last Chance. Had that been an offer of help or an attempted abduction?

What motivated a man like Chandler? Was it money? Could money really be that much more important than friends? Than honor? Hank couldn't understand it. He'd seemed so genuine, and Hank prided himself on being an excellent judge of character. Well, an okay judge of character. There had been a few bad choices. Like that girl in—

Sai stirred in her sleep, and she moved her hand to caress his forehead. Hank closed his eyes and turned slightly to lay his cheek against her leg, enjoying this moment with her. Take the simple pleasures while you may. It was better than dwelling on their situation.

Hank heard the door rattle and open. Sai twisted and nearly spilled Hank to the floor as three large men entered the cell. Hank tried to jump up, but he was still stiff from the stunner blast.

"Come on, girlie. You're getting transported," one man said, making a grab for her.

Sai lashed out with a swift kick to his left kneecap. He fell with a scream, but the other two moved in with batons.

Hank tried to punch the first man, but the guard easily dodged his feeble attack, then smacked Hank in the jaw with his baton. Hank fell to the floor.

Sai tried to wrench herself from the grasp of the other man, but he jabbed her in the gut with the butt of his baton. She fell to her knees.

"Don't even think about it," one of them said to Hank as he struggled to get to his feet. Hank ignored him, pushing himself up. The man shook his head and kicked Hank in the ribs. Hank fell back to the ground, unable to catch his breath. This time he couldn't muster the strength to try again. They dragged Sai from the room, and there wasn't a thing he could do but watch them though his tears.

The man hit Hank one last time across the face, then backed out the door. "Pathetic," he said.

"Where are you taking her?" Hank said.

"None of your business," the man said.

* * *

"Lighting farts in the airlock? Is this the same guy who didn't know the difference between concussion and incendiary charges?" Chandler asked.

"They might be brothers . . . or father and son."

Both men roared in laughter. Even with the tiny sips they'd been drinking, they'd managed to drain the bottle of tequila. And a bit of whiskey as well.

After they both wound down, Chandler looked at Brock. This was a man he knew from war. This was a man he knew from countless days escaping from battle in Confed base bars and back-alley starport dives. He'd had this man cover him as he rushed into hell. He had to risk it. It could go two ways. Either allies to the end, or enemies who would do their damnedest to kill each other.

"So Brock . . ."

Brock turned to Chandler and stared him in the eye. "Mike, let's cut the shit. I know you're not the kind of man who runs around kidnapping folks for blood money."

Chandler nodded. "And I know that you're not the type of guy who would work for pirates."

Brock smiled. "So what the hell are we doing here?"

In a simultaneous motion, both men brought out the pistols they'd been aiming at each other from beneath the table, clicked them on safety, then placed them beside their drinks.

"You first," Chandler said.

Brock sighed and leaned back in his chair. "Confed Secret Service. Deep cover for about a year. The Confed can only protect trade ships in the space directly around major ports of call. That used to be fine, because pirates typically had no way to locate merchant ships except by cruising around randomly in those areas fishing for prey. Thorne changed everything. He's been able to get direct access to shipping routes and timetables. We can't escort every ship. Our only hope of stopping him was to do it from the inside. What about you?"

Chandler took a swig. "Been doing private operative work. My current client is Lord Randol of Nebulaco. His daughter, Helen, was kidnapped. We were in the process of a jailbreak. We have the goods on the operation and how Thorne had been feeding off Nebulaco.

We can shut the whole thing down. If we can make it out of here alive."

"You'll need help to do that."

Chandler nodded. "You in?"

"Damn straight. I'm sick of this rock. All I needed was a way to get the coordinates and get out so I could report them to the Confed."

"Well, we got 'em, and opportunity's knocking on your door right now. Ready to go?"

Brock raised his glass. "All right then." He slammed the last of his drink and stood up. The room spun and he blinked several times. "Give me a minute to let the floor stop moving."

Chandler laughed and pushed himself to his feet. "Still a lightweight, aren't you?"

He went to take a step, then reached for the table to steady himself.

Brock shook his finger at Chandler. "Who's the lightweight now?"

"We can do this."

"Be like our days in the Academy."

Chandler grinned. "Those were the days. Where's the head? I gotta piss like a Dynerian wildebeest."

"Most guys just piss on the wall."

"Yeah, I noticed. That's just disgusting."

"True. Piss in the bottle. We can seal it up and leave it in the galley. They'd probably drink it even if you labeled it *Tequila Piss*."

CHAPTER TWENTY-FIVE

Chandler and Brock marched as straight as they could, considering their condition. Their footfalls echoed through the corridor leading to the cell block. They looked at one another and grinned. Chandler felt pretty invincible, but then, he'd swallowed the worm.

When they reached the cell block, Brock strode right up to the guard's station and slammed a hand down on the desktop. "We're here to pick up some prisoners," he said loudly.

"Oh look, it's Brock," the guard said. "I thought they had you on galley detail."

Brock squinted his eyes and looked at the man. "Don't I know you?"

"Yep," the guard said. "I'm Ray. Ray Larson. Remember? Used to work for Nebulaco. I was the leader of Red Team on Raken. Got fired for that cluster, so I signed on with these guys. The pay is good. They gave me the job of guarding the *important* prisoners."

"Well that explains why they ordered us to move them," Brock said, jabbing Chandler in the ribs with his elbow.

Chandler smiled. "So this is the Larson guy?"

"Yep. He healed up pretty good, didn't he?"

"So what's the story?" Larson asked.

"Like I told you," Brock said. "We're here to transfer Hank Jensen, Sai Collins, and Helen Randol. Glenn wants us to take them to his special secret prison." He gave Larson a wink.

"I didn't hear anything about this."

"No kidding," Brock said. "That's why it's a secret."

Larson checked his log. "Well, it says here the Collins girl has already been transferred."

"Really?" Chandler and Brock shared a concerned look. "Where to?"

"Port Royal, Coulson City."

"When did they transport her?" Brock said.

Ray checked the log again. "Just before I came on duty, about twenty minutes ago."

"You see, Chandler? It never fails around here. They screw everything up. They were supposed to transport them all together."

Chandler nodded. "Yes, it sure looks that way."

"Hey, guys," Larson said. "I wasn't even here."

"Oh no," Brock said. "It's not *your* fault. I understand. Hell, you're too smart to screw up like that. Come on and help me load up these jerks."

Larson shook his head. "Sorry, guys. I can't."

"What?"

"I have to have clearance from upstairs."

Brock threw up his hands. "If that don't beat all. Here I was thinking you were different from these other bozos, and you come up with something like that."

"Sorry. I have to get authorization."

Chandler reached forward and tapped the man on the head with his fist. "Hello! Think about what you're saying."

"What do you mean?"

"Okay. How do you get an authorization?" Chandler said.

Larson shrugged. "They call me on the com?"

Brock and Chandler nodded. "And what's wrong with that?"

Larson's gaze shifted from one expectant face to the other. "I don't know."

Chandler slapped himself on the forehead. "Think! *Anybody* can call you on the com. What does it take to fake a voice? Besides, what if someone tapped the system? How would you keep anything secret? That's why they send us in person for the high-level security transfers. You know who we are, so you aren't going to be fooled."

Larson shook his head. "I don't know, guys. I really think I should call upstairs." He reached for the com control.

"No!" Brock yelled.

Larson looked at him suspiciously.

"Don't you see? If you start broadcasting all over the base, then it won't be a secret anymore. I'm just trying to keep you out of trouble, Ray. For example, how did they handle the transfer of the Collins girl?"

"They called down here on the com."

"See? And that was a mistake. Had they done the proper procedure we would have been able to transport all of them at once. Does it make any sense to use two ships?"

"Well, no."

"Exactly. Now, remember what happened on Raken at that oracle's place?"

"Hey, that should have worked!"

"I know, but did it? Who was there trying to save your butt?" Brock cocked a thumb at himself, trying not to weave too much. "Yep, who's your buddy?"

"You?"

"That's right! Now, I guarantee that if you touch that com and breathe a word about us transferring these prisoners, all hell will break loose."

"Really?"

"Absolutely. I speak with complete certainty."

Larson sighed. "Okay. Let me find the keys."

With Larson's help, Chandler and Brock opened the cell doors. They brought Helen out first. She blinked in the bright light of the hallway. She was filthy—dirty clothes and black fingernails, her blonde hair matted and tangled. As she stepped out, they put her in manacles. She looked frightened and didn't speak or meet their eyes.

She'd gone from corporate princess to slave. Brock tried to nod at her, but she wouldn't look at him.

Hank came next. He'd been beaten. A big welt was swelling up on his jaw. Dried blood crusted around his nostrils. His lips were swollen and split. He looked at Chandler with an expression of pure hate as they placed manacles on him. Chandler winked at him out of Larson's sight, but he thought the motion infuriated more than comforted Hank. He was glad that Hank would be in cuffs for a while, at least until they liberated a ship, and perhaps longer than that based on the looks he was giving.

Chandler and Brock led the pair of prisoners out of the cell block. "Thanks, Ray," Brock said. "Remember, not a word of this over the com. You know those idiots can't keep quiet about anything. You just keep standing guard as if the prisoners are still in there. That's the only way we can keep a lid on this and prevent those morons from spreading the news everywhere."

"You got it, Brock!" Larson smiled, giving him a thumbs-up.

Chandler and Brock looked at each other and grinned.

As soon as they were out of earshot, Chandler moved close to Hank and whispered. "This is a jailbreak."

Hank looked back at him, confused. "Is this another one of your games?"

"Just keep quiet, and leave everything to us," Chandler said, leaning forward, almost knocking Hank over.

"Good god! You smell flammable," Hank said. "What have you been drinking?"

"Tequila, but it's all gone so don't ask," Chandler said.

Hank shook his head. "I really thought you had sold us out. I'm sorry."

Chandler shrugged. "Don't worry about it. I would have felt the same in your boots."

"Now the only person on my shit list is a thawed-out, lying pirate," Hank said.

Helen looked at Chandler. "We've met, haven't we?"

"Yep. Champion beer chugger at your service."

She looked at Brock. "And my waiter is here as well."

"The tips sucked, so I moved up in the world. How you feeling?"

"I've been better. You're really here to save me?"

"That's right. Your father sent us," Chandler said.

"Really? I'm surprised my father even cares."

"Believe it or not, you're the only thing your father does care about. Now keep quiet, do what we say, and we'll get you home to him."

"Does anyone know what happened to Sai?" Hank asked.

Chandler's features clouded. "She's on her way to Port Royal. I figure whoever's behind this whole thing is after what's in her head about the bank accounts."

Hank tried to smile. "At least we know they aren't going to kill her. She's the most valuable woman in the universe to them now."

They followed the hallway to the hangar.

"The way I figure it, we're practically home free," Chandler said. "All we have to do is steal a ship in the middle of a crowded hangar, outrun a couple hundred pirate Marauders, rescue a girl from some bad guys, and save the galaxy before breakfast."

"Been there, done that," Hank said.

CHAPTER TWENTY-SIX

The hangar was not crowded. In fact, it was practically deserted. "I think this is going to be easier than we thought," Brock said.

"Shut up. Every time someone says something like that, it jinxes me," Chandler said.

As they entered the hangar, they retreated to an alcove to remove the manacles from Hank and Helen. Chandler handed Hank his comlink, his pistol, and Sai's whisperblade.

Hank glanced at the whisperblade, then slipped it in his pocket because he had no idea how to use the damn thing. He readied his pistol.

Helen was still scared, but for a different reason. She thought she was no longer in the hands of enemies, but lunatics.

"Stay with us, Helen. We'll get you home," Chandler said.

"Thanks," Helen said.

Hank sneaked a peek out into the hangar and did a head count. "I see only four guys out there, and most of the ships are gone."

"Great," said Brock.

"Not great. That means it will be easier to get a ship, but harder to get away. Those ships are patrolling out there. We blast out and they intercept us. We'd better be ready for a firefight."

They kept to the shadows, moving along the hangar wall to the nearest ship. It was Marauder class, and although it wasn't pretty, it looked functional. It was large enough for three, but it could hold four people if they were friendly. Most importantly, it was fast and already lined up in a launch chute, ready to fly.

It was a simple matter to enter the ship unobserved—the vessels were not guarded. Brock and Helen strapped in while Hank and Chandler got in the cockpit seats and checked out the controls.

Hank had never flown a Marauder, but the layout was typical. He flipped a few switches and checked the status board. Everything looked okay.

"I don't like this ship," Hank said.

"Why?" Chandler asked.

"No cup holder." He glanced back at them. "Are you all ready?"

"As ready as we'll ever be," Brock said.

Helen clutched the arms of her chair with all her might. "I guess," she said.

"Okay, let's go!" Hank reached for the row of engine control buttons. He intended to do a shit-hot takeoff that would hopefully damage the hangar and possibly rupture the air seal on the base. It would be gravy.

He hit the launch control and nothing happened.

"You know," Brock said. "I just thought of something. They probably took all the ships that worked when they left on patrol."

"Remind me to strangle you later," Chandler said.

Suddenly the ship stuttered to life. The engines caught, or tried to.

"Everybody stay strapped in. I think we may be in for an interesting ride."

The engines finally powered up, and the force of the takeoff pressed them into their seats as the ship left the base for clear space. They gained speed, and the base started disappearing in the distance behind them. It looked good.

For a few seconds.

Almost immediately, Hank and Chandler saw the pirate fleet. They were evidently on their way back from patrol. A formation of at least one hundred Marauders approached, led by Glenn's flagship.

"Okay, now what?" asked Hank.

"You're the hotshot pilot," Chandler said. "I did my job back there."

"Thanks."

He took a hard turn to starboard and hit the afterburners, hoping to get a head start. He was sure the alarm had been sounded as soon as their ship left for its unauthorized cruise. Immediately, the fleet turned toward him and moved to intercept.

Hank was familiar with the territory, but unfortunately, so were the pirates, and his memories were almost ten years old. A lot changes in such a chaotic region. He wished he had *Elsa* instead of this junker.

Then he remembered his comlink. "Elsa, this is Hank. Are you out there?"

"Hank! What happened? Where are you?"

"I'd love to chat, but there are about a hundred pirates who want a piece of me," Hank said. "They may be monitoring our transmissions, so I'll meet you at the rendezvous point if I can shake these jerks."

"Got it."

Hank smiled and looked at Chandler. "Contingency plan."

Already the ships were beginning to close in. Even though they weren't yet in range, some of the ships were firing. Glenn's flagship, faster than the others, was gaining.

He had to buy some time. Hank cut around a small asteroid and dove between two intersecting hunks of debris that might once have been the hulls of spacecraft.

He hit the com. "Hey there, pirate scumbags, this is Hank Jensen. I have something that is very important to you on board. You don't want to screw up and hurt Randol's kid. Tell your men to back off."

Glenn's voice answered. "You can't get away, Jensen. We will follow you wherever you go. There is no escape, so why not let us have the girl? I promise that you and your friends will be released."

Hank grinned. "Somehow I doubt your sincerity."

"You might as well trust me, as the alternative isn't pretty. If you force me to chase you, I promise to make you the nightly entertainment for a month."

"Sorry, I don't do stand-up."

"You won't have to do anything but scream."

"Cheerful guy," said Chandler. "I wouldn't piss him off if I were you."

"Now you tell me?" Hank said.

"His name is Glenn," Brock said. "Maybe I can talk to him."

"What the hell is the leader doing out on a patrol?" Chandler asked.

"He's surrounded by idiots, so he's keeping a hands-on approach until he can find a few decent men. He's actually reasonable as pirates go."

"Yeah, he sounded real reasonable," Chandler said. "Let's get out of here quick."

Hank angled around and pushed his thrusters to the limit as they entered the outskirts of the Rift itself. The ship bucked and rocked as it encountered pockets of space-time distortion. Glenn and his men followed, splitting up into two groups, the smaller following directly behind Hank's ship while the other veered to one side to try to maneuver into a pincer formation.

The blaster fire stopped, so apparently his talk with Glenn had at least served to cut down on those itchy trigger fingers.

What he really feared was that Glenn's flagship would get close enough to use its tractor beam. If that happened it would be all over.

Hank dodged rocks and debris, left and right, searching the viewscreen for a landmark in order to get his bearings. He checked the coordinates and knew where he needed to go. Glenn's ship gained ground slowly but steadily.

A few of the other Marauders were entering weapons range, so Hank activated the computer-controlled rear guns. He took one of the vessels by surprise and clipped it across the bow. Most of the other shots missed, but it was the psychological effect that counted. He could shoot them, but they couldn't shoot back. At least not without risking the wrath of their leader. It wasn't fair, but life was rough.

Up ahead, Hank saw what he had been looking for: the chance to ditch some of his pursuers.

Suddenly, the ship was struck hard by something in the debris field. Hank read the severity of the damage in the now-sluggish controls and the warning lights that turned his lime-green status board into a blazing red inferno.

"Shit."

"Is everything all right?" Helen asked.

"No, everything is not all right. The rear guns have overloaded and it looks like we're down to fifty percent power on the drive. Our only weapons are forward and we wouldn't have a chance if we turned to face them head-on."

Hank brought up a tactical display on the viewscreen. It plotted the positions of their ship and the pirate fleet, superimposed against a backdrop of the sensor scan and star map of the area. "The good news is that I know where I am."

"I'll take all the good news I can get," Chandler said.

"Do you see that large derelict?" Hank asked, pointing to the display of a wrecked starcruiser, ten times the size of their ship, that lay drifting nearby.

Chandler nodded. "Yes, it's hard to miss. What about it?"

"In my younger days, I used to prospect for salvage in the Rift. I think I can guide us through a breach in its hull. We can sit in its belly and attach ourselves there with a magnetic anchor."

"Okay," Chandler said. "Now explain why?"

"That's where a little prior knowledge comes in," Hank said with a smile. "Do you see that debris directly ahead? I know for a fact that there is an old-style nuclear drive pod in it, and some unexpended fuel. We used to stay clear of it. There's enough radiation to curb your reproductive ability permanently. No salvage value, but I think I can make some use of it."

"What are you going to do?"

"Trust me," Hank said. "I'm gonna tear them a new one."

Chandler moved in close to Hank and looked him in the eye. "Are you sure it will work?"

Hank looked back. "Truthfully? I have no idea," he said.

There was a pause, then Chandler shrugged. "What the hell, let's go for it. I got nothing better."

"Fair enough. Hold on, y'all." Hank activated the braking thrusters and swerved to port, yelling "Yahoo!" as the ship followed his command. The sudden maneuver overwhelmed the ship's G-force dampers, throwing the passengers around the cockpit.

Helen screamed. "You people are crazy! I think I was safer as a hostage."

Hank imagined he could hear Glenn cursing him as the larger ship passed over Hank's position. He managed to take a fair lead by the time Glenn could turn and follow. Building up every bit of speed he could muster on a straight vector, he prepared for the second turn that would take him to the derelict cruiser.

"Three . . . two . . . one . . . now!"

Hank kicked in the braking thrusters again and took a nosedive toward the derelict. He cut so close to a large piece of space junk that he clenched his teeth, expecting to hear the screech of metal on metal. Quickly, he reversed thrust and made last-second corrections as the derelict loomed huge on a collision course.

The hull breach was where he remembered it. The craft slowed to a crawl, and gently he guided it inside. Hovering in place, he spun the ship around to face the outside.

Hank brought the ship down against the hull with a dull thud. He switched the mags on, anchoring the ship. He fiddled with the forward targeting controls for a moment, then cinched his G-harness tightly about him and crossed his fingers. "You guys really ought to double-check those harnesses. Just a suggestion. Oh, and if there are any cushions back there, I would put them around your head."

Helen and Chandler scrambled to comply.

"Okay, this is going to be bad, isn't it?" Helen said.

"Oh yeah, this is going to suck," Chandler answered.

As the wave of Marauders passed by in front of them, Hank daintily pressed the fire control button. "Bye-bye."

The small ship lurched from the recoil as the forward gun fired. A rolling ball of burning plasma hurtled outward toward the leaking nuclear drive pod.

* * *

Glenn changed course, hoping that his wave of fighters would flush Jensen out. He saw the flash of the gun shoot from the derelict and laughed. It was like a bee stinging a bear's ass. Merely an annoyance.

The plasma round raced ahead with perfect precision, hitting the drive unit of the old vagabond ship dead-on. A chain reaction followed as the unexpended fuel around the drive erupted into nuclear fire. Glenn had only enough time to mutter a surprised curse before half his fleet was engulfed.

The shock waves from the blast buffeted his ship but did no serious damage. "Damn it, Jensen!" Glenn screamed. "That was brilliant! Are you kidding me?"

Everyone looked at him.

He looked around at his bridge crew. "What? Didn't you guys see that? One man in a damned Marauder. Why can't I get people like that?"

He decided right then and there that the informant could go to hell. Daughter of a lord onboard or not, Glenn was going to blast Jensen's ship out of the sky. The so-called informant was not as invulnerable as he seemed, and Glenn was not Thorne; he thought for himself.

Glenn watched and waited. As soon as the blast debris cleared, he was rewarded with the sight of the stolen Marauder sneaking back out of the derelict that Jensen had used as a protective shield.

"Target all weapons on that ship," Glenn ordered.

"Sir?" Hayes, his second-in-command said. "Are you serious? The informant wants the Randol girl alive. Do you know what will happen if you destroy that ship? He'll have your head. There'll be a new pirate lord."

Glenn narrowed his eyes at Hayes. "Yes," he said. "I know exactly what will happen. So"—in a smooth, quick motion Glenn drew his pistol and shot Hayes—"technically, that was self-defense."

The fire control officer watched Hayes fall. He snapped to attention and saluted. "The target is locked on, sir."

Glenn smiled. "Fire at will."

He watched as lances of plasma shot forward and engulfed Jensen's ship. The stolen Marauder exploded, sending bits of debris to scatter and swirl in the eddies of the Outrigger Rift.

He turned back to the crew. "That was a waste of potential." Glenn pointed to Hayes's body. "Someone dump that out the airlock."

Then he pointed to the fire control officer. "You, what's your name?"

"Ken, sir."

Glenn sighed. "Wow, that's actually a worse pirate name than mine. Anyway, good shooting. Consider yourself promoted to number two."

CHAPTER TWENTY-SEVEN

Maxwell had ordered the interrogation equipment placed in an unused storage warehouse near the docks on Port Royal. He would handle everything relating to the datalifter himself. He didn't want to take any chances with his entire financial future on the line.

Stacked crates were scattered across the large room. Tools and other equipment and supplies lay on a worktable, and the girl reclined in the memory probe chair, bound around the ankles, wrists, midsection, and throat. The probe sensors were poised several centimeters above her skull, looking like a crystal crown. She was conscious, but she hadn't spoken a word to Maxwell since she'd been brought in.

"Let me tell you what I'm going to do," Maxwell said. "First, I'm going to perform a complete deconstructive memory probe of your little brain. This will record your every thought, including the account numbers and access codes where you hid my money."

She said nothing, so he shrugged and continued.

"The beautiful thing is that once this process is over, your mind will be essentially gone, and you will be a drooling idiot. I won't let your body go to waste, though. I'll ship it down to the corporate flesh stables where someone with unusual tastes will share his demented fantasies with your shell."

Still, she didn't respond.

"You've caused me a great deal of trouble. But in the end you're insignificant. None of this has been more than a minor setback. I will have my money and my lordship. I will have my organization. And I will have my revenge. You, on the other hand, will have nothing."

"You aren't going to win," Sai said. "You're too greedy, too power-hungry to survive. The lords will find some way to eliminate you. You can't fight them all."

"They are decadent fools. They've lost the vital spark that allowed their ancestors to become lords, carving out empires no matter the cost. I'm claiming what is mine by right of conquest."

He moved to the console and activated the unit. A low hum sounded from within the device, and the probe sensors began to glow in a rhythmic pattern.

Slowly, they descended and touched her skull. She tried to twist her head, but the restraint on her throat tightened, causing her to gag. She had to remain still or the machine would cause her to pass out.

Maxwell stared, licking his lips. It was a lovely sight. The young woman who had caused such trouble for him was powerless, vulnerable, and completely in his control.

The probe started its automated process, and Sai's body writhed under it. Maxwell knew that it was slowly processing her every thought and memory, tearing them from her in chunks, leaving nothing but dull, empty gray matter.

A sound from his wrist com interrupted his enjoyment of the spectacle. Maxwell frowned and looked at the display. It was a notification alert. Glenn had initiated an emergency request for contact by sending a certain coded message to a public forum.

Maxwell walked to the worktable where a full com unit had been installed. He activated the stealthcloak and keyed in Glenn's com code to call him.

An image of Glenn sitting in his command chair sprang to life above the workbench. "Hello."

"This had better be good," Maxwell said.

"I don't know about good, but you certainly need to hear it."

"Yes? What is it?" Maxwell snapped. "You're interrupting me." He cast a glance over to where Sai lay strapped into the mind probe.

"You should know that Chandler, Jensen, and a traitor by the name of Brock made an escape attempt today. They stole a Marauder and we were forced to destroy them and their ship."

"So? I couldn't care less about your petty difficulties."

"I'm afraid that they had the Randol girl with them as well," Glenn said, matter-of-factly.

"Randol's daughter? Dead?" Maxwell said.

"I'm afraid so. There was no other choice. They destroyed more than thirty Marauders in the battle—my men. Moronic as those men were, there was no way that I could let Jensen and the others live after that."

"You ordered their deaths?" Maxwell asked.

"Yes, that's right, and I'd do the same thing over again."

"Who said you could make decisions like that?" Maxwell asked. "You had no right—"

"I had *every* right," Glenn said. "Those were my men."

"No! You and every man on that base belong to me."

"Really? It seems to me that you need me more than I need you."

"You're playing an even more dangerous game, Glenn," Maxwell said.

"You say that, but you see, unlike Thorne, I'm not afraid of you. Together we can have a profitable partnership. You give me information, I make the raids, and we both get rich. Alone I'm just a petty pirate, having to exist on a lucky catch now and then, but you will be nothing more than a powerless man hiding his face, full of dire threats, but unable to carry them out."

"This isn't over, Glenn. You'll live to know how wrong you are. I have other agents. Some much stronger than you. I'll send them against you if I must."

"Bring them on," Glenn said. "You know where to find me. Oh, I'm sorry, that might actually be a bit difficult. I didn't mention this before, but we're relocating. I don't trust you anymore. I know a sinking ship when I see it."

"So that makes you the rat?"

"Rats are survivors. I'm not sure about how you're going to end up," Glenn said, breaking the connection.

* * *

Sai lay with her eyes closed as the probe worked its hell on her mind. She had originally thought she was being taken to her death when they removed her from her cell on the pirate base. As soon as they put her on the spaceship, she understood. Maxwell had discovered that his bank account was a few billion credits short.

Now he thought that the knowledge in her head could get it back for him. Luckily, she knew it meant he wouldn't kill her, at least not for a while. But now, strapped into the mind probe, lost in the world of the probe as it ate into her psyche, her time was running out. Her only hope had been that Hank would find some way to save her.

The probe was programmed to stab into her mind, searching, devouring everything in its path. Normally, it would erase a person's thoughts, synapse by synapse.

Her cyber-psi talent enabled her to control the probe and modify its programming. From all outward appearances it was reporting progress, but the actual probe was not scanning her at all.

It was a painstaking process, requiring concentration, but she managed to keep it under control until she heard Glenn say that Hank was dead.

She froze. The probe bit into her, rending her thoughts. She was on the brink of losing the fight, and a part of her wasn't sure it was worth the effort to win. What would she have left? She would still be Maxwell's prisoner, and Hank wouldn't be there. Oblivion was a tempting destination.

But there was something else to live for. She would fight on, not for victory, not for survival, but for revenge.

* * *

"You little bitch! I don't know how you did this, but you're going to wish that you'd let the mind probe do its work."

The probe had completed its cycle, but when Maxwell called up the results, there was no information from the scan at all. The datalifter had managed to beat the machine. Maxwell had a new respect for the level of her cyber-psi talent. It was no wonder that she had been able to enter the Galactic Bank and wreak havoc with his accounts. The mind probe was useless, but Maxwell had other tools at his disposal.

"All right, young woman. The only reason I use this machine is that for normal people it does a very thorough job and provides much more detailed data than is possible by cruder means. Your talent is obviously very strong, but it won't help you against the blade and the hot fuser. I've actually missed using a more hands-on approach. I'm going to enjoy this immensely."

Sai spoke. "Torture? You would actually resort to getting your hands dirty? I thought that was beneath you."

"I dabble in torture, mostly for pleasure. I am quite good at it, as you will soon see."

"Is this about money? Or sadism?"

"Both."

"Well, if you would settle for your money, I can access it for you. But you have to agree to release me."

Maxwell smiled. "Of course. I'm not a barbarian, Ms. Collins. I'm a businessman. Just tell me what account you diverted the funds to and give me the proper passwords and I'll send you on your way."

Sai smiled. "No, it's not that easy. I didn't just switch around a few deposits; I created a shadow account that's locked in the system, where only I can get to it, and I transferred all the money there. No one else has access; it's as if it doesn't exist. The Galactic Bank is a stickler about security so you'll never get the authority to poke around and try to find it yourself. I have to enter the system to get it for you."

"I don't trust you," Maxwell said.

"The feeling's mutual," Sai said. "I'm the one taking the risk. If I get your money for you, then I'm expendable despite your pretty words. If I'm lying about the money, you still have me, and I'll have to pay the price. You're the one in control."

Maxwell smiled. He liked a woman who knew her place. "Splendid."

It didn't take long to set up the comlink. Maxwell placed the equipment next to Sai and moved to attach a neural lead to Sai's forehead.

"I have limited the device to communications only with the Galactic Bank, Ms. Collins. I will be monitoring your activity. If you try to break my security settings and use this to send a message to anyone, I will send a feedback pulse through the neural lead causing immediate, agonizing pain. I'm no fool." He chuckled. "But then, who would you contact? Jensen is dead."

Sai's eyes turned cold as she glared at Maxwell. "You may get the money, and you may be able to get the stock, but sooner or later you're going to get what you really deserve. It's a solid fact, Maxwell."

"I do hope so. I think I deserve so much more than just Nebulaco. You may proceed, Ms. Collins."

The comlink came to life and the logo of the Galactic Bank unfolded in midair before them. The image rapidly shifted, too fast for Maxwell to process. Countless columns of numbers appeared, interrupted by an occasional challenge for password entry as Sai went deeper into the bank's data. Finally, one number from a multitude expanded in view, then unfolded into a history list of deposits. A large balance figure appeared, floating in front of them in glowing green numerals. It was in the billions.

"Is this the right amount?" Sai asked.

Maxwell smiled. "It certainly seems on the scale I expected. I assume that after you stole my money, you also took all the Nebulaco shares I just bought and then sold them off, forwarding the proceeds of those sales into this account. I stood to make billions, but you cost me a great deal of money by dumping all that stock at the same time. Nebulaco's stock value dropped by ten percent. The rule, my dear, is to buy low and sell high."

"I wasn't doing it for profit," Sai said.

"A life lesson of dubious value at this point, but *always* work for profit. That's why I'm here and you're there. Now, I want all those funds transferred back to the proper accounts." Maxwell keyed his account number into the comlink.

Suddenly, the number in the air began to change, counting down. Slowly at first, then faster. The figure became a blur until finally it rested on a steady line of zeroes with a credit symbol in front.

"Excellent," Maxwell said. Then he entered a command into the comlink to display the balance on his accounts. The display did not change. He repeated the process for each of his accounts, but still no change. It was as if the machine wasn't responding to his commands. "What's wrong with this thing?"

Sai began to laugh. "It's working perfectly."

"What do you mean? The display isn't changing to show my new balance."

"Oh, but it is. That *is* your balance, Maxwell. Zero. Nothing."

"What have you done? Where is my money?"

Sai looked up at Maxwell, her eyes on fire. "I don't know. No one knows. I had the system randomly distribute it amongst the bank's account holders, then I wiped the record of the transactions. I just pulled the lever and flushed your goddamned money to hell."

Maxwell slapped Sai across the face. "Fool! Even this can't stop me! I started life on the streets. I built an empire from nothing and I can do it again." Maxwell towered over her bound form. "But what are you? Filth. You are like an insignificant flea. You have taken a small sip of my blood and think you've destroyed me."

He slapped her again, then paused a few seconds and struck her again, then once more—vicious in his calmness and cold brutality. Blood began to flow from her mouth. "You are going to enter that bank again and you will find those funds."

Sai fought back involuntary tears. "I can't. I disbursed them randomly."

"Then take money from random accounts and put those funds into mine!"

"Fuck you," Sai said.

Maxwell walked to the table and opened a toolbox. He withdrew a fuser. He pressed a button on the side of the slim tool, and the sharp tip turned red with heat. "To motivate you to provide a creative solution with your mind, I will be working on your body with this. I will start with your feet and work my way up to your eyes. And don't worry, if you can't get my money back, I will still have considered this a worthwhile way to spend a few hours."

He pressed the button on the fuser, then bent down and placed it against the flesh on the bottom of her foot. Sai screamed as the red-hot metal broiled her skin and created a sickening hiss and a puff of foul smoke.

The sound of blaster fire erupted over her screams. There was a fight going on just outside the room. Maxwell walked toward the table and reached for a pistol just as the door burst open.

CHAPTER TWENTY-EIGHT

Hank, Chandler, and Brock stormed inside Maxwell's office. Chandler and Brock held pulse rifles while Hank had a blaster pistol in one hand and Sai's whisperblade in the other. Prepared for battle, they found Sai strapped into some sort of machine and Maxwell reaching for a weapon.

"Don't move, Maxwell," Hank said. "We've got you covered."

"Hank!" Sai cried, her voice breaking in shock and exhaustion.

Chandler shot a glance around the squalid room. "Suits you, Maxwell."

Maxwell smiled and made a small movement, then his body shimmered, fading into the background.

"Shit," Chandler said. "Stealthcloak!"

The three looked at each other and ducked down, looking around the room, unsure where to seek cover. A stealthcloak was a tricky thing to fight without special equipment. A blaster shot rang out.

Brock fell back, hit the wall, and slid to the ground, clutching his chest.

Hank and Chandler rolled for cover behind some crates. "Where is he?" Hank asked.

"I don't know. I can't see anything." Chandler glanced over at Brock. "Angus, get out of here!"

Brock crawled toward the door, but instead of leaving, he raised his pulse rifle and fired several shots into different parts of the room. The blasts tore chunks out of the wall but apparently missed Maxwell.

Sai craned her neck and scanned the room with her cyber-psi talent, looking for the stealthcloak's electronic signature. She felt something creeping around the side of the room trying to flank Hank. "Hank! He's coming around your left side."

Hank fired his pistol blindly, fanning shots across the room, hoping for a lucky hit.

"Did I get him?" Hank asked.

"I'm not sure," Sai said. She swept her senses around, trying to again locate the indistinct form.

Maxwell spoke, and his voice seemed to come from everywhere. "I don't know how you managed to survive, but I'm going to make sure you don't leave this room alive."

"What do we do?" Hank asked Chandler.

Chandler shrugged. "You can't shoot what you can't see. We need Sai."

"Hank, he's behind you!" Sai shouted.

Hank rolled, knocking over some equipment. A blaster bolt slammed into the floor where he'd just been. Chandler rose and started shooting into the area behind him while Hank made his way toward Sai.

"Let me get you out of there," he said.

"No, you'll expose yourself," she said.

"Come on, I'm saving that for later," he said with a grin.

"I can see him, he's—" Sai yelled. A blaster bolt came from nowhere and hit her in the shoulder. She cried out in pain.

"Sai!" Hank yelled, rushing forward, heedless of the danger. The wall next to him burst into rocky fragments as he was nearly hit. He tripped and fell, two meters from the mind probe.

Chandler provided cover fire as Hank raced to Sai.

"Hank, throw the whisperblade!" she screamed.

Hank hit the activation button and tossed the weapon through the air, into the middle of the room. Sai took charge of the blade and it changed course, streaking back toward the far right corner, hissing through the air. Maxwell screamed as the whisperblade plunged home, again and again, powered by the thrust of its tiny repulsor beams.

The stealthcloak automatically deactivated when Maxwell's heart stopped, revealing his body—and bright arterial blood leaking from its many gaping wounds.

CHAPTER TWENTY-NINE

The threat gone, Hank rushed to Sai and loosed the restraints that bound her to the mind probe. The shoulder wound looked painful, but not life-threatening. "We need to get you to a doctor," he said.

Chandler walked to the other side of the room to tend to Brock, who was barely conscious but seemed to be breathing okay.

Sai winced as she climbed out of the machine. "How did you escape?"

Hank carried her to Maxwell's desk and sat her atop it. "Easy. Elsa and I used to sit out gravity storms in the belly of this old derelict freighter. It had a hot, old reactor. Stable enough unless you were stupid enough to shoot at it. The backup plan was for us to meet the *Elsa* at the freighter in the Marauder we stole. We played a little trick on the pirates by blowing up the freighter's drive. When the fireworks started, we switched ships, then sent the Marauder back out on automatic for the rest of them to chase. They blasted it to pieces so they thought we'd bought it and didn't even bother to search for another ship."

"But then how did you find me?" Sai asked.

"Elsa is a smart girl. We knew the planet and port thanks to a jailer on the pirate base, so she just monitored the Grid for new dedicated communications to the Galactic Bank when we reached Port Royal. I guess you use a lot of bandwidth. That led us here."

A corporate security squad entered the room with pulse rifles drawn. Hank and Sai raised their hands in the air. "Whoa, now. Let me explain what's going on here," Hank said.

"No need to," Randol said as he entered the room followed by Helen. She stared at the destruction in the room, her eyes settling on Maxwell's body.

"So the cavalry rides in only five minutes too late," Hank said.

"Believe me, we got here as soon as we could. Keeping the communications secret so that Maxwell wouldn't catch wind of it slowed us down. I wish I could have been here to kill him myself."

Chandler called out, "We need a medic over here."

More security and medics entered the office now that the danger was over. The medics started working on Brock and tending to Sai's shoulder. Maxwell was a lost cause, but no one cared.

"Careful," Brock said as a medic cleaned his wound. "That hurts like a son of a bitch."

Chandler sat back and watched the show. He looked over at Hank. "The way I see it, Brock's gonna be fine. Randol has his daughter back, you and Sai have each other, and Elsa, too, for that matter, you lucky bastard," he said, reaching into his pocket for a cigar. He lit it and puffed a cloud of blue smoke into the air. "I got my fee plus expenses, and a great bonus, so I have nothing to complain about. Of course, you didn't get paid like me, but I wouldn't feel too bad about it. After all, you're still breathing. A job is a job, but some jobs I do enjoy more than others." He sat down and put his feet up on a crate to enjoy his cigar.

* * *

Hank and Sai boarded the *Elsa* and took their seats at the main console. Hank started punching buttons to enter the launch sequence. "Where to, milady?" he asked Sai.

"I don't care," Sai said.

"Well, even though the Confed didn't catch Glenn, I doubt we'll have to worry about pirates for a while. Until they develop a new intelligence network, they're going to be picking at scraps, so I figure anywhere we go is pretty safe. Either that or we can expect to see Glenn's Adult Toy Shops start popping up everywhere."

"I'm still battle-damaged," Elsa said. "Our first stop needs to be Brady's Repair over at Matilda next to the Atlas Ship Yards. I want new shields and plating. I also think a second plasma cannon would be a good investment, on the off chance we *do* have to deal with pirates again. Then we're going to upgrade my nav systems at Kylie's Upgrade Shop, and—"

"Whoa," Hank said. "What the hell are you talking about? Do you have any idea how much that will cost?"

"I don't care what it costs," Elsa said. "I'm worth it."

"Of course you are," Sai said. "Isn't she, Hank?"

"And how do you expect us to pay for these upgrades?"

"I've got money."

"Well, maybe, but not that kind of money," Hank said.

"Actually, I have plenty. More than enough to completely refurbish myself from stem to stern," Elsa said.

Sai nodded and grinned.

"Are you in on this, too? How did you . . . ?"

"When Sai entered that sell order to trigger those accounts to dump their assets into the hidden account, we figured that it would only make sense to charge a tiny handling fee for all those transactions. It certainly isn't billions, but you'd be surprised at how quickly fees can add up."

"You sneaky, wonderful, cybernetic wonder woman! You mean we're rich?" Hank asked, smiling.

"I mean *I'm* rich," she said. "It's my own account. We also created one for Sai."

"What about me? I mean, you made one for me, right?"

"Well, Hank, we were the ones doing all the work. We handled the transfers. We couldn't really charge a fee for work not performed. That would be unethical."

"Unethical? Well no, I suppose we would hate to be unethical. So what about me? Am I going to be your butler now?"

"No," said Sai. "Certainly not. You are a professional pilot and deserve to be paid. In fact, we have agreed that all you have to do is ask us and we will occasionally give you an allowance for approved purchases. After all, we are a family."

"An allowance? Why not just an account with a big pot of cash in it like you guys have? You can prepay for my piloting services that way."

"We can't trust you with too much money. You'd spend it all on liquor and wild parties and drellskin boots and gambling."

"Hell yeah, I would! What's the point of being rich if you don't enjoy it? And what about Chandler and Brock? Did you guys give them accounts, too?"

Elsa laughed. "No. I'm sorry, Chandler is too honorable. He'd want to give it all back or some fool thing like that. That said, he will be somewhat surprised when he checks the balance of the mortgage on his ship. He'll likely assume that Lord Randol paid it off for him."

"And Brock?"

"We didn't know about him then, but even if we had, it seems like a conflict of interest. It would be like offering a Confed officer a bribe. Highly irregular," Sai said.

"And he might turn you in," Hank said.

"That too," Elsa said.

"So I'm really going to have to beg you for every credit?"

"Well," Elsa said, "I wouldn't say *beg*. Just convince me that the purchase is reasonable."

"In that case, let me tell you about the incredible durability and practicality of drellskin boots . . ."

ABOUT THE AUTHORS

Gary Jonas is the author of the Jonathan Shade fantasy series, the novel *One Way Ticket to Midnight* (his debut), the story collection *Quick Shots*, and the novella *Night Marshal: A Tale of the Undead West*, the first in a new vampire western series that will be penned by various authors. His short fiction has appeared in numerous anthologies and magazines. Gary was born in Japan and has since lived in Ohio, Florida, Oklahoma, and Colorado, where he now resides.

Bill D. Allen is the author of two previous novels, *Shadow Heart* and *Gods and Other Children*. His short fiction has appeared in numerous publications, including *Personal Demons* and *Small Bites*. He is a native of Tulsa, Oklahoma, where he still lives and works. In addition to his writing, he is a die-hard motorcycle enthusiast and a proud recipient of multiple "Iron Butt" certifications, granted to those who travel over one thousand miles in twenty-four hours by motorcycle.

Kindle Serials

This book was originally released in Episodes as a Kindle Serial. Kindle Serials launched in 2012 as a new way to experience serialized books. Kindle Serials allow readers to enjoy the story as the author creates it, purchasing once and receiving all existing Episodes immediately, followed by future Episodes as they are published. To find out more about Kindle Serials and to see the current selection of Serials titles, visit www.amazon.com/kindleserials.

Made in the USA
San Bernardino, CA
25 January 2014